# Train Whistle in the Distance

*A Collection of Stories*

by

Dan O'Sullivan

TRAIN WHISTLE IN THE DISTANCE

*A Collection of Stories*

Lulu Enterprises, Inc.

www.lulu.com


ISBN: 978-0-557-36675-0


Printed in the United States of America

Visit Dan O'Sullivan on the web at

www.dan-osullivan.com

# Introduction

Tickets, please. Tickets, please.

Sorry. I just couldn't resist. For I, Dan O'Sullivan, will be your conductor aboard this one-way train to the strange, the beautiful and the wondrous. And it could only begin with a book title inspired from the memory of a growing boy on his bed in that house on Bridgeman Road where the soothing late-night sound of a distant train whistle signaled the endless boundaries and possibilities of where the imagination could be taken.

Your first stop aboard this collection of whimsical tales will be a lesson that sometimes the road less traveled doesn't always make all the difference when love, hate, revenge and guilt collide for a young man on an emotional journey with unforeseen repercussions to finding out the truth behind a legendary monster living in forbidden woods in "An Eye for an Eye, a Heart for a Heart" — which to make note of has been delivered to you straight from a personal dream where the events you will read will only be strictly nothing short of the descriptive imagery that occurred one night inside this author's head.

Your next stop, should you brave yourself to continue, will be "The Chosen", where a woman drawn to a strange object buried within an abandoned mine gains superpowers that ultimately start to turn her against the city she has come to protect.

Then, in "Horizon", an eighteenth-century man makes a deal with a mysterious stranger to live immortally throughout the centuries and continually save the woman he loves in her reincarnated lives but pay the price of having to immediately leave her all over again in each.

In "May Fortune Smile Upon You", a new student at a small town high school acquires a ring that grants its possessor five wishes, but as he uses each to try to win the affection of the most popular girl, he learns first-hand the age-old warning to be careful what you wish for.

In "Double Back", a young woman finds herself repeatedly getting sent back in time to the same moment leading to the disastrous events caused by the psychopathic bank robber she and her estranged sister picked up during a road trip home to see their dying mother.

And finally, your last destination is scheduled to be "Nightlife", where a car-thieving insomniac becomes infatuatedly paranoid when he suspects the new girl in the apartment at the end of the hall is following him with an unclear nocturnal agenda of her own.

So I welcome you all aboard and can only thank you for partaking in this journey with me to distant places only truly limitless imagination can bring you.

# Table of Contents

# AN EYE FOR AN EYE, A HEART FOR A HEART

Monsters... are not real.

From the moment we escape the womb, we are bred to believe that the only terrible things in this world lurk under your bed. That if you go out at night alone, you will surely not return. But these are notions that we soon abandon when we reach those later stages of adolescence into early adulthood, where fiction turns into fact, and you realize that gullibility has gotten the best of you as a child. Parents only say there are monsters beneath your bed to make you clean under it. They tell you a monster will snatch you up if you go out alone at night simply because they're being protective of your well-being to the strangers of these lands that may have far worse agendas than any fang-toothed beast.

Monsters, in any time, any language, any place, have always been the center of grand and wondrous, if not scary, stories around occasional campfires, handed down generation to generation. A good pipe-smoking story, my grandfather would probably call it. But if every ounce of fiction comes from some line of fact, then what of the monster? What of a beast, so vicious and well-hidden to its fairy tale existence, managing to hide for so long of a time that its presence could never really be unfolded to open any true eyes? The only existence of this atrocity has appeared merely through floating words in the air out of some poor jokester's own mouth.

But perhaps that's where the fact comes in. Perhaps this monster *did* exist somewhere nestled deep in these woods, but has eluded most other life presence to the point where its stature has shaped into a story. Perhaps these stories have only been derived because the people that have come fully across its path were never seen again, allowing its horrifying snarl to be masked in secrecy by idiotic tales. After all, every pound of rumor comes from some quantity of truth.

I was twenty-three-years-old the first time I saw a monster.

And only at the start of our group's long trek into the forever-stretching woods did I begin to question my own gullibility toward this monster's existence.


Life in the village was simple. Hard work at times, maybe, navigating the crops to their full potential, but it was our way. Nobody ever really had one specific job, which is what generally made things so easy. Everyone would pitch in and do a little bit of everything and anything. The men would even occasionally scrub the laundry while the women carried the baskets of wheat or hay from the fields. But through the daily chores, tiresome projects and standard ways of life, one must find a single thing to get them out of bed everyday. Something to lift their spirits and fuel the motivation of moving onward. That something for me — was her.

And her name was Tristan.

*Such a beautiful name*, I would think in the back of my mind every time it ran through. Like the bold name of an ancient goddess across the seas. That's exactly what she was to me, too — a breathtaking goddess of both inner and outer beauty, which as much as I could try to describe, would end up being nearly impossible. I could leave it to the basic points, and tell you that her soft brown hair always seemed structurally weighed just delicately enough for the light breezes to fit through. I could tell you that her smile — oh, that smile — could rumble a quake across the lands for as long as they stretched. But her eyes were my favorite. Anything I could ever want to know or tell from her came from those doe eyes. And the fact of knowing they were always on *me*, that they were always *for* me, made it an even better feeling.

I had known Tristan practically all of my life, meeting her around the age of eight, which in the grand scheme of mental time seemed like yesterday. My mother had died in childbirth, so it had always been just my father and I, usually taking one of the smaller wagons down the trails to the nearby neighboring villages for supplies and trades. It was at one of those neighboring villages I had met her for the first time. Even then, when true beauty in an eight-year-old boy's mind was limited to the extent of a newly-carved toy, she had captured my attention. Perhaps most other of the boys in the village could have seen her merely as a "girl", as that great portion of their prepubescent mind was not yet unlocked to the mysteries of the female inner anatomy. *But my God, that girl was beautiful.*

She was easy to talk to, in fact, she had spoken the first words. Only Tristan and I had never really needed words. And as I sat there on that seat, her body curled on my lap under the shades of the forest canopy above us those fifteen years later, I was reminded yet again of the beauty of that very rare and mutual occurrence. Most lovers or spouses always had their own particular private practices that made them as a couple unique to all of the others around them. When a woman might come home to her man and engage in the daily ritual of a conversation of how the day went, Tristan and I would simply just hold each other. Her eyes would stare up into mine as the tips of her fingers worked gently on my chin. She'd kiss my neck, nuzzle her nose into it and maybe often fall into a deep sleep. Those were the conversations I liked best. Together we communicated from our insides, privileged in the otherworldly powers of appreciating the rarest and truest love.

Often times one of my good friends Thomas would sit on a stump nearby simply for his odd likeness to being that off-skew third-wheel to us. He would always tuck his hair out of his eyes and chew from his bread loaf, admiring Tristan and I as if we were some sort of painting or art sculpture. When Tristan would sneak a kiss or two to my lips, his true nature would always unravel to jokingly kissing his bread loaf in a mocking passion, which always curved a blushing smile onto Tristan's face. She had more often than not attempted to find him a matching partner of his own from her selection of friends, our village and the next, but as much as he appreciated the finer aspects of a woman's indulgent touch, he preferred the single man's life. A life I had never really known, nor ever really wanted, for that matter.

I can't say much more about the cosmic colliding of Tristan and I and the kinship we seemed to develop other than the lamentably unfortunate circumstances that brought us together. It always seems to happen that way. Something bad must happen by sacrificing itself for the better good of something to come. It was in the death of Tristan's parents that I thought this to be possibly true, even though I regret it happening both for her sake and the sake of two loving people who treated me like their own offspring. But like the changing of seasons or aging of a child, the sickness that landed her parents into their eternal beds when she was still living back at her village as a child could not be stopped.

I remember going into their hut when they were on their deathbeds, the inside dark and dreary, allowing only select beams of white light from outside to pour in at various points in the structure. My steps were slow and cautious, wary of the mood sifting through. The doctor was standing in the far corner, hands wrapped together at his front with an essence of powerless ability to his face; his knowledge and craft failing to prevail in what he had so many times with so many people been able to mend. I remember my father's hands sliding off my shoulders from behind as I made those steps now alone toward the beds. Even for a young mind, I sensed melancholy ached through the hut, and the feeling of death seemed to ride the gentle breeze coming in through the sunlight holes. I walked up to her mother's side of the bed; the father's eyes were shut as he occasionally would deliver rhythmic coughs. Her mother pried her eyes open at the sight of me standing next to her.

I remember Tristan had her mother's eyes.

She weakly managed to lift her arm and enveloped a cold, coarse hand over mine, shunning a very meticulously short smile as she gently pulled me closer. "You have to take care of her now," she quietly whispered into my ear. The words were delivered with a softness and care I had then not known about. The words were meaningful, packaged with a warm responsibility even a young wandering mind could hang onto. And the words were her last.

Since Tristan had no other immediate family relatives and had grown such a closeness to me, it was decided that she would come back to our village to stay with us, and her village had given her a proper send-off. With a snap of the reins, the horses clunked forward, pulling the wooden cart packed with supplies and what few belongings she now owned brought down to her by inheritance. We sat at the edge on the back, our short legs dangling over the side. I looked over to her and saw her face — for the first time since meeting her, it was one I had never seen. One with a hiding hint of desolation and change. Her eyes would streak across the muddy road beneath as it emerged from under the wagon and then up to her home. Her home village which saw her caring neighbors giving gentle waves as they grew shorter in the distance. I had never seen this emotional side of her. And being young, it was awkward to relate or pass off some kind of compassion to someone in need, especially the same age. So I did the only thing I could think of, and reached behind me to one of the smaller open boxes, pulling out a carved wooden wolf — a toy. One of my favorites. With a graceful gesture, I held it out to her, saying nothing. Her eyes took a moment to find it, and her mind silently registered the offer. She carefully took it from me, inspecting and looking it over in her hands, rubbing the edges. She didn't say "thank you", or smile, or start hopping it around, but simply held it close as the wagon slightly bounced and rocked its way into the forest.

Now over the years, when kids begin to grow, there's a sense of territorial gender dispute, especially when it comes to boys and girls socially accepting one another. One of those many ways this social symbiotic relationship is nurtured is by that ever-so-timeless game of boys chasing girls, or sometimes vice versa. Perhaps it's a test of power, the boys wanting to be champions of hunting down and tagging their prey and the girls wanting the equal gender strength of dodging those finds by smartly eluding their predator. So many times I had played this game with the other children of the village, hopping and running, circling around the huts and trying to slip past the constantly moving and working adults, who more often seemed not to mind us getting in the way by affection of a short smile and pat on the head, remembering those similar long-ago days of their own.

It was with Tristan that the game had changed for me. Now, instead of discovering a giggling girl hiding in the brush and throwing a pair of victorious fists into the air, the girls would make it a point to be easily found. And instead of turning a corner to see Tristan cowering behind a hut, she was standing in plain view. She wouldn't run, or scream, or laugh — she would take a few steps toward me, maybe a hint of shyness in them. And I wouldn't yell out, "Found you!" or try to tag her for she had me mesmerized under some strange spell to which my feet were sinking in the ground, unable to move as she zeroed in toward me. She would gently touch her fingertips under my chin and close her eyes, dipping her face forward to land her soft lips on mine. Maybe it was indeed the spell of a first kiss, or perhaps a growing boy's curiosity, but I wasn't able to move. *This isn't how you play*, I could remember myself thinking at that particular shattering moment. But when it had ended, she would merely try to hide an emerging smile by biting her lower lip and turning to run in the opposite direction, continuing with the game as if it had never ceased activity.

And it's at that moment when you look at girls differently. No longer do you try to punch them, or make fun of them for not being physically built as strong or fast as you. Something in your heart changes. As if it were in a cocoon and has now evolved into something much more beautiful. You want to look back at a moment where, perhaps, you felt her pain sitting on the back of a wagon and attempted to offer solace by giving up something of your own care to see that she was happy again. You feel the incredible, unstoppable need to keep giving her things as a show of affection. You feel the need while playing the chase game to, when she falls while running and scrapes her knee, not stop and laugh with a pointing finger or take advantage by tagging her and yelling, "Got you, got you!" but instead fall to your own and brush the dirt off hers. To, if it bleeds, tear off a piece of your clothing and wrap it around for a mend.

And it's at that moment when you're sitting in a chair on a peaceful day, cradling her in your lap while the golden sunlight trickles through the foliage above to shine down upon her fluttering eyes as they veer up to you, to feel in your heart the power of noticing what an extraordinary woman she's become.


From time to time, particularly seasonal, there is a need for the village to acquire harvesting supplies and necessities that the neighboring villages simply can't offer. Thus, there is a need to venture out across the lands to further establishments — our primary life support being the Far Village of the North. The journey itself took the entirety of three days round trip, a day and a half there and a day and a half back by wagon, and when a seasonal mishap like the unexpected crash of weather took a toll on the village and harvesting supplies were already low, the importance and quickness of the trip was all the more significant as to keep our way of life strong and ongoing. Many of the villagers, especially the younger ones, didn't seem to properly understand the repercussions of a botched Far Village of the North trip. Infinite little things played part in a strand of life that flowed through our way. If we leave too early or too late, we might miss the seasonal rains that cause the seeds to grow. If the seeds don't grow, the special turnips that the pigs will only eat won't grow. If those don't grow, the pigs will willingly starve themselves. If the pigs die, we'll lose a significant portion of the food supply for us. All because of certain seeds we didn't get or got too late. It wasn't as if the neighboring villages wouldn't lend a helping hand or open their doors to our needs, but one has to understand the fragile system between villages. I've heard stories before about far villages completely failing because of these chain reaction effects. Those who left the village would overpopulate neighboring establishments and throw off their control. Those who stayed simply wouldn't have the manpower or personal power to keep the way of life going. The village would slump into a dying, deserted decay. Families would abandon their huts and become nomads, drifting across the lands in search of a new village that would rarely have the room and life support to sustain their sudden appearance.

It was about survival. It was about working together in a repetitive daily pattern that as long as we followed would dare not bring doom to all we knew.

And that time for the journey had come up. Generally it was a small group, maybe seven people at the most, my father usually at the helm. But for some reason, at this particular time, a small fire had broken out that spread and destroyed a good number of supplies in addition to a few huts, leaving some individuals or families to temporarily shelter with others. My father, being the leader that everyone seemed to appoint and look up to him as, had a great deal of responsibility in keeping control of this situation.

So in that, I found my opportunity. Like a growing boy who insisted he was old enough to walk to the neighboring villages through the woods path in the dark, I had offered to take up lead of the wagon on the trip to the Far Village of the North so my father could stay and better control our small-scale catastrophic situation. Almost immediately he was opposed to the notion, making judgments and cases that even at twenty-three I was still too young and inexperienced to lead the caravan for such an important and vital journey. And, almost immediately, I had retorted with facts that I *was* indeed old enough, had known the trip from accompanying it so many times before, and felt I was mature enough in the eyes of the village to take on such a large task.

Actually... it was more for Tristan. Even with her undying and un-parting love for me, I still felt the need to impress, much like a younger teenager attempting to marvel the girl he's trying to constantly woo into his arms and onto his lips, and eventually, into his bed, for lack of stating a more typical motive to the minds of most young men. Except that Tristan was already mine. I saw in her sparkling eyes that there was never any need to impress her, that there was never any fear of losing her to a better looking rival. And for the most part, I was comfortable with that. Except now that marriage wasn't too far off, and larger responsibilities were peeking over the horizon, I felt this tiny little need within myself to really prove to her once and for all that I could truly go beyond the person she wanted and expected me to be. That I could do the wish of a dying parent some justice and solidifying comfort. Or perhaps it was simply just the egotistical persistence in my male genes.

Nevertheless, after my endless nagging and cases that I refused to give up, my father finally turned, laid his hand on my shoulder, and said in a finally-agreeing and sighing tone as he had trusted me with many times before, "Yes."

I really did believe that the village needed him at this time, and although somebody else could have more easily and properly harnessed the trip, it was finally an opportunity to rise above myself. When I had told Tristan about the decision, she seemed a bit reluctant at first, of course trying to convince me that if it were indeed a tactic to prove something, it was unnecessary. "I don't know how anyone else in this world could dare be as gentle yet strong as you've always been for me," she said. "Please know, that no matter what happens, no matter where we go, your heart will always be strong enough to protect me. The only work I'll ever need of you to support me with is the strength to open your eyes in the morning when you wake to meet mine next to you. That and that alone will be more than enough to give us power to make it through each day."

She's always been the optimist. She would never yell at me, or disallow me to touch her when she was angry over something else. I had once built a small stable for one horse by my lone self; the wood was cracked, the rope could have been tied better, and the roof didn't quite sit right. I even caught a few instances when our horse seemed a bit reluctant to enter, as if somehow thinking in its simplistic mind, *This has got to be a joke.* But even in my own sheepish reveling of accomplishment, Tristan had walked over to me, curled an arm around mine and gave a nod to the potentially-hazardous structure. "It's absolutely perfect," she supported with a kiss to the cheek. "If it weren't for the horse, it could be our marveling kingdom that I would be honored to grow old inside with you."

She had a way to doing that, and at times I could tell a certain statement was more sarcastic and joking merely to play around with me, but there was always her heart buried somewhere within, like a mother encouraging her small child on what a wonderful drawing he had done when in fact it was just a series of scribbles and odd shapes.

Tristan had accompanied my father and I only a few times over the years we had made the trip to the Far Village of the North, simply because she couldn't stand a three-day absence that had taken me away from her eyesight. "Anything could happen," she always worriedly insisted when I went. "The wagon could fall off a cliff or a storm could wipe you out or pillagers could come from nowhere and thieve all of your supplies on the way back, leaving you all dead. I feel as if I have no way to protect you while you're gone."

And sometimes she did in fact convince me to sit out on some of the trips, but others she knew just how fascinating the long voyage was to my adventurous mind. It was something different than the everyday experiences back at the village; not that I at all minded the boredom of said activities. So in light of my impending leadership, she wanted to come along, perhaps for that reason of simply being with me, or maybe she was indeed intrigued by this giant step I was taking toward responsibility.

Nevertheless, there was the issue... of the monster.

In order to get to the Far Village of the North, you had to follow the trail that led through a deep valley and across the river, which accumulated the day and a half trip. On the other hand — there was the trail leading through the West Woods. The trail that by design skipped the massive gulping mouth of the valley and went alongside the river. The trail that cut that day and a half expensive nearly fifty percent. The trail through the woods — where the monster dwelled.

Not much was known or hardly spoken, to that matter, of this so-called beast that supposedly roamed the uninhabited West Woods. Its presence was merely a story around campfires for me, but to the others of the village and neighboring villages across the lands, it was superstitious truth in the highest form. No one ever dared to step foot an inch into those West Woods. If two children were playing near the edges of its boundaries, they were immediately scolded by their adults and given a wary earful never to go near it again. Legends and theoretically unsound stories always circulated around the actuality of this monster to some degree, but they were usually all the same — someone goes in, and doesn't come out. In fact, despite the seriousness surrounding the subject, many of the villagers generally took a light outlook toward the legends, since they themselves would never really have the atrocity to go seek the truth. Kids would often dare each other to enter the woods, or take a single bounding step within its endless perimeters, but no one would ever really get too far, and those teasing them for their cowardly retraction would soon stop laughing at the thought that they themselves wouldn't even hold the bravery to try it.

When I was around ten, a drifter had come into our village from the east. He was older, short, dark-skinned and walked with a cane that balanced the limping of his right leg, which was probably all the more reason my father and the other villagers had so easily agreed with a shade of sympathy to give him shelter and food in exchange for a helping hand in the daily activities. He had actually stayed around for quite some time, always squinting in the sun as he worked in the wheat fields, occasionally tipping up that strange straw hat he wore to wipe the sweat from his forehead. He was a trickster of sorts, always dazzling the children with unique illusionist magic and an aging smile that always blocked out his true motives on his road through life. When it had come time that he announced he was departing and would be heading toward the Far Village of the North by way of the West Woods trail, the villagers insisted he take the long route through the valley instead. The legends and stories of the monster of course sprang up, and with each little fabricated detail that made most everybody else shudder in coldness, the drifter had given a warm, skeptical smile. I was the last person to see him off as he headed for the trail to the West Woods despite the failed attempts to steer him differently. When I had curiously asked him why he was going to face the monster, he gave that same warm sun-reflecting smile, crouched down more to my level and told me, "Without fear, anything in this world is possible."

Our next trip to the Far Village of the North revealed that he had never arrived. He never came back to our village. No one had ever seen him again.

I'm not quite sure if my father ever truly believed in the monster, but his response to my notion of taking the West Woods trail to cut time had been as firm as it would get. "You're better off just sticking to the valley trail," he told me, as if trying to scour some justification not relating to any superstition. "We've been taking the valley trail for ages. We know it well and you know it well. Monster or no monster, there's no sense in endangering the trip by going down a hardly-used path. No one knows what kind of shape it's in. I've already agreed to let you lead the group. I have strong judgmental faith in you for that and I hold the same for you to be able to respect my answer on this matter."

When word of this had broken out between the small group readying the trip, I had suddenly become an unfavorable part of the equation. "He's crazy, he is!" Bixley, a balding older man had mentioned in response. "This isn't some walk down the road to get hay. This is an important acquisition of goods from a journey that this entire village depends on! We don't need some young fool at the reins trying to impress a girl!"

I wanted to chime in with my defense, but Tristan was there to hold me back, guiding my attention to her face. "Everything will go all right. Your father has been leading them for years. It's natural for them to be hesitant, but they'll see. They will see how responsible you truly are and you'll soon gain their trust," she said. "I believe in you." She kissed my forehead and nuzzled my cheek with her thumb, going off to help load the wagon.

As my father had always done so well before, the group was convinced that everything was on schedule and going according to plan, and flaring emotions were quickly eased. The large wooden wagon was loaded with the supplies we could use to trade for our needed goods; two strong horses at the reining helm in front. Bixley and two other older men climbed into the back, accompanied by Thomas, who seemed positively delighted to not only be a part of the trip but to be going on it with me, his best friend, as I led it for the first time. "A sense of wandering adventure in a new age," was how he put it exactly, trying to come off as being intellectually supportive. "Besides — if someone with true restraining authority doesn't come along, you and Tristan might find the need to stop every hour to retreat to some secluded bushes in privacy."

Tristan giggled at the remark, casually hiding her blushed red face and I playfully nudged for him to get into the wagon. "Good thing we have you to come along," I had replied boldly to him. "We'll be needing *someone* of squirrel intellect to interpret to the animals that won't move out of the path."

He grinned and shook his head.

So we were off not long after that; our ancient guiding stallions clacking and thunking their hooves into the dirt below as the wagon garnered a smooth riding rhythm for Bixley and the two older men. Thomas, of course, felt the need to show off a sense of venturesome arrogance by preferring to walk alongside for most of the time. I was sitting up front along with Tristan, who seemed to preserve her outlook of a relaxing sightsee by occasionally curling up close beside me when she wasn't assisting with the reins. At one point we had even stopped for a short half hour or so alongside a thin and shallow portion of the river to load up an adequate water supply for the journey, as the majority of the trek wouldn't have allowed us the opportunity to do so if suddenly by chance needed.

As I recall, I had taken a few minutes to stroll down the stream a bit, stopping by the water's edge to suck up nature's true elegance. There was always a sense of peace away from the villages. Time was but a whisper in the breeze through the foliage. I had usually liked to steal a glance at the mountains while they were still far away and mysterious, boasting their royalty like barriers to entirely new worlds. But out of everything this great green world had to offer me, I most enjoyed catching the sun spots skipping across the water. It was better at sunset, but even at that particular point in the aging day the river was given a sparkled illuminating essence that guided my wandering eyesight to my beautiful Tristan, who not too far away was crouched tempting the river's delight with the wash of her hands and arms. She turned her head and spotted me, simply calling out with a deafening warm smile. True beauty is hard to find in this world, and true beauty that holds an appreciative notice to you and you alone is nearly impossible. A few years back, after our makeshifts had made that progressive leap into adulthood, I had once accidentally walked in on her in the bathing hut. She hadn't noticed at first, only because my footsteps were silenced by my awe of the atmospheric flickering candlelight that bounced an angelic glow of her silhouette in the tub behind the silk curtains.

Any other boy my age, or older, for that matter, may have just about lunged into a scientific and experimenting curiosity determining the measurable proportions of an additional person jumping into the tub. But I was never like that. And I never became that. To me, she sat in the silence of a calm night's comfort, maybe giving a soothing musical hum as she soaked the cloth and ran it over her shoulder, letting the drops roll down her arched bare back. It was at that moment that my heart skipped. I was not a wandering young man who had seen and persisted to spy on a beautifully-crafted woman within a porcelain white tub. I was a young man who for the first time was privileged to see a woman in her utmost perfect tranquility with herself, swarmed by an array of dancing candlelight firefly flickers that guided tenderly lenient eyes to lay on me as her chin laid on the pedestal of a graceful shoulder. She didn't jump. She didn't cover herself, or yell, or scream. She manifested a simple, bashful smile and continued welcoming the cloth of a soundless evening's personal perfection.

And again my heart skipped to that flawless construction of a woman's soul as she caressed and washed her hands in the river; her eyes being mercifully carried by the current to my heart. She saw me as me. She saw my hand as a dancing invitation to run out in the middle of the night through a forest of fantastical rapture and leap with her off a cliff into a lake, blanketing each other with only the entanglement of our arms and the floating buoyancy of passionate kisses under a twilight's roof of stars.

We went to that place often.

That place of soulful sincerity and boundless dependency.

That place of love.

And love is a place where all of us belong.


It was at the fork when Bixley had started barking out obscenities over my sudden declaring stop of the wagon. "It's a right, in case you've forgotten," he seemed to snip with superior tone.

"I'm well aware of that," I blurted back to him.

"Then why are we stopped? We just took a rest an hour ago," he added.

"Well aware of that also," I noted. "But you see, the thing about going right is that it has this history of taking a long time."

One of the other men huffed out with, "As it's the only way, we really can't help that. Unless you've managed to find the secret to making this wagon fly."

The other man broke out a quick witted chuckle. I nodded my head to the path on the left. "How about going left?" I gestured.

The chuckling stopped. A turtle cracking a twig with its foot a mile away could've been heard in the silence that followed. Even Tristan looked at me with a flat face. "You're not serious," she said, hinting with a waiting notion that I was joking.

"Of course he isn't serious; he's damn well *crazy* if he thinks he's leading us that way," Bixley snapped.

"Why? Because of this "monster"? Who's really crazy here?" I pointed out.

"Your father was very explicit to stick to the long trail," Thomas reminded me, as if acting like a nagging conscience. "No detours or risks along the way."

"This isn't a damn risk, Thomas. It's fact. Going left through the West Woods is shorter and will cut our time in half. We can be at the Far Village of the North tonight instead of tomorrow afternoon and bypass any idiotic hindrance of this so-called monster — which is *not* fact," I sharply explained.

"No! Absolutely not! I will not enter those woods!" one of the men said, as if a frightened stir began to ring out between everyone.

"The West Woods is inhabited by the monster, and those who have not returned from their exploring curiosity have further proven its existence," Bixley stated. "Plenty of men have sat in the very spot you abuse now and pondered what you're thinking. Those who have gone left — have never returned."

"*There is no monster!*" I yelled with my annoyance getting the best of me. "You've all been fooled by these pathetic bedtime tales that some jokester put into effect ages ago and has since been the sole responsible guilty party of costing us years of lost time and energy by going through the valley. Well, I'm through with that! I'm sick and tired of being the laughing stock of myself by ever having allowed my mind to accept such an absurd lunacy!"

Tristan had laid a concerned hand onto my arm as if trying to transfer some of her calming energy into my body. "Perhaps there is nothing there," she suggested. "But the valley is safer. We know it. Besides — I like the valley. It's so pretty this time of year."

She was trying to get me to keel over to her girlish persuasions. And although many a thousand times I had succumbed to her, it just wasn't going to work.

"Look," I firmly spoke out with, "this isn't about reputation or beliefs. I'm trying to improve the journey so that life can be better for everyone back at the village. Somebody had to do it sometime."

"But the monster!" one of the two other men shimmered out with.

I cleared my throat and took a commanding grip to the reins. "This wagon is going left. Through the West Woods. Where it will arrive back to the village with all of our supplies earlier than expected," I said with authority. "Anyone who still wishes to be childish is free to get off. I'll go to the Far Village of the North by myself, if I have to, and then everyone — including all of you — will see that I was right all along. You'll miss being part of the defining trip that will change how we do things."

There was another rumble of silence, almost as if they were contemplating their decision. I looked at Tristan. I didn't want it to be this way. I really didn't. And of course I wouldn't just leave her behind, but this entire notion was ridiculous. I only wanted her to see that. She arched a sheepish expression over to me as her soft eyes sifted into mine. "You know I'll go where you go," she quietly answered.

It didn't take any further argument to get the horses and wagon moving again. Left. Toward the West Woods. Toward the monster that had forever seemed to plague a handicap onto our way of life.


I only wanted to help the village.

And sure, maybe come back out of the situation as a hero. As the one individual who defied the laws of beliefs by shifting into the no-nonsense approach to travel. I had envisioned arriving back home with a wagon full of our needed goods far ahead of schedule, the villagers inquisitively popping their heads out of their huts or stopping their raking of the fields to see how in the world that was possible. Thomas and the other men would gallantly jump off the wagon and go running toward them with laughing smiles, excitedly unraveling explanations of our West Woods trip through and back and how we dodged the menacing jaws of the monster with the weapon of gullibility to its false existence. Even Bixley would feel a bit burned by finally realizing that I was right all along. Maybe he would even try to play it off. "It made a damn good legend at least. It probably *was* really alive years ago and died, so we're just lucky," he would grumble, continuing to be the sour sore-loser. Tristan would shower me with kisses and affection of being the one who took the shovel and buried the rumors for good. "So brave," she would playfully congratulate, nuzzling her nose into my neck. My father of course would scold me by not following through with his orders, giving the whole "you-could-have-put-everything-and-everyone-in-jeopardy-by-taking-that-chance" line, even though I would retort as the son who positively would keep declaring, "But we made it, didn't we? Everything *did* go well, didn't it?" I knew that in his mind he would be glad everything went well and I took that chance, since it would better improve our village travel. And once the word spread! Boy, what a feeling that would be! The villagers revealing to the neighboring villages that the West Woods was now a safe haven. And I was the one who made it that way. Life would be changed all across the lands. Emotional tensions would finally be given slack. Maybe I wouldn't be carried by everyone in celebration, but I would certainly receive more "hello's" everywhere I went. A tale over many campfires to my grandchildren with Tristan — I was the hero who slain the monster perception with bravery, and she would shimmer an aged smile that could only be thinking, "And I was there with him to witness."

Left. I should've gone right. In life, there are many forks in the road. Sometimes we know where one direction leads while the other holds the temptation of new frontiers. And when we take one of those directions, we get to more forks, which in turn lead us to chains of different paths through life — all with endless combinational possibilities that could have simply been changed by turning down the other direction just one of those times.

The West Woods were dreary. I had never been inside its perimeters, as of all my other riding companions. There was nothing too out of the ordinary for its presence. The trees and bushes were as green as they could be. Maybe an occasional bird chirped here and there. The sunlight even brightly found its way by shading plenty of daylight through the plush foliage roof above.

But still — there was something dreary, and when I was beginning to feel pretty good about my decision, I had noticed Bixley and the two other men constantly turning their heads in a state of wary uneasiness. Even Thomas appeared to be off his hinges, slowly walking alongside the wagon as it rolled down the path. I saw that his left hand was tightly gripped to the edge, surprised that he wasn't being privy to splinters. It was in the face of Tristan that my skepticism began to rapidly decline. Her eyes were scanning the forest. Her body was stiff, hands folded in her lap. The sound of a pin dropping could have sent her off the wagon. I wanted to playfully tickle her hip and make note of what a great place it would have made for a picnic.

But my regret started to fill. They were all in a lurid state, riding with the feeling of an animal sensing an approaching storm. The animals always know. Humans only lose the majority of that sense from their intellectualism. But even we know when something's not right. And it's easiest to tell from the person you love. It's not about knowing the person better than yourself, knowing what scares them, knowing what mood they're in — it's about the symbiotic relationship you share together. That you're so well-connected you can feel them inside you.

And something was scaring her.

The woods seemed to go forever, and since none of us had any true record of how far it was to the other side, it was difficult to guesstimate how much longer it would be, even if the overall outcome *was* known and proven to be shorter than the valley approach. I wanted to ease their edginess by saying we would be out soon, or maybe give a casual pick-up-the-pace snap-of-the-reins for the horses so that we could physically move faster, but even the horses seemed a bit reclusive.

That's when they stopped. A sudden jolt of the wagon and everyone was on the edge of insanity. The horses neighed and jerked back, jumping upright as I tried to pull the reins and keep them from escaping. "Something's gotten into them," Thomas noted.

Bixley jolted his body from side to side, clutching the wagon. "It's the monster!"

"Everyone just settle down," I told them, trying to keep a rational state.

"God help us," one of the men blurted. "We should have never gone in here! We should've kept to the valley road. *We should have never gone in here!*"

The roar erupted through the forest.

It was unlike anything I had ever heard before. There was a sickeningly echoing inhuman quality to it. Tristan gasped; her breathing starting to fluctuate rapidly as her jaw quivered. She gave a scared squeak, huddling into me as her body trembled.

"The monster," Bixley gulped with a softer, unbelievable tone.

Everyone shot their heads in different directions, trying to locate the source as the ground shook with a tremor. And then another. And another. The rumbles were like thunder, stomping their way closer and closer. "Where is it?!" one of the men irrationally shouted, looking into the endless greenery.

"Get us out of here!" Thomas ordered, trying to slap some sense into me.

The horses went berserk. I couldn't hang onto the reins any longer for fear of literally getting yanked out of my seat, and they neighed loudly, giving a trollop to freedom as they broke free and away from our wagon.

The monster came fast. Due to its massive size, it was unapparent at how we couldn't spot it coming from a mile away, but I suppose it used the bulk of the trees and forest to hide itself until it was in approachable distance. It was at least thirty feet tall, covered from head to toe in a brown and maroon-shaded reptilian skin and muscle. It didn't seem to have much of a neck, as the bulkiness of its round head seemed to sit hunched on its shoulders with a flattened face. That of course didn't hinder its anatomy for containing a massive mouth to which it immediately bellowed a roaring snarl with, menacingly threatening a good amount of randomly spaced jagged fangs that seemed more like spikes at their size. Thick, oozing saliva would cascade from the corners as if making tiny waterfalls. With a simple backhanded long-armed motion from one of its clawed gigantic hands, it took out a tree as splinters and leaves trickled like rain. Everything about it was immensely colossal. In fact, its two black beady eyes were its only real true smaller feature, but even those glistened with a nightmarish trance.

Tristan screamed at the top of her lungs. I had never heard her scream like that before. Bixley, Thomas and the other two men cowered back. My mouth hung open as my eyes stared up toward the horrible monstrosity, sheltering Tristan behind me.

"My God in heaven!" Bixley cried with astonishment, jumping off the wagon.

The other two men wasted no time following as I quickly urged Tristan to do the same. As we had all exited the wooden wagon, the monster swung a hand down and strongly batted it through the air and into some trees, making it shatter into a million pieces upon lavish impact. The items and goods inside flew everywhere, broken.

Natural immediate instinct had plundered me that our only option was to run, but the monster was too quick. It barked another roar and backhanded one of the men, knocking him to the ground. It reached forward and grabbed Thomas as if he were a small doll in its hand, but he wiggled his way free of its deadly grasp and fell to the ground below, cracking his leg with a painful holler.

The monster turned to Tristan and I. I tried to keep her behind me, picking up some rocks and throwing them, but they merely bounced off as a nuisance. The creature snarled and snapped its jaws as it swiped a hand down toward me. I managed to dip out of its path, bringing Tristan down to the ground with me. But the monster had rebounded its attempt quickly, turning to scoop her up within its claws. There was nothing I could do to stop it. "No!" I cried out, trying to jump in hopes of catching at least her foot.

It was at this point that Bixley, among the other men, had shifted his attitude into not running or protecting his well-being but actually fighting back as he picked up a rock and heaved it at the monster's stomach. The other two men began to do the same, grabbing rocks and hurling with all their might trying to be careful not to hit Tristan, who at the top of her fear screamed out, calling my name to her aid.

"*Nooo! Put her down!*" I wildly screamed, rushing toward the beast.

The monster, in all of its unsympathetic form, persisted on clutching and squeezing her tightly as it used its other free arm to fend off the incoming rocks. Bixley and the other two men had managed to get to the wagon wreckage and pulled a few spears, now inching closer to the monster as they poked and prodded. The creature roared, stepping back and fumbling about in its stomping footsteps in response to the pricks the blades dully gave its skin. It was probably more than likely the spears would be enough in bringing down the monstrosity but it was more of an issue of actually getting in a good shot, as the size of the monster and its constant defensive motors made it difficult, much like a raving lion would act.

Tristan was swung all over as if in its defense the monster had forgotten she was a toy in its grasp. I couldn't take it anymore. I felt so helpless. The only thing I could think to do was hurry over to the wreckage, where I found a sharp knife. Gripping its handle and clenching my teeth, I ran full speed toward and behind the beast as it was backed into a series of trees. I climbed my hardest. And if it weren't for the branches and natural foot holes, it most likely would have taken me much longer to get up to height and increased my chances of the monster moving away or even simply turning to bat me down. I wasn't thinking. I was acting. And my intuition signaled for me to take a leaping jump from the thick branches onto the monster's back, where I gripped and rode its round neckless head. The men continued to holler as they poked their spears, but the monster's attention was now mostly diverted to me — the itch on its back that even with long arms it couldn't seem to scratch. It swayed and tried to turn, making for a ride as I gripped its cold scaly skin tightly with one hand and the knife in a downward pointing manner in the other. I started to stab. At first I was just hitting its back and lower head, sputtering some blood as it yelped and attempted to shake me free. I thrust my hand repeatedly faster and faster as more blood flew.

The monster roared. It had now thrown Tristan out of its hand like a rag doll. I didn't see where she had landed or how far, but it was the final ignition to a fiery inner rage. I screamed and climbed higher onto his head, bringing the knife into its beady black eye. It shrieked an indescribably insane cry as its black puss splattered and sputtered. I kept thrusting the knife, unsatisfied. It was getting harder to hang on. After I had done all I could do with that eye, I moved to the next and stabbed, repeating my angry strike as it arched back and howled.

I just remember finally being tossed off and hitting the ground hard; the weeping sounds of the beast getting further and further away as it painfully trudged through the forest, covering its eyes with one arm as it held forward the other to prevent it from bumping into trees. I coughed and winced. Luckily I had landed right and nothing seemed broken. Aside from some cuts and bruises, I was in adequate shape as Bixley and the two men jogged over and helped me to my feet. My head swam with a rush of blood as I took a quick moment to come to my senses.

And I saw her.

Lying within the brush close by.

I gasped as my breathing froze, eyes going wide and unblinking as I pushed past the men. I slid to a stop in front of her, slowly dropping to my knees.

She didn't move. And although apart from the bruises and injuries her body obtained, she looked unharmed, but she didn't move. I didn't know what to think. I gave her a shake, lightly patting her cheek. She didn't respond. I put my head down to her chest and listened. There was no soothing breath. There was no heartbeat. So many times before I had laid my ear upon her life center as she would caress fingers softly through my hair. "It's beating for *you*," she would whisper.

But I felt nothing. A tiny optimistic part of me kept saying that in a second or two she would weakly open her eyes. Her chest would rise with a sudden intake of air. She would maybe ask for some water.

Her eyes never opened.

Bixley stood nearby watching with some remorse as the other two men tended to the injured condition of Thomas. My eyes glistened as my jaw and cheeks quivered. This couldn't be happening. This wasn't right. I scooped my arms under her legs and back and lifted her into me, cradling her close as I streamed some fingers across her still face. A thousand thoughts and emotions raced through my head that I could not tame or control. *Please. Don't let this be it.* I would gladly have cut my limbs off or detached any needed interior organs if that were the case. I just wanted her to open her eyes, so the world could start moving again. And following the delusion of hope came an immediate and immensely unwanted acknowledgment of acceptance. *But it couldn't be like this.* Don't let it be like this without any kind of proper goodbye. It wasn't fair. My insides dried out like a forgotten well. I felt cold. I felt nauseous. I didn't want to let her go.

But she was gone.

She never woke up.

Her eyes never opened.


It was sundown when we had finally arrived back at the village; golden light from an aged day shedding across the lands under a purple sky. The villagers had popped their heads out of their huts or stopped working in the fields to the surprise of our return on foot. But no one had cheered. No one had come rushing over to us in surprised excitement. Instead, they stood and watched as Bixley carried what materials he could salvage from the wagon wreck, followed by the other two men carrying a poorly-constructed stretcher that held Thomas and his injured leg. It was then that the villagers had broken from their statuesque state and began to swarm around them, immediately asking questions and aiding to Thomas. Among them, my father watched and turned his attention back to the trail.

I had arrived last; Tristan wrapped within a tattered white bed sheet as I carried her in my arms.


I remember my father always telling me that a hero was the everyday man who would work hard to provide for himself, his family and the well-being of his village. A hero accomplished an amazing task because he had to, not because he wanted to.

Nobody had carried me on their shoulders. Nobody began to whirl astonishing stories of marvel that spread from place to place. Because of the West Woods incident, our materials and goods from the Far Village of the North weren't acquired in time, and before anyone had the chance to reorganize another expedition, the rain season hit. And it hit hard. At first only a few of the villagers had packed up and left in fear of the impending and inevitable life support failure, but it wasn't long after that the others began to follow. Proper crops were not planted in time. Food for the animals was not received in the proper quantity and many did not last the rains.

The rains.

Often at times it was bad enough that I had trouble sleeping at night, but now that the rains had arrived, I would sit up in my bed and stare outside, occasionally glancing down to an empty spot beside me. That spot was always warm and inviting. And she would always awaken to my distraught sleeplessness to lightly tug at my shirt, guiding me back down as she cradled my head into her neck. "Shhh," she would gently hush, laying her plush lips onto my forehead. "Sleep. Just listen to the rain... Just listen to the rain... Our dreams are in the rain..."

I have since cried more tears than a thousand rains could bring.

The bad weather season did eventually tide over and went away, but there were still no cheers. The village was emptier now. Quieter. I would often work in the hay and wheat fields, scraping and raking the rocks and seeds as to be alone and unbothered. No one ever said "hello" when they passed by. There were no exciting stories around what campfires managed to surface. Occasionally within the village from time to time I had seen Thomas lingering about, limping his way around on crutches as he provided what work he could. He would give me an expressionless glance. I always wanted to say something, but the moment of opportunity always passed too quickly, and he was back on his way. But the place I spent the most time at was with her. Far off from the village on a grassy hill mound where others before us had laid, overlooking the vast mountainous possibilities in the distance. I would spend hours or even all day there, huddled against her gravestone as if trying to be some watcher or protector from eons of land-shifting changes that might threaten to break apart that only spot of solace and comfort I had remaining for me. There's always a sense of assuage in the places your loved ones have been. A room may seem ghostly from the memories of times spent within. A particular tree may seem sacred from the fact that you once guided one another to a slumbering summer's day sleep beneath its shielding and shaded leaves. And a hill may seem like your Mecca because it's just high enough to touch the heavens of the skies with your fingertips. The closest you can be to her.

It was the end of summer when the day came that I had slipped into a brown hooded robe and sharpened my spear. The air was getting cooler with a sense that fall was kissing the tips of the breeze. Soon the leaves would morph into their bright yellow, brown and orange colors that would illuminate the forests with a beautiful glowing era of change. The floating drop of every colored leaf to the ground seemed to always hint at the remembrance of a world once known and the precognition of one to emerge forward.

As I had walked down the path out of the village, my father was waiting for me. I stopped when I had reached him and didn't say anything, instead waiting for whatever bold parental authority he would try to block me with. He had stared at me firmly for a long dragging moment, until finally only saying, "It won't bring her back."

There was no retorting. No arguments, or cases made for the feelings inside me that I couldn't begin to speak out to him in words. So I simply passed him and walked onward.

It took me quite a while to walk, following the left path in the fork that led into the West Woods. The forest was as still as it had been before; giving off that false assurance of peaceful and beautifully safe tranquility I was so foolish to adhere to before. With each step, my heart thumped harder in anger. My hands gripped around the strong sturdy wood of the spear's long handle. It was more than enough. I didn't need an army of mobbing villagers to accompany me and help secure a definite victory. I wanted to do this alone. I felt it was the only proper way. The only proper justice. My eyes narrowed within the green foliage, scanning for any movement. I remembered the suddenness of the nightmare the last time and was all the more prepared for it this time. I would find it. Hunt it down. Find whatever deep, black, heartless cave it probably dwelled within and give it the thrust of an end that it so probably for a long time deserved. I would scour these West Woods for weeks if I had to.

But I didn't need to search for weeks. I didn't need to drag it out of its homestead. And I didn't need to prepare myself for a blindsided attack out of nowhere.

The monster was already there. Up ahead within the trees, I spotted it sitting; its back resting against the trunks with its stubby legs lying outward. *Perfect.* The best word to describe my response at that moment. In this case, I didn't have to charge forward like some kind of ancient crazed warrior. I could sneak up behind it and catch it by surprise. Oh, the satisfaction behind initiating a burning revenge that way. It wouldn't even see it coming. How scared it would be, in its massive towering size and power being taken down by a simple human. It probably had all sorts of plans, if monsters indeed had any, for that particular day — to terrorize helpless other smaller creatures, to lazily sleep within the confines of its comfortable cave, to bask in the coolness of the rushing river water as its own giant personal bathtub. And I would destroy all of those schemes, feeling all the more proud.

So I crept quietly closer and closer toward the beast. It may have been sleeping, but at my position I couldn't quite tell. *All the easier,* I would motivate myself by thinking. I was extremely careful as to where I stepped, as a tiny twig cracking or brush of leaves would give up my plan, not that it would make my attack any less desirable.

My breathing got faster. My adrenaline was pumping. I suppose a strike from behind may have been easier on the angle of surprise, but I wanted more than that. I wanted a strike to the heart, or the throat, or any of the other infinite places of choice on its front side that could allow me the sweet savoring taste of a faster victory. So I circled around and faced the beast as my jaw stiffly locked. My eyebrows bent down, and flames overtook the position of my pupils. *This was the damned beast that took my entire life out from under me.* I kept seeing the image of Tristan flash in my mind. Her ability to gesture in her small eleven-year-old hand the rest of her bread after I had finished mine. Her approach to not minding the sickness she would catch herself after spending so much time taking care of me whenever I was ill. Her charitable nature of tucking me with just a little bit more of the blanket on a cold winter's night. This monster knew nothing of her. *You don't know anything of her. You know nothing of what I had. You had no right.*

I stood before it, holding my spear at the ready. The monster was not asleep. But it didn't jump up and roar. It didn't lunge for me. It didn't growl, or swipe down with its razor-sharp claws. It merely perked its head at the sound of my presence, holding to listen. It gave a soft snort, slightly turning its body. I wanted to drive the spear into its chest while I had the chance. But there was something odd about its reluctance to striking such an easy prey before it. And that's when I noticed the eyes. The spots where they should have been, bolstering their beady black evil darkness, were now scarred and patched up with the natural overtake of time and skin growth. It couldn't see me. It could sense I was there, but it couldn't see me.

It was blind.

Tactical warfare immediately shot through my mind. I couldn't wish for an opportunity better than this. Sneaking wasn't even necessary. All I had to do was take a few casual steps up to it and drive the spear into its heart. I even had the time now to perfectly climb onto its legs and mark a target spot if I wanted.

But I hesitated. Something kept me frozen as I stood and studied the creature. Surely over time its remaining senses would have developed to at least some better level, but it seemed... distraught. Sad. It turned its upper body, veering its neckless head to listen for a moment. One of its clawed hands slightly moved but set back down resting on its legs as it took a deep breath and gave a long, sagging sigh, shoulders sinking as its head veered down.

Mixed emotions overcame me. I stiffened my position and held my spear ready, holding back the onslaught of a tearful cry. "You took her away from me," I said aloud, grinding my teeth. "You took *everything* away from me!"

Even to the sound of my voice, the monster didn't reply or spring up. It merely continued its steady depressed breathing. I took a gallant step forward, poking its leg with the spear. "*I hate you!*" I shouted, flipping the spear around and whacking it over and over with the blunt wooden handle. "Get up! Get up and fight me, damn it! Come on! I'm right here!"

The monster still sat there, letting me hit it again and again, letting out a wheezing soft murmur. I stopped hitting when the tears began to flow, helplessly dropping the spear as I fell on my hands and knees. The realization had only then hit me. The monster never killed Tristan.

I had killed her.

I put her in danger by bringing her out to these woods despite her objections. But she loved me enough to trust me. To trust me with her life, and what had I done? Jesus, what had I done? I had taken it away from her. My arrogance and cockiness had gotten the best of me. If only I had taken that right in the fork. Spent that extra time on the trail and gotten our supplies from the Far Village of the North. No one would be congratulating me for braving a successful incursion into the West Woods, but instead complimenting me on a first-run job that replenished the goodness of our way of life. Thomas wouldn't need his crutches to hike about the village. And Tristan would be safe.

My father was right. Killing the monster wouldn't have brought her back or made me feel any better. I saw what I had done to the beast, and a sense of remorse and pity overcame me inside as I got back to my feet. I should have the right to hate this monster. And maybe I did. But the damage had been done. There was nothing more for me there in those woods. I wiped the wetness from my eyes and turned, leaving the spear on the ground as I began to walk back the way I came.

The monster continued to sit there, softly breathing in its state of repentance.


I was twenty-three-years-old the first time I saw a monster.

And for the first time, I now felt like one. I don't know what it was that hit my heart inside — seeing the blind monster there punish itself with its helplessness. Maybe it was guilty for what it had done. Or perhaps maybe its greatest weapon, its eyesight, was taken away from it. It felt handicapped. Rabbits or squirrels could now taunt it just as it had terrorized them. What place would it have in this world now? What purpose?

And what place would *I* have? What would I do now? Where could I go but back to where I felt the warmth of her love on that hill overlooking the lands. The pain subsides a little every day, but it will always be there, as with the guilt of what I had done. What I fool I had been. I often wondered if she would ever forgive me, and that thought always seemed to circle back to the notion of who she was in life. She was forgiving. In my restless dreams I see her come to me and lay that forgiving hand against my cheek. Perhaps assuring myself that she would forgive me if she knew what happened to her made me feel even worse and more guilty sometimes.

There are all kinds of monsters in this world. They just appear differently on the outside. The terror one monster can wreck with its appearance, another can wreck with its emotions.

I wasn't a monster. But I felt like one. I knew the anguish of a monster's rage, and the pain of the turmoil from its repercussions. Perhaps with that, we can all show no fear, and anything in this world is possible. If in some way every monster can each feel another monster's suffering, then maybe we can all learn something from each other.

# THE CHOSEN

"Sela..."

And this time, Sela sat upright in bed with a short gasp, clutching the entanglement of sheets to her chest. She was absolutely sure she heard it this time because now she was awake, and although she wasn't *wide* awake, she was still positive it wasn't just her ears playing tricks on her. "What?" she had sleepily and softly asked, turning her head so her dazed eyes could scan the dark room.

Her breathing calmed down a bit as she swiped the back of her hand across her forehead, which glistened with the aftermath sweat that only a nightmare or disturbing dream could deliver. But she wasn't dreaming. She had heard it again. "Dale?" she called out, raising her voice a little higher.

She finally unwrapped herself and swung her feet off the bed and onto the floor, walking through the darkness as she planted her hands against the walls for balance until she reached the living room, where Dale was asleep on the couch.

"Dale," she strongly whispered, circling around it.

When he didn't wake, she bent down and shook him, repeating his name at a higher volume until he snorted awake and looked around. "W-What?" he mumbled, trying to get a grip within those first few seconds of lucidness.

"Did you call my name?" she asked him.

He rubbed his eyes and scratched his head. "What?"

"My name. I heard you calling my name," she insistently told him.

"I've been sleeping," he groaned, clearing his throat. "You're hearing things; go back to bed."

"I heard it. You were calling my name, and telling me to go to the mine north of town. This is the third night in a row."

Dale turned on the couch, shifting the uncomfortable pillow as he tried to tuck himself back into a sleeping position. "I didn't say anything. You were probably dreaming," he attempted to convince her.

"But I heard it," she repeated, now growing as an annoyance to him.

"Then *I* was dreaming and talking in my sleep," he blurted, giving in.

She sat there for some long dragging moments, of course, as most persistent wives would, until he had fallen back asleep within moments. She gave a sigh, as if waiting for him to wake back up and notice that she was still upset. But he didn't budge. He didn't care. His own wife could be going crazy for all he knew and he didn't give a damn.

At least she didn't think she was going crazy. She was sure of what she heard.

Someone was calling her name, in the middle of the night, for the third night in a row.




Sela hated psychologists. Shrinks. To her, they were the highest form of offense on Earth. What kind of person charged another person to listen to their problems? They just sat there, elbow sitting on the armrest of their high and mighty chair with their fist balled under their chin, listening and listening. Constantly repeating, "Yes... Yes... Uh-huh. Yes. I see. Tell me more." For Sela, help meant enlisting in the advice from friends or family, the *real* people to go to, that actually gave a damn about you. She was more than certain that shrinks really got off on the power they had sitting on that chair. Of course the people hashing out their problems are damaged and hurting. The shrink knew that whatever they told them to do was the final word on things. "I'm a professional and this is what I think of your problem, so I'm right. Pay me now." Sure, the psychologist might actually want to genuinely help people, which is a good quality to find in any individual, but to take advantage of them by charging them for it — charging them an outrageous price — was ridiculous.

But, Sela knew as well as any other married woman that sometimes keeping a marriage together meant asking for help. And that's why she was sitting there in that boring room with Dale. It wasn't like she didn't want things to get better between them, but she certainly figured they could do it without emptying their bank account in the process.

"Sela?" Dr. Connelly spoke out with.

Sela glanced to Dale, who scratched his hair as he waited in the chair next to her.

"How do you feel about that?" Dr. Connelly further added, crossing her legs in the seat across from them.

"How do I feel about what?" Sela wondered.

Dale grumbled, lightly tossing a hand in the air. "And here's that part about not listening I was referring to."

Sela closed her eyes and rubbed her face. "I'm listening. I just... I didn't get much sleep again last night."

"Oh, yeah — the voices in the dark," Dale huffed, shaking his head.

"Not voices. Voice," she immediately corrected him. "Jesus Christ; you make it sound like I'm having a conversation with an imaginary person in our room at night."

"What "voice", Sela?" Dr. Connelly inquisitively asked.

Sela sighed. Dale perked his eyebrows. "She says she's heard someone calling her name the past few nights," he told her.

"Look, I wasn't dreaming, and I'm not crazy," she insisted. "I keep hearing someone say my name and tell me to go to the mine outside of town."

"Was it a woman's voice or a man's?" Dr. Connelly noted.

"I... I dunno... I can't tell," Sela answered.

"This mine — have you ever been there?"

"Never. I never even knew we had one until I looked it up," Sela added.

Dr. Connelly gave a soft nod, jotting something down in her notes. "Uh-huh," she mumbled. There it was — the psychologist "Uh-huh". Dr. Connelly lightly tapped her pen against her jaw. "Tell me something, Sela, and don't think that this is my deduction, but — are you still on your anti-depressants?"

Sela darted her eyes to Dale. How arrogant of her to ask! How dare her to even use her professionalism in a manner of logically assuming that she was crazy. Dale looked away, trailing his eyes through the office until they landed on Dr. Connelly's legs. Sela noticed. She knew what he was thinking. It was obvious. Even without their marital problems laid out on the table, he was a guy, and she was good-looking. Probably even better looking in her suit, with that crafty intelligence showing behind her glasses rather than in her breasts. Sela snapped her thoughts back to the issue at hand and gave a careless shrug. "It's not the medication, if that's what you're implying."

"I didn't mean to imply anything," Dr. Connelly kindly retorted. "Maybe this voice or sound you're hearing is just an effect of your surroundings, like a rotating fan or something."

"My fucking fan is not talking to me," Sela snapped, rigidly narrowing her eyes on her. "I don't even know why we're talking about this. This is not what we're paying to be here for."

"You're here for you," Dr. Connelly calmly reminded her. "If you weren't concerned about yourself and Dale then you wouldn't be here, so you're already making great progress just by doing that."

Sela slightly rolled her eyes, shifting in her seat.

Dr. Connelly turned a page in her notes. "Let's get back to talking about adoption."

"I don't want someone else's kid," Sela bluntly stated. "I want my own baby. From *me*."

Dr. Connelly licked her lips as if trying to come up with the correct reply approach without upsetting her further. "I understand that, Sela. And Dale understands that also. But sometimes... we just have to reach a point where you have to accept what's happening and... consider seeking alternatives."

"What? I have to just sit back and accept what a couple doctors say over a few measly tests? I'm twenty-seven-years-old. I still have lots of time. There's still a chance," she presented. She firmly stood up. "I'm gonna have a baby. And no one with any fancy medical degree, or PhD, or plaque on the wall is gonna assure me otherwise."

With that, she stormed out of the room, leaving Dale to take an exasperated breath. He gave a tired gesture and said, "That's what it's been like with her."

"She's hurting, Dale," Dr. Connelly implied. "She's hearing all these people tell her she won't ever be able to have the one thing she wants. And denial is a reaction you have to counteract with continuing support and love. You have to stay positive, and keep encouraging her. She may not show it, but she needs you now more than ever."

Dale bobbed his head and casually stood up. "Thanks, Dr. Connelly. We'll see you next week."

He left out of her office and exited the building to see Sela sitting on a bench outside, joining her and letting the traffic of the street in front of them be their only source of sound. "I'm trying my best," he opened up with. "But I don't know what you want from me, because you won't let me in."

"You're giving up too easily," she stated.

"I'm not giving up, Sela," he disagreed. "I'm just... preparing myself for the harsh reality being presented to us. I don't wanna accept it any more than you but the longer we hold onto a hope that has no cause, the more we're gonna hurt down the road. The doctors said that it's probably not going to happen."

She stiffened her jaw and held back a pair of watery eyes. "How many times do I have to say that I don't care what the doctors think they know? We can keep trying."

"Yeah, on the bed with you or on the couch with me?"

"I never said you had to stay out there."

"You said you wanted your space and I'm trying to give it to you. And then you say you wanna keep trying. So which is it? Just tell me what to do, and I'll do it. I love you, Sela. You can't push me away forever," he explained, laying a comforting hand on her shoulder.

She slowly moved aside, letting it slip off as she stood up and rubbed her nose. Dale regrettably sighed, giving up and letting his hands flop into his lap as he pulled out his keys and walked away.

It was a ride home in silence they were both all too familiar with.

They had later arrived at their one-story house outside of the city. A section of it was still unfinished and it definitely needed to be repainted. And judging from the back of Dale's carpenter pickup truck they had arrived in, it was a job that increasingly got held back from being finished, no doubt from other issues they were presently and more importantly busy trying to handle. But Dale was always chipping away at it bit by bit, most likely as a personal excuse to escape from those issues. And as he got out of the truck and reached into the back to grab a paint can, Sela circled around to meet him. "Can I use the truck?" she asked, holding a waiting hand out.

"Where are you going?" he asked.

"I just wanna be alone right now," she told him. "I'll be home for dinner."

He was strongly hesitant, and it showed in his face as her mood became a bit more sympathetic. "I'm not gonna drive off a cliff," she smoothly assured him.

He reached into his pocket and gave her the keys without any arguments or further questioning, turning as he carried the paint can toward the house. "Dale?" she called out, making him stop and re-face her as he waited for her to continue.

But she didn't say anything. She opened her mouth to say something, but held back as if changing her mind. Instead, she took a few wary steps over to him and laid a soft kiss onto his lips. "I just..." she began, fumbling with her emotions, "I haven't done that in a while, and... I wanted to do that."

He gave her a flat look. It was understanding and mutual, but somewhat heartbroken and reminiscing, as if they both took it as it was and left it at that. So he continued walking to the house as she hopped into the truck and drove off.

Sela pulled to a stop, kicking up some dust in front of the old abandoned mine entrance located within the jagged and rocky cliffs of the desert. She got out and took a look around, secure with the fact that she was practically in the middle of nowhere with no soul in sight. The entrance was gated off, chained with a thick padlock along with an accompanying sign that threateningly read with bold letters, "DANGER — MINE CLOSED. KEEP OUT!"

She wasn't sure what the mine was used for exactly or why it had been closed, only that it had been closed for quite a few decades based on her limited research. And she wasn't going to let any menacing sign or gate keep her away from discovering why that voice had mentioned for her to go there. As she dug through the back of the pickup truck for a large hammer, she was wondering if she *was* in fact crazy. There she was, about to break into an abandoned mine based on the command of some voice she had heard for three nights in a row. It was probably all in her head, or based on some side-effect of her medication. She wasn't stupid. She knew those were the most logical reasons, even if she didn't want to admit it to Dale and Dr. Connelly. But she was stubborn, and *something* in her gut was telling her to go into that mine. She figured if anything, going inside and seeing a whole lot of nothing would at least solve the problem and put her mind at ease.

So with a flashlight in one hand and gripping the hammer tightly in the other, she walked over to the gate and peeked through the bars, then struck the old rusted padlock with a heavy swing. It took three or four tries, but it finally broke loose as she unhooked it and unraveled the snake-like chain so she could push her way forward into the tunnel. A part of her felt a bit odd about the breaking-and-entering aspect of the ordeal, as she was never the type to even jaywalk, but her guilty conscience was put at ease with the thought that no one would even ever come out there to notice let alone care. Based on the age of the rusted lock and chains, it was evident that if no teenagers itching for a party spot had attempted to bust in by now, then no one would give a worry on whether or not the mine was still secure and not tampered with.

She clicked on her flashlight and began to follow the old railroad track line that sloped downward, spotting a control box on the wall. She stepped over and inspected it, pulling the large lever up as electricity sparked and geared on throughout the tunnel, still able to generate power after all that time unused. Of course, the flashlight still helped as she trekked onward down the tunnel, ducking under various rotted wooden beams and swiping her way through dusty cobwebs. She pointed her light in every nook and cranny, but only saw what she expected to see — old tools, boxes, stacked beams and various cars on the track every now and then. She felt as if she were walking for quite a while, and limited her turns as to not get lost, even though there were old faded maps pinned to the walls in every section. It was quiet and eerie, with the exception of the occasional light dripping of water from pipes above or the ghostly whistling of air coming from various shafts. She thought she spotted a rat scurry into the wall through the brief beam of her light, which disturbed her even more. And she was nearly ready to give up and turn back around when a faint green light began to pour between the cracks and openings of a boarded room behind her.

She turned and confusingly cocked her eyebrows, shining her flashlight. At first, she thought it may have been a trick of light, perhaps a section of the electricity was starting to die out or short-circuit. It was unlikely that the workers would have purposely used a color filter for their light down there, but then again, she didn't know a thing about mining or mine tunnels, and perhaps it had something to do with that particular area or maybe even a safety issue. No, that wasn't it. This light was green. Green. A very out of place abnormal green. It seemed to get brighter as she crept closer to the boards. Her stomach turned. A fear coiled inside her. And even though her lucid brain was telling her to run out of there, something was gnawing at her to get inside. It wasn't just curiosity. She *had* to get into that room.

Sela started hammering away at some of the boards, prying and ripping them off until eventually creating an opening large enough for her to slip through. She ducked her way into the small room, a bit in awe at the sight before her. The object was egg-shaped and set within the rocky wall, the only thing in the room. And it was definitely the source of the green glow, although it didn't appear to be electronic in any way. She took slow and small steps toward it, brushing some hanging cobwebs out of her path. A slight low-level hum came from the object, perhaps not too noticeable but definitely supplying a lifelike essence as she moved closer, stretching out her hand as her unblinking eyes stared. As Sela reached closer, the object gave a stronger breath of more green light, causing her to slightly retract. She started moving her hand forward again, and the light pulsated in soft repetitions like it were a slow heartbeat.

The object was solid, a bit bumpy and somewhat metallic as she skimmed her fingers over it and through the surrounding cobwebs. That's when she felt its power. She closed her eyes and let it flow through her. She wasn't sure what was happening, but she liked it. It was as if she were rejuvenated. Her skin tingled. She could feel the life of her blood flowing through her. Her breaths were perfect in every way. It was like being purified. She reopened her eyes and turned her head. The green light faded, but was still evident within and surrounding the oval object. She wasn't sure what to make of it.

And she certainly wasn't sure what to tell Dale later that night when she was home preparing dinner. It was on the tip of her tongue to immediately blurt it out the second she got home, but for some reason she held back as he hammered away on the unfinished section. She had thought it over while she was cooking, especially when he finally came inside to wash up, but that's when the first incident occurred. She was over at the sink prepping the meal and moved her hand past the front of the microwave to reach for the cupboard above when it abruptly turned on; the light illuminating the interior as the plate inside slowly spun. She gave a strange look, moving her hand away as it turned off just as quickly. Assuming it had malfunctioned, she repeated her attempt to reach for the cupboard above when it once again turned back on with the passing of her hand. She froze and slowly dragged it away, seeing the device shut off. And with a curious reach, she touched the tips of her fingers to the top as it whirled back to life, startling her with a small gasp as she yanked her hand away. She looked back to Dale as he untied his boots near the door and suspiciously zeroed her eyes to the microwave, coasting her hand to push the button for the door to open when it exploded with a sparking burst, causing her to shriek and hop back.

Dale quickly jetted over, grabbing her hips and guiding her away. "Jesus," he murmured with an astonished expression. "Are you okay?"

She swallowed and nodded, warily looking over to the microwave. He stepped closer, opening a nearby window and waving the smoke as the last remaining sparks died out. He cautiously grabbed the door and pried it back open, peeking inside with a playful attempt at a grin. "Did you put a hotdog inside or something?" he wondered. He clutched the sides, zipping his hands away from the leftover heat. "Thing's gotta be older than *us* for Christ's sake."

After he was assured that she was okay and they were finally settled at the table eating their dinner, the second incident occurred. Dale had been chewing away at his pasta watching TV off to the side as Sela poked her fork into her salad bowl. He glanced over to her and spoke out with, "Everything okay?"

"Yeah. Fine," she answered with a zombie-like enthusiasm.

"You're quiet. You seem a little out of it," he noted.

She took a breath and ran a hand through her hair, plucking some lettuce onto her fork. "I'm — just tired, I guess. Probably go to bed early."

Dale nodded and took a sip of his beer, returning his eyes back to the TV. "All right. Think I'm gonna meet some of the guys for a drink in a bit," he mentioned.

She reached across the table for the pepper shaker as it wobbled in place, making her freeze her hand. The shaker stopped moving, and when she went to reach for it again, it tilted. She slightly bent her fingers, and it veered to the side. She waved her fingers back, and the shaker leaned the other way. Positioning her hand more upright like a wave, she slowly moved it forward as the shaker completely flew off the table on its own and fell to the floor, making her gasp as she quickly pulled her hand away, burying it in her lap. Dale turned, leaning out of his chair to pick the shaker up off the floor and set it back onto the table as he continued watching the TV.

But perhaps it was the third incident that finally gave Sela the notion that things weren't quite right with herself. She had gone to bed early like she had said she would while Dale retreated to join his friends for some drinks. She did remember waking up at one point later in the night when he eventually fumbled home, but fell back asleep as soon as his movement had settled onto the couch. Only she felt a bit drowsy, as if her head was plugged full of a cold that she tried to subside by taking the nighttime pills that would knock her out. Her eyelids were heavy every time she had opened them, and when they were closed, she felt as if she were dizzily spinning. And then a cool, relaxing feeling started to flow through her that wiped all that away. She felt comfortable and light. The bed was so soft that she couldn't even feel it anymore. She stretched her arms out and let them drop. It was as if she were floating.

Then she opened her eyes.

She *was* floating.

Her safety net of comfort was immediately replaced by fear-stricken panic as she turned her head all around, waving her hands and feet. She was a good height above the bed, nearly to the ceiling when she started to scream for Dale over and over. He groggily grumbled and slinked his way into the bedroom, tiredly stopping at the threshold. "What?" he had almost annoyingly asked. "What did you hear this time?"

His hand slapped against the wall beside him, clawing for the light switch until hitting it with a flick. His eyes lit up as bright as the lights that illuminated the room at the sight of Sela floating above her bed. "Jesus Christ!" he stammered, backing against the wall in surprise.

Sela dropped to the bed and landed with a bounce, kicking the sheets as she cowered against the backboard. Dale was speechless as he stared at her, mouth ajar. He kept looking back and forth from her to the ceiling above. She tried to catch her breath, clutching her chest as if someone had knocked the wind out of her. "Sela — what the hell just happened?! What the hell *was* that?!" Dale blurted.

She seemed just as confused and bewildered as him. And after a few minutes of calming down, when Dale was finally sitting on the bed beside her, she spilled it all out. "It was in the mine," she started, staring to the floor as she recollected in her head. "I just... I couldn't take it anymore. The voice that kept calling me and telling me to go there. I had to go and find out if I was crazy. So after we got home from Dr. Connelly's earlier and I went back out, I went there. I broke through the gate and went inside."

"Jesus, Sela," Dale upsettingly scolded. "You went down in there alone? Especially without telling anybody? You could've gotten hurt, and nobody would've been able to get to you."

"Would you have let me gone if I told you I was going there?"

Dale didn't have an answer for her. Perhaps she had a small point. She sat a little closer, dressing her face with a more serious expression as she looked at him. "Listen to me — when I was down there, I found this, this... thing. This thing in this room that was closed and boarded off. I don't know what it is or why it's there, but it... did something to me."

"What do you mean, "something"?" he wondered.

"I think it gave me some kind of... powers. These abilities. I mean, shit, Dale — I was *flying* over my bed."

"It was more like floating," he corrected, trying to throw some unfitting humor in.

"This isn't funny," she stiffly said. "I can fly, Dale. I know I can."

"What else can you do?"

Her eyes looked around the room until finding a picture of them framed on the dresser. She put her hand out and concentrated, slowly lifting it up in the air. Dale couldn't believe his eyes as she used her hand to float it across the room and set it on the nightstand beside them. "Is that all?" he asked, trying to recapture his breath.

So she took him outside to the driveway and walked over to the pickup truck, stopping before its front end. He wanted to say something and showed concern at what he thought she was about to do, but said nothing as she did it anyway. Tucking her hands underneath the bumper, she lifted the entire truck's front end as if it were a light lawn chair, softly setting it back down and turning to reface him. "Have you done that before?" he asked her.

She shook her head. "It's like when you wake up after a great night's sleep, or you're hyped up on caffeine, and you just feel like you can lift a million pounds. It's like that, only something inside me doesn't *feel* like I can do it. I *know* I can do it."

Dale stared at the truck for a long moment, swallowing the lump in his throat. He tried to search for words to explain it all, but he only ended up saying, "Take me to it. I wanna see it."

It was a short while later after they had gotten dressed that Dale and Sela found themselves pulling the truck up to the abandoned mine entrance in the middle of the night. They clicked on their flashlights as Sela led him through the gate and inside, descending and twisting down the shaft for quite a while until she stopped and pointed her flashlight in various directions, growing a bit bothered. "I know it's around here," she noted, but the tone in her voice was unsure.

Dale turned, directing his light in another direction. "Maybe we took a wrong turn?"

"No," she insisted. "I'm sure it was here. I'm not making this up, Dale."

"After watching you fly around a room and practically lift a truck over your head, I don't doubt you are," he convinced her.

She walked forward and stopped, freezing her eyes down a tunnel that slowly began to glow to life with green. "Here," she blurted in a trance-like manner. "We're here."

She led him down the tunnel and to the hole in the wall she had created, slipping inside and helping him through as he marveled at the egg-shaped object in front of them. He paced around it, confounded by its mysterious presence as it lightly gave its breathing hum. "My God," he mumbled. "What the hell is this thing? You just found it in here like this?"

"Yeah," she simply said.

"Why is it glowing? Did you turn it on or something?"

She shook her head. "No. It just started doing that when I came near it in the tunnel."

"What did you do?"

"I just touched it. Something made me feel like I had to touch it. Like something came over me," she replied. She closed her eyes and steadily breathed in with an essence of euphoria. "Don't you feel that?"

He looked at the object and then at her. "Feel what?"

"You don't feel that?"

"No. What does it feel like?"

"Like... like a dream. Like I'm at peace. Like a drug is flowing through my body. It's more pure than anything I've ever felt," she described, reopening her eyes. She looked at him. "Maybe if you touch it."

He gave the object a hesitant look. "Look, Sela — we don't know what this thing is or what it's doing to you."

"It's okay. You can touch it, honey," she calmly convinced. "It's safe."

He licked his lips and reluctantly extended his fingers out, slowly coasting them toward it until softly planting the tips against its grainy and rough surface. She cocked a hopeful half-smile, as if waiting for something to happen. "Do you feel anything?" she wondered.

Dale planted his hand more flatly against the object and began to feel around, shaking his head. "No," he said.

She stepped closer and did the same, planting her hand on its base as it seemed to pump more full of green life, making Dale step back and warily watch. "I can," she stated, letting the feelings surge into her.

"It seems to have quite the, uh... connection to you in particular," he then added. Something had caught his eye on the side of it as he zeroed in for a closer look. "What's this?"

She looked over to see the small round button he was pointing to. "I don't know. I didn't notice it before. It looks like some kind of button." She stuck her index finger forward, ready to plant it against the button as he suddenly grabbed her hand.

"What are you doing? Don't touch it," he ordered. "We have no idea what this thing is."

"And we won't know unless we push it," she suggested.

Dale sighed and placed his hands on his hips, turning and pacing away. "We shouldn't mess with this thing, Sela. I say we go find someone right now and tell 'em about it. And get you checked out, too."

"Are you kidding?" she outstandingly asked. "We can't tell *anybody* about this. This is the find of the century; maybe of all time! Haven't you seen what it's doing to me?"

"We have no fucking clue what it's doing to you!" he hastily retorted. "But frankly it's scaring the shit out of me! Something about this thing isn't right. I mean, it's not so much the fact of what it is, where it came from, or what it's doing to you, but why it's sitting buried and hidden in a room down in a closed mine after all this time."

"We can't let anyone take it away," she argued.

Dale gave a shrug. "It didn't do anything for me; maybe it'll work on someone else. Maybe it only works on women."

"Do you want doctors and scientists to start poking and cutting me up on some table? Huh?"

Dale took a deep breath. She stepped over to him, laying her hands on his arms as her sympathetic eyes met his. "Please, Dale. Just let me figure this out. Let's just see what happens, okay?"

He wanted to argue against it, he really did. His only initial instinct at that moment was to alert somebody — anybody — for her own safety. But, as she had done many times before, she got the best of him with a simple pleading look, and they retreated back to the house.

Perhaps if Dale didn't have to go into the city the next morning for some construction supplies, things may have gone differently. Perhaps if she didn't even go with him, they could've had more time to assess their strange situation. And perhaps if those small tree logs hadn't fallen off of that oncoming truck, she would never have garnered the position she was granted. But it did happen, regardless of the many endless combinations that could've changed their fates that simple Sunday morning. Neither got much sleep after returning from the mine, nor did they attempt to use their day off from her teaching and his carpentry construction to stay in bed longer and catch up. Dale thought he actually nodded off for a bit on the couch, and after he had snapped awake a handful of minutes later, tried to convince himself that what he had seen that night was just a dream after a bad evening of drinks with companions. But delusion was a luxury he wasn't giving himself, and his hopes were diminished when Sela had retrieved the coffee can — from across the kitchen.

As usual, he was going to set her out of his mind (this time for an actual decent reason) by doing some more work on the house, but he had needed a few supplies in the city. Sela decided to tag along, which was rare in their current state of relationship, as the complexities of scoring second grade test papers wasn't going to take up her entire day. The possible thought had crossed his mind that she didn't want to be alone after divulging her secret to him, so she hopped into the truck with him and they were on their way, both wordless to one another but both obviously itching to find the right way to bring up the topic of her newfound abilities.

They had just arrived onto the large suspension bridge that loomed into the city when an oncoming log truck down the road had lost some of its cargo off its back, bouncing a few stump-sized logs onto the road. The first car had swerved and dodged the small mess, but the minivan containing the soccer mom and seven rambunctious kids behind it was given little time to react. She had jerked the wheel to the right, screaming as she lost control of the vehicle and veered through the side guardrail of the bridge, bursting through and braking just enough so the van turned and tipped over the side, balancing for dear life. The vehicles behind had all screeched to a halt, with patrons immediately jumping out of their cars with concern.

"Holy shit," Dale had blurted from behind the wheel of his pickup as he firmly stopped. He got out of the truck with Sela as they started to walk forward with others.

The kids inside the minivan were scared, crying and tearing up as the mother attempted to quiet them down and keep them still. Those starting to surround the van warily crept forward, being cautious in their steps to approach it while finding the best and fastest way to aid it without sending it over, for the slightest wrong touch could do it in. That's when Dale and Sela looked at each other. They knew they were thinking the same thing, but neither could bring the words out of their mouths. Sela simply hurried off toward the minivan, leaving Dale to call out her name in a manner that was halting, encouraging and confusing at the same time.

The van started to tip more as the children pleaded from behind the windows, causing those who were trying to help to do whatever they could by slapping their hands on the van and pulling it back. But no matter how many people there were, the weight, position and angle of the minivan was far too great for their attempt, and its front end began to give way as it tipped off the bridge. Bystanders let out screams and cries.

Sela wasn't thinking. She didn't just feel what to do. She had *known* what she *could* do. So she ran and jumped onto the side barrier as the van completely tipped off the side, beginning to drop. But then it stopped, jerking the children and mother as they gripped tightly to their seats. Confusion began to replace their fear. They should've been in the water by now. And then the van started to back up, getting pushed onto the bridge as they looked all around.

The crowd above was just as baffled as they stepped back to allow the van room. A few of the bystanders had run over to the side to peer over, when one of them pointed and shouted for them to look.

Sela was free-floating beneath the van, pushing the front end up with both of her hands as the crowd unbelievably watched. As a matter of fact, they seemed to be more interested in a young woman floating in the air and pushing a two-ton minivan back up onto a bridge with her bare hands rather than the van itself and its inhabitants. Within moments, Sela had completely wheeled the van back up onto the bridge and back a safe enough distance from the edge. The mother and seven children immediately piled out, greeted by the aid of those around who weren't applauding as Sela softly soared up onto the bridge ledge and stepped down. They accumulated around her, talking in awe and treating her with their eyes like a visual marvel.

Dale was the only one outside of the crowd, watching with an absent enthusiasm.


After the proper authorities and medical personnel had arrived to the scene, Dale and Sela had been cordially escorted to the downtown precinct where the questions started flinging to Sela about her not-so-common traits. Dale was of course all too ready to start spilling the beans on the mine and what had happened to her, but she convinced him otherwise, calmly taking the matter into her own hands. It had been arranged for her to appear at a press conference later that afternoon with the mayor of the city, where she could shed some light. A press conference? It made her feel like some sort of sports athlete, or celebrity. No one seemed ready with their knives to cut her up. No mysterious government men threw her into the back of a dark Sedan. Sure, they were interested in knowing everything, but the fact that she had saved that entire minivan full of little sportsters in front of a hefty crowd of pleased witnesses gave her quite the leverage in tranquility. She insisted that she meant no harm and that her superhuman anatomy was her own business, which is exactly what she mentioned at the press conference.

The mayor of course spun his election propaganda by siding with her and saying nothing but positive remarks, even giving her some kind of city civilian award. "How did you get your powers?" one reporter eagerly asked. "Were you born with them?" another chimed in. "What else can you do?" a third wondered. It seemed very overwhelming, especially in the constantly flashing lights of the cameras.

The mayor had smiled ear-to-ear, stepping beside her at the podium as he placed a supporting hand on her shoulder. "My fellow citizens," he began, "the fact is not how she acquired these abilities or when, but how she chose to use them. This amazing young woman went above and beyond her call of duty as a simple civilian of this great city by using these incredible gifts to rescue people in an extreme situation. Let us not focus on the origins and motivations behind what has happened, but what they stand for. And to me, this woman is a standing example of not only the good that this city represents, but the good in what this world represents that many of us have forgotten."

They ate it up. It was a buffet line of shining promotion. And sure, it didn't stop the questions from still being asked, but Sela had been awarded an instant celebrity status. She and Dale were even lucky enough to get back home without being followed, although that didn't stop the mayor from insisting a patrol car to keep watch outside their house anyway.

"Can you believe this?" Sela asked as she waitressed Dale's plate of dinner over to him at the kitchen table, watching the news on TV. "Are they actually calling me a superhero?"

"Isn't the politically correct term "superheroine"?" Dale wondered with the perk of his eyebrows.

"Whatever it is, it's weird," she added, bringing her own plate over and sitting down. "It's like the mayor is trying to spin me into some kind of city watchdog or something."

Dale chewed some food and poked at the rest with his fork. "Look, uh... you did the right thing, you know," he said in a more serious fashion. "By helping them, and exposing yourself like that before even *we* could know what to make of what's happening to you. I know last night we had talked about not telling anyone until we knew what was going on, but... if it weren't for you, all those kids would be dead."

She thought it over with a warm, thankful grin. "Yeah. I mean, I just felt like I had to do it. Like I had to act, no matter what the consequences. It felt right."

"Well, it's certainly put other things going on in our lives out of our minds," Dale added, taking a sip of his drink.

She had realized that he was right, and although it had only been over twenty-four hours, she felt as if she had been distanced from their problems for weeks. But that still didn't change the fact that those problems were still there, and from Sela's lack of speech after the comment, Dale wondered if he had said the right thing. So he scratched his head and tried to lighten the situation by continuing with, "So, you gonna come up with a name?"

"A name?" Sela strangely asked.

"Yeah. If the mayor really wants to employ you fulltime as the city's official superhero, you should probably come up with a catchy name or something, since everyone already knows your real one."

"I think Super Girl and Wonder Woman are already taken, so I guess that leaves me with Super Shit-Out-of-Luck," she noted with a smirk.

Dale grinned. It felt nice to act like that again with her. It was something he missed. Something that reminded him of a time when things were good and right between them. She rested her chin on her fist and looked down to her food. "You really think that's what I should do? Help people? Maybe that's... Maybe that's why all this is happening. Maybe it's what I'm meant to do," she simply stated. "I don't need a fancy name for that. I just wanna be me. Sela. Just... Sela."

He didn't have an answer to that. He didn't really know what to say then. Because herself is all he ever wanted her to be...


Despite her new popularity and options, Sela still maintained her ego as a simple second grade teacher, and returned to school that Monday morning like any other weekday. Of course, she was instantly famous among her faculty and colleagues, even the ones she had never talked with much. The principal was giving her special brownnosing treatment, which should have really been the other way around. Even the district superintendent showed up for a bit to extend his congratulations. Nevertheless, she kept a cool mind about it, simply smiling and thanking everyone for their attention and comments as she went off to her class, who gave her the most pomposity. In the mind of a wondrous second grader, she was quite the stature for awesomeness, which she did get a kick out of. Especially when she showed them a few of her tricks, like opening the blinds to the windows with the wave of her hand or force-pushing an empty desk to the side of the room with the gesture of her fingers. She didn't feel like a teacher that day. More like a special guest magician, dazzling and razzling their bright eyes. It made it difficult to stay on track with her usual lesson plans, but then again, how often do students really pay attention to their teacher? She had their complete and utter observation as she stood up front. "Can you really fly?" one little boy asked. Another upgraded the question with, "How high can you fly? Can you go into outer space?"

A girl had asked, "Can you lift a school bus?"

The boy in front of her turned around and shot back, "Of course she can! I watched her lift that van on the news! She can lift anything!"

"My favorite superhero is Batman!" another boy chimed out with.

"Mine is Superman!" his friend added. "My favorite cartoon is when Batman and Superman fight!" He hopped out of his seat and started to act out a fighting scene as his peers giggled and laughed at the class clown material.

Sela even snickered herself, trying to calm and quiet them all down as she urged to get back to their lesson plan. "Could you beat Superman and Batman in a fight?" one boy wondered, ignoring her request.

"Sure she could!" the class clown retorted. "Superman and Batman are just comic book and TV heroes. All she would need is an eraser and remote!"

The class broke out in wild laughter again as the boy hyped up his popularity with the waving of his arms, then giving a bow. Sela smiled and just watched them. She felt closer to them now — more connected. And since it was on a more personal level, it made her teaching seem more meaningful.

She excitedly recapped her day to Dale later on that evening at the house. It was an exuberance he hadn't seen from her in a long time. "They were so excited. You should've seen their faces! They were actually paying attention for once," she told him. "I would do these incentives, like moving something through the air across the room onto their desks for every correct answer. I don't think I've ever seen so many hands raised at once."

Dale smiled and took her by the arm. "Come on. I wanna show you something," he said as he started to lead her into the bedroom. Once inside, she stopped and gave a confused look to the black-and-gray-colored spandex one-piece uniform and gloves lying on the bed.

"What is this?" she asked with a strange grin.

Dale gave a light shrug and scratched his hair. "Well, this whole thing has kinda got you on cloud nine — literally — and it's really bringing out something in you. I figured, if you're really serious about this whole helping the city thing, I wanna be behind you. So why not make it official and have some kind of uniform?"

She cocked a ridiculous smirk as she stepped over and picked it up, skimming her fingers along the sides with a quick chuckle. "Are you for real? You really think I'd actually wear this thing out in public?" she asked.

"Why not? Wouldn't want you ruining all your favorite tee-shirts."

"Look at it. It's ridiculous," she added. "Besides — all that was just talk. Me? An official superhero? If anything, the mayor will probably only ever call me to rescue a cat from a tall tree. You're the one who's supposed to be talking me *out* of this."

"I know, but... I just want you to be happy."

Her grinning shifted more into a warm, comforting smile as she raised her eyebrows and held the uniform up. "You just wanna see me in spandex."

"Well, I'd rather see you flying around in Victoria's Secret lingerie, but I don't think it would be too appropriate for the kids watching at home," he joked.

She laughed. They were laughing together. But their conversational debate was frozen from being continued any further with a ringing phone interruption. Dale walked over to the nightstand and answered it, listening for a moment. "Uh, yeah. Hang on, please," he said into it with a bit of confusion, gesturing it to Sela. "It's for you. It's the mayor."

Sela took the phone and put it to her ear. "Hello?" she asked, listening for a long moment. "Oh my God, that's terrible," she responded, growing more concerned. She listened and then more promptly spoke out with, "Yeah. Yeah, yeah. Of course! I'll be right there." She hung it up and looked at Dale. "He said that both the brakes and emergency brake system went out on a passenger Amtrak train outside of the city and is gonna derail if it's not stopped soon."

"Jesus," Dale murmured. He exchanged a look with her similar to the one they had given each other on the bridge with the minivan. Suddenly his enthusiasm about her helping hands didn't seem too plausible to him. "Sela... are you sure you...?"

"I can do this," she flatly told him. She stepped closer and gave his lips a kiss. "I'll be okay."

With that, she turned and ran out of the room and out of the house, leaving him to look at the uniform sprawled out on the bed.


It wasn't as if Dale didn't want her to go help, but a part of him didn't necessarily *want* her to go, either. He really didn't think that it would all begin this way so quickly, or at all, for that matter. He only expected her to be called upon for more questioning or "cat-out-of-tall-tree" emergencies, as Sela herself noted. He didn't expect to be watching clips of her that night, only a night after the bridge incident, on the eleven o'clock news — where helicopters were lucky enough to grace intrigued viewers with floating aerial shots of her saving the speeding Amtrak from eminent doom. Her shoes glided along on the rails of the track as she firmly pushed against the front end of the engine, eventually slowing it to a safe and cushy stop. And then of course the news hour turned into two hours, supplying plenty of aftermath footage of the countless passengers being escorted off the train by medical personnel they had no need for. Sela was interviewed with the same dozen questions over and over, explaining how she did it as her supporters endlessly cheered and hoorayed her heroics. That was hours ago, and by the time she had arrived home at some ungodly hour, Dale was asleep on the couch in the dark — or at least he pretended to be asleep. He could sense that she was rustling around on purpose, as if trying to wake him and form some sort of apology for her press conference after-party tardiness. But he wouldn't budge, and she went into the bedroom, closing the door behind her.

It had become almost like a second full-time job. It wasn't like she went out after dinner every night to prowl the dark city streets and alleys for muggers and purse-snatchers, like some cliché caped knight. But there always seemed to be something happening that basic law enforcement or medics couldn't handle themselves, extending a hand out for her useful abilities, whether it was getting a call to help out people stranded in a flood or rescue them from a small retirement home fire. And then there was her celebrity status. Aside from her teaching and occasional catching of bad guys, she found herself heavily participating in charitable events and award ceremonies. She had become the new symbol of the city, and that of course didn't stop numerous other cities from across the country to wave big dollar bills in front of her in attempts to steal and employ her as a salaried exterminator of their own problems. Dale didn't even know how she could physically do it all, from waking up early in the morning to go teach rowdy second graders to lift a crashed Mack truck pinning its driver down to cutting some ribbon for a new park — all evidently in her now-trademarked sleek black-and-gray spandex uniform. But she certainly did it all in the following few weeks, as physicality for her didn't seem to be an issue. He felt as if he wasn't seeing much of her because of her schedule, so he responded the easiest way he could by putting his feelings and problems aside and working on the house. She even offered to help him then, as her strength could be put to good use and they would finally have it finished after so long. But he insisted he wanted to do it the "old-fashioned and hard-earned way" and that those said abilities would best be left for the cameras and spotlights. The comment upset her, and she had stormed back into the house where she slammed the door so hard, it broke and shattered off its hinges, nearly hitting the truck in the driveway. "Now you can fix *that!*" she screamed from within the kitchen.

There was, however, the incident with the toddler on the high-rise balcony. It was one of those uptown buildings that towered to the heavens featuring only the most superiorly disdainful and their fat checkbooks. Sela was already in the area at the time when someone had begun screaming that a toddler had wandered out through the open doors onto the balcony high above. Perhaps the maid was busy with the husband, or the wife was chatting on the phone, but when it was apparent that no one from within the apartment was coming out to snatch the little tike any time soon, the bystanders nervously watching below called upon Sela for help. The toddler had fumbled on his feet and split through the bars of the gate, free-falling with only the horrifying screams of those below to land on. Sela took a leaping jump into the air, flying upward a good forty or so stories to catch him in her arms as the spectators gasped with breaths of relief, soon followed by the usual accompaniment of claps and cheers.

When Dale heard her shuffle through the darkness of the living room to leave out the front door later that night, he knew something was up, so after throwing on some clothes, he hopped into the pickup and drove until arriving at the entrance of the abandoned mine. Clicking his flashlight on as he got out, he entered inside to see the power already turned on and made his way down the tunnels, until being guided by the familiar green glow of the sealed-off room and its mysterious content. She was inside, sitting on a ledge in front of the egg-shaped object as it hummed and softly pumped its lifelike glow. "Thought I'd find you here," he said after finding no other way to start the conversation.

"I didn't want to take the truck and wake you so I took Sela Airways," she murmured, joking without a single evident trace of any smile whatsoever.

He sighed and leaned against a rock. "You wanna talk about it?" he then wondered.

"If I had wanted to talk about it with you, I would've stayed home and woken you up," she almost snobbishly replied.

Dale unbelievably shook his head and tossed a hand in the air, turning to duck out through the hole in the wall. "Glad I could help," he blurted. "See you in the morning."

"He was so small," he heard her say behind him, causing him to pause in his retreat. He turned back around and looked at her as she stared at the dirt ground in thought. "He was so small in my hands. And I looked at his face while I carried him down... and he didn't even know what had happened. He didn't have any comprehension of what had just happened to him. Of what *could* have happened..."

Dale stepped more fully back into the room, silently staring at her as she began to tear up. "What kind of people would not care enough to watch their baby every second?" she continued. "To soak up every precious moment of their face, and sit down just to watch them to play? How can there be people in this world who don't appreciate what they have?"

"It was an accident," Dale chimed in with. "Sometimes things just happen that are out of our control. But you took control. And he's alive because of you."

She sniffled and wiped her eyes. "What do they know about loss? What do they know about not having? I can save every baby that falls out of a window in the world and see how grateful and appreciative they are to have it back, but they don't know. They'll never know..."

"You can't think like that, Sela," he said with sympathetic support. "You said it yourself — maybe this is your calling. Maybe the reason all of this is happening is so you can help others."

"Right. I can't have a baby so I'm forced to save everyone else's and watch them happily appreciate what they've been ignoring."

"I didn't say that," he told her.

"No, you didn't say it that *way*," she huffed, getting to her feet.

He shrugged, extending his arms. "What do you want me to do? Huh? Tell me, and I'll do it." She turned her back on him, rubbing her face and not answering. "I miss you, Sela. Sometimes I wonder if this whole thing has happened for the best. You're never around anymore, you haven't come with me to see Dr. Connelly — how am I supposed to work on fixing us when you're too busy fixing other people?"

"Maybe we're not meant to be fixed," she mumbled under her breath.

"Oh, come on — I know you don't mean that."

She turned back around to look at him. "You think you know what I'm feeling? You think I don't know what *you're* feeling? Why don't you ever have the balls to just tell me that you'd rather be with someone else? That you'd rather not put up with all this bullshit and go off and knock up some other woman who will be able to give you seven kids and a nice home and a happily ever after?"

He couldn't believe his own ears. "Jesus Christ... how do you say something like that to me? How can you stand there and even *attempt* to think that's how I feel? I want *you*, Sela. That's all I've ever wanted. I know you know that. I'm with you, for better or for worse; that's what this ring stands for. And I know you're scared, and you wanna push me away, but I'm not going anywhere. Because we're gonna work this out, and no fancy ability that you develop is ever gonna be strong enough to push me away."

He stepped over and placed his hands on her shoulders as she lightly squirmed to break him free, choking back more tears. "Don't touch me," she urged.

"Just hold me," he requested. "Like you used to. Just love me. Give me a hug, for shit's sake. Please — let's start *somewhere*."

She brought her glassy eyes to his, swallowing. "Every morning I wake up as the hero who saves people and every night I go to sleep as the wife who fails you..."

She pushed her way past him and ducked out through the hole in the boarded wall.


Dale wished that things could have gotten better from that point on. He wished that with the more people she saved and the more she had gone through with her superhero status, they could leap over the hurdle that eternally seemed to haunt their relationship. He would have even settled for things to stay flat and neutral, accepting that the silence between them while he worked on the house and she cooked dinner was the worst of it. But she became more aggressive. She stayed out later. She actually *looked* for trouble, and it was not difficult to find it on a regular basis. She was not only appointing herself the personal task of rescuing people, but of stopping them in their crimes as well. She was now dealing with the likes of muggers and thieves, cocky in her bullet-deflecting upsets of their illegal activities. The jailhouses were becoming fully booked, and cops were now spending the majority of their shifts taste-testing all of the different daily donut flavors.

It was on a Saturday afternoon that she received word about the bank robbery in progress. The group of three ski-masked fiends had successfully made off with quite a bit of money stacked neatly into duffel bags straight from the vaults and hopped into their own personal waiting chopper on the roof of a neighboring building. She had flown up to the helicopter and popped inside to the surprise of the celebrating bandits. Perhaps they were out-of-towners who were unfamiliar or unbelieving of her territorial status, or perhaps they were locals who had the proper genital strength to dare a folly from her of their heist, but if one thing was for sure, it was that she was now there with them, and none of their incoming bullets threatened a departure for her. She merely grabbed their guns and bent the barrels as if they were plastic toys, ordering them to land or she would do it for them. The pilot veered the chopper in an attempt to shake her loose, and by initial instinct, she grabbed one of the thieves for leverage and managed to pull him right out of his seatbelt as he fell out of the chopper and clung onto her arm for dear life. He shouted and pleaded for help as she blankly stared down to him.

Then something happened within her. Something boiled and brewed in the deepest region of her emotional abyss. It's not like she let go. She did hold on. But she certainly didn't pull. And his grip of her arm quickly became her wrist and shortly after became nothing but air as he fell to the city streets far below. She brought her body back into the chopper and gave a steely look as the other two thieves held their hands up in defense, giving in to her authority.

"It's been a while, Sela," Dr. Connelly said as she sat across from her and Dale in the tidy office. "You seem to have become quite the celebrity since the last time we met."

"Yeah, well, you already have my autograph on paperwork," Sela dully responded. "Look, if you don't mind, I kinda don't wanna talk about that."

"What would you like to talk about?" Dr. Connelly wondered in an offering manner.

Dale looked over to Sela and added, "I'm interested in knowing that myself, seeing as how you've never been one for choice of topic here."

Sela sharpened her eyes as she crossed her arms. "What is *that* supposed to mean?"

Dale shrugged. "It means the only chance I get to talk to you lately is when we're paying for it."

"I don't believe this," she huffed in return. "I'm out there working my ass off, going to school everyday and then flying around saving this city until the sun comes back up, and this is the thanks I get from the one person who's supposed to be supporting me most."

"Hey, who do you think got you that now-famous outfit you prance around in?" he shot back.

Sela tightly clenched her mouth, actually finding the strength to not argue back. Dr. Connelly pointed her pen, striking an idea. "Why don't we talk about that, then? This whole "superhero job" ordeal with Sela is obviously stemming some communicational issues between the two of you."

"Gee, nothing gets past you, Doctor," Sela blurted, rolling her eyes.

"What's the matter with you? That's rude," Dale sternly scolded.

"Well, excuse me for having a bad weekend," she stated.

"What happened, Sela?" Dr. Connelly asked.

Sela sighed, turning her head away. Dale looked at her and then shifted his eyes to Dr. Connelly. "She was trying to stop a helicopter full of bank robbers and one of them fell out," he answered.

"I heard about that," Dr. Connelly said, sitting a bit forward to give Sela a more serious approach. "Listen, Sela — a death can be traumatizing, even in the smallest way. Especially for someone who's become so used to saving people."

"I'm not shedding any tears for a dead bank robber," she noted. "He put himself into that position in the first place."

"Well, Dale certainly seems to think it's having some sort of emotional affect on you," Dr. Connelly conjured. "It wasn't your fault, you know."

"That's just it," Sela began to say, eyes pasted to the floor. "It *was* my fault."

"I know you want to think that, but remember who you are, and what you've done for this city in so little time. You can't save everyone, Sela," Dr. Connelly declared.

"I couldn't save him because I didn't *want* to save him..."

Dale's look grew a little more concerned as he shifted in his seat. "What are you talking about?" he pondered.

"I could've pulled up, but I didn't. He didn't slip," she remarked. "I just didn't pull him up."

"You — dropped him?" Dale surprisingly asked.

"I never said I dropped him. I said I didn't pull him up."

"I don't really see the difference," Dale strangely affirmed.

Sela's stare continued to stab into the floor with her thoughts. "I looked at him as he was dangling from my arm and I wondered if the world would be better off without him. Who knows what drugs or weapons or terrorism he would condone if he had gotten away with all that stolen money."

"That still doesn't give you the right to choose whether someone should live or die," Dale blurted. "He was a human being. Whatever his crimes were, whatever kind of person he was, he still deserved a fair trial. What if he was stealing it to pay for a desperate operation for his sick brother? Would you still have let him go?"

"I just fucking told you that *he* was the one that let go! All he had to do was hang on!"

"What if a guy lost his job, and his car, and his house, and he was so desperate to feed his wife that he stole bread from a grocery store? Would you judge his penalty with immediate death then?"

Sela promptly stood up, shaking her head as she waved her arms. "This is ridiculous; I can't do this."

"Sela, please," Dr. Connelly rationally pleaded. "Let's just calm down and talk this through."

Sela spun around and shot her eyes wide, pointing a guilty finger at her. "All you wanna *do* is talk! And you *charge* people for it! You sit there and nod and come up with all these bullshit rubber band remarks to everything everyone says so *nothing* gets solved and we have to keep coming back here and pay you more! What do you know about *doing* anything? You sit in a chair and you listen. You're not a doer. What do you know about helping people?"

"I realize you're upset, Sela," Dr. Connelly began, "and I understand how you can get the notion I might live an easy life by getting paid to sit in a chair and talk in fifty-minute increments. But please don't think I'm here for a payment from you. I'm here to *help* you, because I *want* to help you. Some people help with special powers, and some people help with talking. That's all I'd like to do. And if you don't think that talking is the solution to your problems, then that's fine. The important thing is that we find out what that solution is."

"You really wanna help me? Then why don't you give that speech to me again when you're in labor. We'll see what good it does for me then," Sela snipped. "As a matter a fact, my husband's probably looking for an able-bodied bitch to knock up. I'm sure he wants to bang you anyway."

Dale shot out of the chair to his feet like a rocket. "Hey!" he shouted to Sela with an intensity he never used on her before. "Let's go; outside! Now!"

Sela wasted no time charging for the door, but not before stopping to look over her shoulder at Dr. Connelly, saying, "Someday... you'll be somewhere calling for *my* help... and I'll gladly tell you to schedule a paid appointment."

She pushed her way out as Dale sternly followed behind, stopping at the threshold to turn back to Dr. Connelly with an attempted sympathy. "I'm so sorry."

She shook her head, showing no offense whatsoever as she waved him on. "Dale, just — go after her. I'm fine. Don't worry about me."

He nodded and continued onward, hurrying through the hallways and outside of the building to see Sela sourly walking away down the sidewalk. He jogged after her, clutching her arm to stop her when he caught up. "This isn't you," he firmly told her. "Something's not right."

"All that money wasted on the good doctor and you're just realizing this now?" she asked, perking her eyebrows.

"I'm not talking about us; this isn't about us anymore. Something's happening to you. You're changing. You're turning into some kind of emotional monster. I can't even see the girl I married. It's that damn thing you found!"

"You can't have it! It's mine!" she yelled. "It chose *me*, not you! It gave the powers to *me*, not anyone else! And no one's gonna take it away from me! This is the one thing *I* get to have!"

"*Sela. We — can't — have — a baby.* I'm sorry. I don't want to think about it or accept it any more than you. But that's the way it is. That's it. If I could do anything or give anything to change that, I would in a heartbeat. I just don't know what other way to convince you. I don't know what to do anymore. We can't keep trying and hoping and deluding ourselves that some kind of miracle will float along and catch us, because this is the real world, and I'm losing you. Please. Help me find our way back to each other. Stay away from that thing and come back to *me*."

"That *thing* is the only thing that's made life worth living," she noted.

He took a deep breath and softly responded with, "I remember when you used to say that about *me*..."

And with that, he turned and walked away, leaving her alone. She tried to hold back her tears, stiffening her jaw as she instead took it out on the wooden bench next to her, blasting it to woodchips with a shockwave force from her hand.


The death toll rose. It wasn't an absurd number, but Sela was certainly doing her part to make sure plenty of the city's criminals wouldn't make it to the court room. At first, it was very subtle — an accident here, an accident there, but then the witnesses and bystanders she was protecting in those instances began to make note of her unorthodox methods to cleaning up the crime. The mayor himself even eventually began to frown upon it, gazing upon her like a disobedient child or a policy-breaking employee. She was losing stock in her fan base, and soon the nightly news clips of her latest heroics became moral debates on how she could have handled those challenges in a safer method. Of course, there was the pro side of the column to which it was always heavily noted, especially by her in her own defense, that the majority of those criminals and law-breakers she was giving the fatal boot to were murderers, rapists, and thugs who had no ethics for their own lives let alone the lives of the innocents around them. Still, she was reckless, despite the attempts Dale tried to make at getting her to take a step back.

But they didn't talk much nor see much of each other in those following weeks, as she had distanced herself from the house, sometimes being gone for days. Her students at school had lost interest in her once-magical powers and returned to their disruptive chattering, not stopping even when she tried to re-capture their eyes with the use of some of her powers. It was as if she had become invisible to them. She had become invisible to the city.

And then the bridge disaster occurred.

It's strange how things always seem to end where they began. But this time, instead of a tipping minivan over the edge, it was *all* of the vehicles on the bridge when it began to collapse. The actual cause of the structure's downfall was never determined, but it began with the snap of a cable, and then the crack of a beam, followed by the crumble of some concrete, providing all of the proper mathematics for a disaster equation during rush hour of all times. Perhaps all of the weight on the bridge played an intricate part in its structure finally giving in to its age. Or perhaps the cable that first broke was not secured correctly to begin with. Whatever the first domino had been, Sela was conveniently in the area to counteract with the cries and screams for help as she flew her way onto the bridge and over to a man in a business suit who had retreated from his car and lost his footing over the edge, barely hanging on. She was gripping his hand tightly and beginning to pull when those somber thoughts had popped into her head...

Why should she help them?

What had they done for her?

Nothing. And that's exactly what they were to Sela. All of them. Just hoards of people going about their pointless lives without any admiration or appreciation for the things they had. Why should they deserve to get what they want? Good things do not happen to those who wait. And good things especially do not happen to those who choose not to wait by working hard to acquire them.

No. Sela was finished helping them. They didn't care about her, or about anything she had ever gone through. They didn't understand, because they always got what they wanted. They only called for her when they needed something. It was always one-sided. Always selfish. They always wanted help, and never had any intention of offering it. The man in the sharp business suit was the epitome of all they represented to Sela as he hung onto her gloved hand. And as he cried for help and dangled for his dear, pathetic life, she could only stare at him through the bangs of her softy-spiked razor-cut mid-length black hair, piercing a look of revulsion that terrified him even more than the fatal fall to the water below. He attempted to claw his way up her wrist, but she merely stood there and did nothing, clenching her jaw as his grip began to slide from the arm of her black-and-gray one-piece spandex uniform.

And then he fell, fell far to the watery depths below the bridge with a bottomless scream that faded from her earshot long before he had even let go. She leaned back upright over the side and turned, tightening her leather gloves as she began to steadily walk down the collapsing bridge, sickened by the cries and pleas coming from the people behind her who tried to escape their cars as the center structure collapsed into the water even more. A Buick had coasted backwards past her with its passengers banging on the windows. She ignored it as it toppled off the end and upside down toward the water below. A truck was rolling toward her, but she merely caught it by the front end and picked it up, heaving it out of her way as it spun through the air and off the bridge. She simply hopped up onto the hood of the next car as it coasted by down in her path and took a flying leap, soaring herself with a gentle land on her feet to the safety at the end of the bridge, where the plethora of police cruisers, ambulances and other crowds of bystanders watched in awe.

She could hear everyone yelling and screaming, asking her what she was doing, asking her why she wasn't helping, but were *they* helping? No. They were at the end of the bridge, like cowards. Comfortable with their silver platter lives, waiting until they were ushered home to dinner so they could forget it overnight until the next thing happened they could gossip over.

Sela turned to re-face the bridge and cocked her head up as another cable snapped. Another dozen vehicles had slipped off the edge as the roadway collapsed even more, and those who had managed to actually escape on foot went down with them. The steam built up inside of her like a pipe ready to blow as she watched the chaos of the bridge collapse ensue. She began to breathe deeply; her jaw tightly shut as she slowly raised her hands forward. Backing them to her chest, she then strongly pushed forward, sending a massive blast of shockwave power into the bridge beams as the entire structure ripped and blew apart, sending vehicles off into the air as others fell with the road into the water or were crushed by the toppling debris.

She turned to the screaming crowd behind her who had all begun to scurry and stampede into the city. She was doing them a favor, really. If they were really thinking as free and clear as she was, they would be thanking her. Thanking her for letting her show them the errors of their arrogant ways. The only ones that stayed behind were the authority figures, huddled behind their flashing cars with mouths dropped. And as they watched her slowly walk toward them, readily raising her hands, they drew their guns in a useless defense to the next shockwave that blasted them and their vehicular shields through the air. She turned to her left and blasted a crowd of running people into a building. She picked up a car and bashed it into the side of an ambulance, crushing the paramedics inside as if it were an aluminum can.

There was no stopping her. She was in no need to rush after those who had gotten away. She simply raised her hand and blew another shockwave into the bottom of a tall building as it bent forward and collapsed onto a terrified group of people with an aftermath storm of dirt and smoke. A policeman held his arms up in self-defense as she walked by and gripped the collar of his uniform, jerking him up as she flew into the air and tossed him like a rag doll, gently landing herself on her feet five dozen yards ahead. Buildings were destroyed like sandcastles. Cars were smashed like Matchbox toys. Sela noticed herself on TV in a store window and looked upward to see a news helicopter floating nearby. She walked over to a parked motorcycle and picked it up, throwing it at the chopper and knocking it off-course as it swayed and lost control, finally plowing into the side of a skyscraper with a shattering explosion.

The SWAT and special unit vans were approaching now, stopping some-odd distance before reaching her as the armored and helmeted enforcers piled out. They began to return a rapid wave of automatic gunfire, but the countless bullets merely bounced off of her body like rubber as she continued her stroll forth. She arched her arms back, as if accumulating a massive charge of power, and then surged them forward to forcefully blast the group of armed protectors away, clearing the streets ahead. Another helicopter approached and shot a small missile, but she merely used the power of her hands to slow it down and arch its direction around, sending it full-force to a building in the center of the square as it rumbled and demolished.

It wasn't long beyond that when Dale's speeding pickup truck had screeched to a halt before her as he jumped out. She turned and aimed her hands, causing him to duck beside the side-view mirror as she held back from using her powers.

"Sela! Sela, it's me!" he yelled.

She just stood there, not replying as he held his hands up and inched his way toward her, mouth dropping while he inspected the apocalypse of the city she had created around her. "My God," he unbelievably mumbled, shaking his head. "Sela — Sela what have you done?"

"They deserved it," she answered. "They don't care about me. They were using me."

"That's not true!" he argued. "That still doesn't give you the right to do this!"

"They can't have it! It's mine! I found it!" she screamed back. "They won't take it from me! Dale, if they find it and take it, I'll lose everything!"

56

He stared at her, unblinking, and began to slowly shake his head again. "This has got to end, Sela. I'm sorry. You leave me no choice," he told her as he turned and started to head back for the truck.

"Where are you going?" she called out.

"I'm going to do something I should have done a long time ago," he said, jumping into the truck.

"Dale! Don't do it!" she ordered as he turned the truck around and drove off.

She clenched her jaw and held her hand out, preparing to use her powers, but had second thoughts as she flew up into the air and out of the city.

Dale had nearly lost control of the truck as he halted it to a stop in front of the mine entrance a short while later, getting out and grabbing the sledgehammer from the back. He determinedly carried it with him as he pushed his way through the gate and walked into the mine. He knew she was there, and not because the electricity was already on. He hiked and made his way through the tunnels until ducking through the hole in the boarded wall, where Sela was already waiting in front of the green-glowing egg-shaped object. Her eyes darted to the sledgehammer. "Move," he finally said after a dragging silence.

"I won't let you do it," she said, taking a protective step back.

He gave a shrug. "What are you gonna do, kill me?"

Her firm and steady expression began to slightly downcast. "Please, Dale — don't do this. You don't have to do this," she pleaded.

"That thing has been fucking you up since the second you found it," he reminded her. "Jesus Christ, those... things you were doing to those people... I don't even know who you are anymore."

"I'm still me," she retorted. "I'm just different. I can make this work. I know I can. I've just made some mistakes."

"You were *killing people*, Sela!" he shouted. "Innocent people! You were *killing* them! I'm doing this for *you*. It's the only way. We can show everyone what it was, and how it was changing you! And we can get you some help!"

"Help?! Help?!" she repeated, growing more angry. "It's so easy for you say, isn't it, Dale? It's always been so goddamn easy for you to say that to me! You always think you know the pain I'm going through, but you don't! You'll never know what it's like to be me inside!"

"Then tell me how to help you," he simply replied. "Because all I want to do is fix you."

Her jaw quivered as she fought back the tears. "It already fixed me inside. It understood what I was going through and it gave me purpose. That's why it chose me and made me the way I am. It chose *me*."

"I'm sorry, Sela," he said, shaking his head as he lifted the sledgehammer and took a sturdy step toward the object.

"Noooo!" she screamed, holding up her hand and blasting him with a force so powerful it sent him crashing back through the boarded wall and into the tunnel as the walls and ceiling shook and caved in throughout the area, burying him in a baneful pile of soil, rocks and wood.

After the rumbling of the mine had halted, Sela stood within the small room and slowly dropped her jaw, glancing at her shaking hands. She couldn't believe what she had just done. So she hurried through the newly-created open wall and began to dig her way through the debris. There was so much of it. She just kept digging and digging, throwing pieces of wood and pipe aside. Her fingers clawed through the dirt like a rabid animal. She couldn't breathe. And then she came to one of Dale's hands. She gasped, quickly unburying his remaining body and pulling him out to hold him in her arms. He was beat to hell. She shook him, calling out his name — "Dale?! Dale?!"

But he didn't move. He didn't answer. And he wasn't breathing. Her face pouted as the tears sprung from her eyes. "Dale, no... no, please... I'm sorry... I'm so sorry..."

She hugged and rocked him closely, pulling him away to look at his bruised face as if hoping for some sign of life. But he was gone, and she knew it. All she could do was cry. And after she felt she had poured enough tears, she delicately laid him on the dirt floor, sniffling and wiping her eyes as she stood to her feet. She tightened her mood and noticed the sledgehammer nearby, persistently trotting over to grab it and bring it into the small room as she gazed upon the glowing egg-shaped object. It continued its softly pumping hum as she stared and moved toward it. She grinded her teeth, strongly curling her hands around the sledgehammer and swung it down for the first major blow, cracking the object. She spared no time hitting it over and over, down and sideways, smashing and destroying it as metallic pieces flew. After a spark here and there, the object's glowing began to die, fading away while its humming churned and groaned, whirling to a stop as it were a dying machine breaking down.

Sela tiredly threw the sledgehammer aside, crying more as she backed against the wall next to it and slid to the ground, hanging her ashamed head. But through her sobbing, she thought she heard a faint beeping noise and stopped to listen. She waited, trying to concentrate more between her shaking breaths, and slightly re-positioned herself back onto her feet. She narrowed her eyes to the egg-shaped object, where the small button on the side barely blinked. It was definitely the origin of the beeping sound. So she carefully inched her way toward it, staring at the perplexity of something on it actually still working after what she had put it through. She slowly reached her hand out, pointing her index finger and hesitating before finally pushing the button. A tiny rectangular portion of the egg-shaped object popped out, much like the tray of a CD player, only it didn't seem to be at full-capacity because of the object's overall shape, so it only half-ejected as Sela pondered whether to assist. She reached forward and backed her hand away, then grabbed the sides and finished pulling the tray out as a quick burst of blue light blasted around the object. She gave a startled gasp and warily jumped back.

The blue light flickered and bounced a bit, and then a shape started to come into focus, much like a distorted television image. After a few more moments, the holographic image was clear — it was a good-looking woman, maybe in her late-thirties, dressed in a simple white robe. Sela's mouth hung a bit ajar as she watched the woman begin to speak:

"Greetings, Sela. I appear within this recorded message for you in this form, because it is familiar to that of your race. I come from a place far away among the stars bearing you the gift of opportunity. You are a unique and special individual, and you have been chosen to be the mother of the first child on a new planet ready for life, just as we once chose a mother for your own. The object you have been called to which you are viewing this message on will prepare your body to be sustainable on this new planet but as an effect will temporarily evolve you beyond your species' current capabilities until you have arrived, where the effects will subside. You will find detailed electronic instructions within the object on how to control these abilities, but take great care of it — if the object should break or be destroyed, you will lose your only method to contact us, for our people now only have the ability to travel to your planet if we are summoned, so call upon us when you are ready, and we shall arrive with a welcoming hand of peace and great expectation."

With that, the hologram flickered and bounced, blinking out with an end to leave a quiet stillness in the air. Sela couldn't breathe. Her eyes couldn't budge a blink. A thin line of water rounded the bottom edges, threatening to spew forth unbelievable tears. Her jaw shook, her shoulders dejectedly sunk and her legs grew weak, dropping her to her knees on the dirt as her eyelids slammed shut like heavy garage doors.

# HORIZON

What is immortality to a man but only a series of dreams throughout a series of blinking nights in a man's life?  David was never really truly immortal.  No matter how many centuries he had lived, no matter how many things he had seen or how far man had progressed, he was simply human, and nothing more.  He ate when he got hungry, he bled when he was cut and he cried when he felt that emotional pain.  The emotional pain that he dragged along with him.  That black hole of empty loneliness that he seemed to forever fall down every year that passed.  Albert Einstein's theory of relativity, for all simplicity, stated that sometimes an hour could seem to last a second and sometimes a second could seem to last an hour.  But of course Einstein wasn't alive in 1792, so as much as anyone could maybe hold that notion in their own personal experiences, David would evidently come to encounter its meaning firsthand.

It was particularly those hours he spent with her under that giant oak tree in the far field beyond his house.  The hours that would often seem to last a second.  Just gone and disappeared, in the blink of an eye.  It was never the other way around, like anyone could hope, because if those seconds seemed like hours, he could save and cherish them more preciously.  It just went by too quickly, that's all.  One hundred years, two hundred years — it didn't matter.  All could easily be construed as mere seconds of memories that dissolved upon a finger's reaching touch.

He could never really explain it.  Not in words, not in writing, although not for lack of effort, he did try.  Can anyone in love ever really truly describe why or how they felt for that special person?  That one soul whose purpose on this great planet of life was to bear a majestic role of indescribable perfection.  And she was perfect to him.  How could she not be?  How could she not be perfect to *everyone?*  Perfect in every way, inside and out.  From her batting eyes to that small, adorable mole on her left cheek.  Her flowing golden brown hair with the accompanying smile.  A person fit for a pedestal.  Of course, she wasn't really the type of girl who would care about being lifted up there, but who would take the helping hand and instead lead him to run off into the woods.

She had smooth, perfect skin.  Unbreakable yet delicate as silk.  Her fingers were as thin as her figure and crafted to interlock perfectly within those of David's.  And when they weren't joined, they were always touching him, always affectionate, streaming along his face as he slept.  Tickling that spot on his side that only she was privy to know about.  Caressing her hand through his short, wavy hair while her forehand balanced against his.  But that was all exterior.  Interior, well — David had worn many a quill pens down writing about that.  And even when the technology of computer keyboards finally presented themselves, he still preferred an old-fashioned ink pen to continue forth in his handwritten journal. A journal that detailed the very fibers of her inner soul, for those were the details he could describe the best. The best details in a woman were always the ones that could not be physically seen by the naked eye. Only sensed and felt. And he felt every inch of her. Every beat of her heart pulsating who she was.

Her name back then was Simone.

And David loved her.

Nothing was going to stop that. He wouldn't let it. *They* wouldn't let it. It was the two of them, intertwined in each other's starry paths of destiny, welcomed by the support of friends and family. Some good work lined up, a house of their own someday with some children that would be protected by the guarding gate of two loving hearts... and perhaps a white picket fence. But the coughing started. She was getting sick. No common medicine seemed to help. It would interrupt meals, sleeping, work, and that calming, precious time spent beneath the giant oak tree. There were more and more spats of blood within her faded white handkerchief that seemed more and more impossible to wash out. She was only twenty-one, but she coughed like she was seventy-one. "Tuberculosis," the doctor had eventually diagnosed while pinching his scraggily-thin mustache. "Incurable."

Nothing is ever incurable with a little bit of hope. Or deniability, in David's case. His inner seams were torn, and all needles of the world seemed long lost. Despite the constant prayer from those family members, friends and townspeople, the determination of an unfair and unjust world was the evidential conclusion in his mind every time he looked at her lying in bed. Her face was pale, her hair was flat, and her eyes seemed dimmed of the light that once sparked her essence. He would sit beside her and hold her hand most of the time, occasionally assisting with new handkerchiefs for her coughs. She never said much, and aside from the obvious reasons why, David knew deep down she didn't have to. She would occasionally apologize for putting him through this, and he would merely shake his head in nonsense and spark some tears to which she would always reach out and thumb away. The doctor had given her a month. But what would that month be to David but a mere passing of seconds? Or perhaps that month would seem like many with the agony and pain of watching her wither away before his eyes.

The giant oak tree seemed lonely when he passed it on his way to Simone's house. Its leaves were dying and its bark was rougher than usual. She would ask him to go there for her whenever he wasn't taking care of her, and that wasn't often. Only circumstantial thoughts entered his head whenever he passed it. That when she was gone, he would fence off a good unnecessary mile of the land beneath its roots simply to protect it from the changes of the growing world around it.

David would often sit at night crying at the edge of the wooden bridge over the creek. One teardrop for every star that seemed to be out. It would've been any time then. Any moment. The month had passed and she was slipping away. David could only sit there and imagine himself slipping into the water to float downstream. Softly and gently to a place and time back when beauty knew nothing of the shattered world that he resided in.

He didn't see, or even hear, for that matter, the mysterious man who seemed to just appear out of nowhere next to him there on the bridge. The man was older, maybe in his fifties with salt-and-pepper hair, tall, neat and orderly with his long black overcoat and a firm undertone expression on his face that read as if he had been standing there next to David all along. "Despite what you may think, wanting and wishing are two very different things," the man said as he stared out into the creek. "Wishing can only give you hope for something, but wanting can actually give it to you."

David looked at the mysterious man with a bit of curiosity and confusion, turning his head to look around for any explanation to the sudden arrival of the stranger. "I'm sorry?" he asked.

The mysterious man stepped closer and comfortably sat himself down with ease on the ledge next to David. "You can't save her by wishing for her to live, David," the man continued.

"Who are you? How do you know my name? Do I know you?" David began to interrogate.

"But if you want her to live — if you *really* want her to live — then you just may be able to get it," the man said.

"Simone? Are you speaking of Simone?" David wondered. "How do you know of her? What are you speaking of?"

"What if I told you she could live? A happy, full life. Free of the tuberculosis eating away at her lungs?"

David stared at him for a moment and then looked back to the creek below. "The doctor said it's incurable. We've tried everything. She could go any time now," he replied with a tone of dejection. "Listen, I... I don't know who you are or what you want with me, but unless you're God Himself offering a solution, then I'd like to be left alone, please."

"I can save her, David," the man simply said. "For something in return."

David twisted his head back to him, shaping suspicious eyebrows. "I don't have much money," David flatly said.

"Money is of no use to me. As it is to those who value other things in life, like yourself. And I'm not God," the man confirmed. "Or the devil, looking at your soul for trade, if that's what you're thinking. I suppose you could say I'm a curious magician, of sorts. I'm just someone offering to help. If you want it."

"And you... can save her."

"I can cure her tonight. As if she never had it to begin with," he stated.

A slight shockwave of interested enthusiasm blasted through David as he turned more toward the man. "You're serious," he said. "How? Tell me how. I'll do anything."

"It's very simple, David. I will save her this time. But the next time will be up to you. In her next life."

"In her what?" David asked, the confusion slamming back into him.

"Imagine someone telling you that you live lives on top of lives, one after the other. That you have no knowledge or memories of any of the prior ones to your current. And that one person you love, the one person you care for — will die young in each one of those lives," the man explained. "Now imagine that someone giving you the opportunity... the power... to stop that. Every time."

"I don't understand."

"The terms are simple, David. In each of her lives, she will die sometime within the age she is now. I can grant you the power to walk through those lives, to skip starting over. You will not age. You will not get sick. You will retain all your memories and knowledge. But you will only meet her sometime within that year. Once you have, and once you have saved her, you must move on. You cannot stay with her. You will wait until you meet her in her next life where you will have the chance to save her again."

David's expression grew more serious this time as he hopped in reverse from the bridge's ledge and took a cautious step or two back from the man. "Who the hell are you?" he wondered with a shaky tone.

"I told you. Someone who wants to help you. But you have to want it to get it."

"What you're saying... is not possible," David blurted, slowly shaking his head.

The man stepped back from the ledge and crossed his hands in front of him. "Anything is possible," he merely retorted.

"If what you tell is true, then you can make me... immortal?"

"Not quite immortal. You can only die by taking your life under your own willpower."

"And say I did take my life. What then?" David challenged.

"Our deal would end. You would start over in your next life. You will meet her again, be with her, and she will die, but you will not have the knowledge or memories to see it coming, or to prevent it."

"Then what is the point of this illustrious offer? That the only time I can be with her is for a short time only to save her and move on?"

The man perked his eyebrows. "There is one method in which you may be able to take your life that may hold the power to change the course of her fate in future lives. But it's not my liberty to speak of that method. Perhaps that is up to you to figure out, if and when you feel the opportunity is fit to present itself. What you really have to ask yourself is — can you reject this offer knowing now what you know and go into your next life without it? Could you go forth and live a million lives having her die in your arms a million different ways, wishing a million different times that you could have seen it coming so you could have prevented it? Experiencing that empty stomach-gnawing pain over and over? There doesn't have to be any more wishing. You can save her, David. You just can't have her."

David quickly shook his head and waved him off, starting to walk away. "No. No. I don't believe you. What you speak of is not possible. It's madness. I don't know who you are, but stay away from me."

"Go back to her, David," the man called out as David quickened his steps down the road. "You'll see all is well. And then you'll see how much of a difference there is between wishing and wanting."

David didn't look back. Frankly, he was upset. The mysterious man had shaken an uneasy feeling through his bones. There was something strange about him indeed. Not necessarily wrong, or evil, but different. Something he couldn't put his finger on. All he wanted to do at that moment was get back to Simone. To get back to her comforting soft hand and nurturing presence. And when he did — she was well. She was upright in bed, surrounded by the excited and overjoyed support of family and friends. Her coughing had disappeared. She spoke clearly and unstopped. Her beautiful golden brown hair had volume. The rings beneath her eyes were gone. David couldn't speak. His eyes merely welled up with tears. He climbed into the bed with her and wrapped his loving arms around her body, engaging himself within the soothing songs of her healthy breathing. She didn't say anything in return. Soul mates like David and Simone never had to. She kissed his head and closed her eyes, bolding a small, warm smile. The doctor said it was a miracle. All traces of the tuberculosis had seemed to disappear. "A medical miracle" was the official declaration he gave.

The crowd of friends and family had retired for the night, leaving them alone. Of course, David couldn't sleep a wink, not just because of the excitement of having her recuperated, but because of those thoughts of the mysterious man and all he had spoken of. It was while David was taking a walk through the house during the middle of the night that he had spotted him outside from a window. He was standing by a fence, hands planted deep within the pockets of the large black overcoat shadowing him, simply staring at David. David was almost tempted to go out and confront him with a million questions, but before he could muster up the ability to do so, the mysterious man had turned and begun to walk away down the road.

And that's when David knew. That's when he realized it. The only reason Simone was deep asleep without the fits of coughing at that moment was because of that man. He had now only needed to face it.

So the next day, when the sun was beaming more beautiful promise down onto the Earth than ever before, David had taken Simone up to the giant oak tree. She had told him as soon as they got there that she wanted to make love to him underneath it, and hold him for hours as they basked under its towering branches with the gratefulness of a second chance. But he could only sink his head down and tell her that he had to leave. "W-What? Why? What do you mean?" Simone had managed to muster out, immediately overcome by fearful and confused anguish.

"I can't tell you," David answered. "I wish I could. And I don't want to leave you. But if I don't, you'll get sick again."

She didn't understand. She had quickly rebounded with the fact that she was plainly back in excellent health, and that what they had was special, and it was their strength together that given them that miracle of extended time. "Wherever you're going, I'm coming with you," she had insisted.

"You'll be with me," he assured her as his tears dropped onto her hands he held. "I don't know if I'll ever be able to tell you why, but I have to do this for you. It's the only way. I have to do this. I have to do this for *you*. Any trust you've ever had in me, you have to put in me now."

Her breaths grew rapid and shaky as her glassy eyes gleamed back to him. She began to quickly shake her head and step back, plunging herself into extreme denial. He stepped toward her and placed a hand on her face, pulling her into him. She hugged him and pouted into his chest. He kissed her forehead and closed his eyes, speaking out with, "Just please know one thing... If you should ever happen to wake up one morning and feel the beauty of being alive, it's because I love you."

He cupped her face within his hands, took one last long drink of her soft, precious lips, and turned to walk away from her. His jaw shook. He tried to fight back the onslaught of tears. He wanted to spin around and run back to her, telling her he had made a mistake. But every fiber in his soul told him that this was the right thing to do. The only thing to do.

For her.

And so she stood, beneath that giant oak tree in the field. Alone. Watching him leave.

*June 13, 1943.*

*So many faces... so many places... And now here I am... taking to the skies to find you this time. In a world that's gone to war with itself, I'm lost without the warmth of your presence again. I used to believe that the only thing this world went to war for was love... and now these blue skies are filled with red. Our green fields of sanctuary we used to lie in are littered with the bodies of those who are lost in their own confused hatred and insanity.*

*How I wish I was lying there with you again...*

*On top of that soft and bright green grassy field with that single towering oak tree. You would gently strum your fingers along my cheek as my head rested in your lap. The setting sunlight would flutter gold across your beautiful face.*

*I regret that choice I made to leave you that first time. And to leave you the second time. And the third. So many times I've walked away from you now... Waiting for the next time. Asking myself if I could do it again. If I could step away just so it means you can be safe... I wonder... when I see you again, will it be different? Can I save you and not walk away? Is there a life of yours I'll be able to continue sharing? In a world that's gone mad within itself, is it still possible to find you this time? I wonder... if I sift through an aerial graveyard, crawl through a trench of endless corpses, muddle through rivers of drowning hopes — will you be there waiting for me again? Will you be there waiting for me to save you?*

David pulled back on the control stick, veering the plane up as the German fighter roared past beneath its belly. Henry, sitting behind him, gripped the handles to the turret and pulled the trigger as countless bullets chased after the enemy plane through the air. He swung the turret around, aiming for another coming from their right side.

Another American fighter plane had dipped into their view, taking out a German with fiery balls of explosion. Within seconds, the favor was returned, as the American plane was targeted and taken down by passing bullets. David sharply jerked the plane, flushing through the thick gray smoke and barely missing the flying debris.

The sound of a German fighter had roared past as Henry grit his teeth and unleashed a fury of more bullets, only puncturing the air at its tail. Bullets from another direction had rattled and ripped into their plane's side, cracking the glass to Henry's portion of the windowed hatch roof. David stretched his head back. There was no movement coming from Henry's seat as more firepower blasted into their side.

Smoke began to filter as the buzzers and emergency beeps went off. David's control board flashed and blinked like the Fourth of July. He held onto the control stick tightly and bounced in his seat as the plane began to wildly shake, quickly losing altitude. It dipped and dipped, soaring downward as it grazed the tops of the trees below, finally crashing on its stomach as it skipped forward and tore through the grassy ground below, snapping through a few thin trees as if they were toothpicks. David cracked his left shoulder against the side and barked out in pain.

It finally teetered to a stop as the smoke filtered all around. David panted out of breath, taking a moment to recollect. He was careful to undo his safety belt as he held his left arm. Reaching forward, he began to push various buttons on the control board, but nothing appeared to be working, especially the radio. So reaching upward, he pushed open his hatch as he worked on pulling himself out of the plane, prying off his helmet as it bounced off the side and rolled across the ground. He slid and leaned against the side, pulling his right arm out of his jacket so he could more easily take it off of his left. He hollered in pain, finally getting it off so he could inspect the shoulder. It was dislocated, and he had immediately considered whacking it against the side of the plane to pop it back in, but held back on the account that he wasn't quite sure if he could do it correctly.

After he had made sure the rest of him was okay and intact, he moved to the rear section of the plane and opened that part of the hatch as well. "Henry," he said, reaching inside and giving him a light shake.

Henry didn't move. He sat there immobile and unresponsive, slouched to the side in his seat as his open eyes lifelessly stared down. Blood had shaded his curly sandy-brown hair with a mixture of red. David felt for a pulse on his neck as if hoping for some sort of reviving chance, but when it was clear that Henry had officially taken his last flight to the skies, David gave a soft, regrettable sigh and reached to his face, closing his eyelids as if closing shades to windows of life. And when he was about to push himself out of the cockpit, something on Henry's dashboard had caught his eye — a taped photograph of a pretty blonde girl.

David fell into thoughts as he stared at the picture, and one of those particular thoughts reverted him to a recent memory when he and Henry were camping out next to a fire at night with other fellow soldiers. They were all scattered about the woodsy area, sleeping, talking or smoking cigarettes, but Henry and David seemed to have a little patch to themselves, both resting their heads on small backpacks next to their fire.

"Hey, David?" Henry had asked with his southern accent after a long while of silence.

David, still awake, replied with a simple, "Yeah."

"You got a gal waitin' for ya back home or what?" Henry curiously inquired.

"I don't really have a home," David simply stated.

"Well — you got a gal waitin' for ya *anywhere*, then?" Henry reformatted the question.

David didn't quite answer right away, and when he did, it was with a soft, emotion-filled, "Yeah. Somewhere..."

"So what's she doin' while you're playin' flyboy in this worldwide hell?"

"I'm not sure, really," he answered. "I haven't seen her for a long time. She was a gypsy the last time I saw her."

"A gypsy?" Henry awkwardly wondered, not sure if he heard him correctly. "Is that one of those girls that wears all the bead necklaces and veils over their face and dances or tells fortunes?"

"Something like that," David mumbled.

Henry flashed a quick smile. "That's different," he said. "My Annabelle — she's workin' in her daddy's sewing factory right now." He dug into his pack and rustled through some items until pulling out a photograph of her, leaning over and holding it out to David. "That's her right there."

David took the photo and held it up so the fire could illuminate her pretty face. "She's pretty," he said.

"She's my own lil' piece of southern comfort back in 'bama," Henry proudly proclaimed as David handed it back to him. He gazed over it himself, streaming his fingers across her face. "Yeah, when the war is over and I get back, my Annabelle's gonna cook up some kids for me and gimme that whole white fence thing. She's good like that. Ya know, even sometimes she sends me some good ol' nudie shots of her to keep me motivated." He rolled over and put the picture away, continuing with, "I'm sure you'll understand if I don't feel so inclined to pull those out for ya."

David stared up at the starry sky.

"You got a picture of your girl?" Henry asked in return.

"No," he responded.

"No? How can you not have a picture of her?"

"I didn't think of it, I guess..."

Henry smirked. "Didn't think of it? Well, hell, man — at least tell me what she looks like. Gimme *somethin'*, here."

David's eyes were still frozen to the sea of stars above. "I guess I could tell you that her face never changes. There's always the same sense of... security... and... safety... in her eyes, and in the way she smiles or laughs. I could tell you that the tones and frequencies in her voice combine more beautifully than any symphony you've ever heard. That her hands are crafted so perfectly you'd feel you were getting touched by the fingers of God if they were to even accidentally find any part of you. And I could tell you that a picture is worth a thousand words. But that would never be enough, because there are not nearly enough words in the English language to even begin to describe her. So, no — I didn't think of a picture... because I've never needed one."

"Damn," Henry huffed, curling as he turned on his side. "She sounds like quite a find."

"Yeah... she is," David quietly agreed, eyes glistening. "Every time I find her."

David transcended back into reality from his thoughts, veering his eyes from Annabelle's picture on the control panel dashboard to Henry in the seat. He took another breath and glanced back to the picture, plucking it off and neatly tucking it into Henry's inner breast jacket pocket with a small, secure pat. "You'll see her again someday," he told him.

So David started to walk away from the plane, holding his dislocated arm to his chest. He wasn't quite sure where exactly in Germany he was aside from the loose coordinates he had mustered at some point while up in the air, but the fact that he was in Germany itself let alone just participating in an aerial attack not too far back was unsettling enough for his currently stranded situation. Of course he was trained to follow protocols should situations like this occur to a soldier behind enemy lines, but they were all set up to be carried out at the soldier's discretion depending on what resources were available to them at the time. And in David's case, his plane's radio was busted, so he had no form of direct communication to any aiding United States help. He couldn't speak German, even if he wanted to ask someone for a phone or a radio — and even that was contingent on happening to ask the right or wrong person, and if it were the latter, he had at least some security in the sense that his trusty fully-loaded pistol was tucked within the back of his pants.

His own discretion, however, alerted him that he really had no other choice but to trek to the nearest town in order to find a phone or radio so that he could rendezvous with a squadron or camp that would hitch him a ride back to his base of origin. In that case, he was better off removing his jacket anyway, as the arrangement of patches, emblems, stars and the U.S. flag itself might call too much attention to himself once he had reached that town. His clothing beneath was a bit more conspicuous but he still wanted to establish communication as quickly as possible.

The town he had stumbled upon around sunset after hours in the woods and fields was quaint and crumbling at every stone, even noticeably before its present war-shaken role. Still, it was nice, and had David not been in such a fix, it was one he would have considered sightseeing more leisurely. Despite its appearance and condensed size, the town was bustling in the streets with merchants and folk going about their daily business, and he immediately lost himself within them as he searched for the proper place to make a call. But as his eyes floated across the stores, stands and people, they stopped to the group of five marching soldiers coming toward him down the street — complete with the bold red swastika bands wrapped around their uniformed arms. If anyone on the street didn't make a noticeable fuss about his attire, the soldiers surely would.

He quietly looked around for some sort of escape route into temporary solitude but only saw the few paintings on easels behind him, ducking behind the art for cover and letting them pass down the street. After they were gone, he took a breath of relief only to lose it again with a small gasp.

She came out from fixing one of the easel legs and brought her brown eyes to his. Whatever sat on the easels was surely not crafted as magnificently as the motif of her face. It was the same as the last time he had seen it, and times before that, and of course, that regrettable day of his first departure from her beneath the giant oak tree, with the exception that her brown hair had a curled bounce to it, falling on her hooded shoulders delicately. She didn't say anything at first, returning his wondrous stare and snapping herself back to life by mustering a friendly smirk as she gestured to the paintings around them. "Ein Anstrich auf Ihrer Wand würde aussehen nett, Nahrung nett in meinem Magen so auch aussehen würde," she said.

David blinked and glanced to the paintings, then back to her. "Oh — uh... I-I don't speak German," he told her.

She immediately grew more cautious and took a step back, sizing him up in his clothes and turning her head to look around. She veered her attention back and lowered her German-accented voice this time to say, "You are... American. American soldier."

"Yes," he answered after slight surprise.

She took another wary look around, spotting more Nazis. "This is wrong place for you to be, American soldier."

He didn't quite know what to say, as he was in an awkward spot, but she noticed his left arm held against his chest and pointed it out. "You are hurt...?" she wondered.

David dropped his eyes to the arm but stood in an almost sheepish silence. The soldiers started to walk toward them down the street, and a tiny portion was telling himself that she might surely turn him in, but she didn't. Instead, she hesitatingly laid a hand on his good arm, saying, "Come. I live up here. We get you inside."

He cocked his head to the approaching threat and took her waiting hand as she walked him through the threshold of the thin apartment building they were in front of. The intimidating Nazis passed by and continued onward. He followed her up the series of rickety and creaking stairs to the second floor. The building appeared to be in older shape than the town itself, but David wasn't one to judge, as he had lived in worse places himself.

She led him to the end of the hallway and pulled out her key, twisting and turning it into the lock of her door. She pushed it forward as it wobbled on its hinges and led him inside, closing it behind with a workable push. It was very small, packed wall-to-wall with the kitchen, bed, dresser and bathtub that gave very thin walking space between. A closet in the corner seemed viable enough to hold only one article of clothing, and the only open space the entire apartment had to offer based on its set-up was taken up by painting materials and two easels, one of which contained a blank canvas ready to be born with colors and the other covered by a small drape. There wasn't even an eating table.

She pulled her coat off as David took in the living quarters. "Sit," she gestured to the cot.

He slowly sunk himself down as she came over and crouched in front, inspecting his arm with very gentle touches. He watched her fingers as they streamed up and down; his eyes were lost in the silence of her face. "I think it's dislocated," he managed to inform her.

"Yes," she agreed. "I must push it back in."

"Do you know how to fix —"

There was a sudden sharp snap as she pushed his arm up, and he cringed forward clenching his teeth in searing pain. "Sorry," she muttered somewhat sympathetically. "It was the easiest way without telling you first."

He held his arm and took a few calming breaths. "Thank you," he said as she stood up and began to clean her small kitchen countertops. "And thank you for... helping me... down there."

She looked over her shoulder to him but didn't speak.

"You speak English well," he noted as if searching for a topic-starter.

"When the entire world is killing each other, it does not make sense to speak only one language," she replied.

"I suppose you're right."

"So what brought you here, Mr. Soldier?" she next inquired.

"I'm a pilot, actually," he corrected. "My plane went down outside of town. My gunman was killed and my radio was destroyed, so I thought I would head to the nearest town to call for help."

She wiped her hands on a raggedy dishtowel, turning to face him. "Must be scary. Not knowing where to go, not knowing who to trust."

He dropped his head lower, softly responding with, "There are much worse things, I assure you." After a moment of dragging silence, he then asked, "What is your name?"

"Emma," she flatly replied after some hesitation.

"Emma," David repeated. "That's a pretty name. I'm David."

She poured a glass of water and gave it to him, once again not saying anything as he drank it. He turned his head and scanned his eyes up and down the room until spotting the painting area. "So you paint?" he asked.

"Yes. I work at a bakery on the corner but it is still not enough money, so I must try to sell my paintings just to keep my apartment," she told him.

David realized something and gestured to the door. "Oh — they're still on the street. Someone might take them."

"I should be so lucky," she huffed. "I cannot even give them away for free. Sometimes I wonder why I even still do it."

He got up off the cot and slinked his way over to the easels. "You should do what makes you happy in life. Regardless of how much money it brings you," he said.

"Sometimes I forget to think like that. Perhaps it is why I am painting this one," she said, stepping to the easel with the drape over it. She removed it to reveal a nearly-finished painting of a giant oak tree in a field, bold and beautiful with colors that sprang forward. David's heart skipped a beat as his face grew soft. He slowly coasted toward it, eyes sinking into the emotionally-haunting yet peaceful tranquility it surged into him. "It is not finished," Emma continued, "but this one is special to me. This one — I will never sell..."

David's fingers reluctantly floated toward it. He wasn't sure what to say from there and as much as he didn't want to deep down, he thanked her and suggested to leave as to not burden her with further trouble. But she mentioned that he'd have nowhere to go or stay for the night, and she could have easily pointed him in the direction of a telephone or radio, but perhaps she didn't want him to leave, either. Perhaps she felt an unspoken sense of safety and comfort in this foreign stranger that had suddenly arrived in her life and on her side of that warring chaos.

So David stayed.

He stayed that night, sleeping on the floor, and stayed the next night after that, and the night beyond that, until the nights turned to weeks. He had assisted her around the apartment, fixing the little things that the landlord never got to or never would get to, and in return she had used a tiny sum of her weekly earnings between the bakery and her paintings to buy him some basic clothes so he wouldn't have to paint a target mark on his forehead wearing his tattered U.S. flyboy attire. She had grown a trusting fondness for him in a matter of short time, just as she had the moment she met him. David had no plan, no goal, no aim — but to be with her. To be near her. When she worked at the bakery, he would never stray too far from her and her tiring hours within the corner shop. At one point she had asked him if his army would come looking for him or acknowledge his disappearance but he merely concluded that they would plausibly assume he was dead, killed in action. It would be better that way, for he certainly didn't wish to return to his patriotic role. "Better to think I'm dead because of the kind of life I live," he had told her. When she asked what kind that was, of course, he added, "The kind that makes it easier for you to move around a lot when people think you're dead."

He had assimilated his livelihood into hers then, leaving behind any place he was going and any place he had been. The moment was her and her alone, and he knew that in what limited fateful time he had with her, whether the weeks would continue into months or merely end on any particular day, she was all that mattered. And although he treasured those countless hours sitting at one of the few tables inside the corner bakery, watching her behind the counter as the aroma of bread and other baked goods warmed him like a coat, it was those nights at her apartment watching her paint that truly captured his affection. In most instances he would merely just sit and watch as he scribbled in his journal, but in others she would actually take delight in letting him paint on the easel beside her, teaching him the ropes of using a colorful hand. He would never try to paint anything specific or serious, sometimes even turning in place to playfully swipe her nose with the end of his blue-bristled paintbrush to fish for a giggle out of her.

But he always loved to watch, especially when she worked on her oak tree. He would always pause dabbling with whatever atrocity he was working on and glance over to her as she would gently skim her brush along the trunk of the tree and give the leaves speckled patters. Her eyes would frequently get lost in the painting, and her brush would freeze mid-air as if she had fallen into a sudden trance of forgotten memories and familiarity.

One particular night well into their companionship, David had been lying on the hardwood floor next to her bed with his pillow and blanket as usual when the sound of her gentle German voice spoke out with, "David? Are you still awake?"

He opened his eyes and turned in attempt to see her through the darkness. "Yeah," he answered. "Is anything wrong?"

"Nothing is wrong," she told him without immediately continuing. "Except... making you sleep on the floor after all this time."

"I'm okay, really," he insisted. "It's not bad. I'm used to it."

"There is plenty of room on here," she noted as he heard her slightly shift over.

"That isn't necessary, but thank you."

"Nonsense. You have been living here as my guest, helping me. If I did not trust you by now, you would not be here now. You are my friend," she explained.

David thought for a long minute and got up, shuffling through the dark and crawling onto one side as she allowed room and lifted the blankets. The bed did indeed easily fit the both of them, but it surely was a tight fit, and in David's case, much more comfortable. Once they had settled in, they lied within the silence of the room for a short while until Emma once again interrupted with, "David? Would you mind if I...?"

"What?" he wondered.

There was an ambivalent tone buried within her sentence when she carried on with, "Would you mind if I put my arm around you?"

The request made his stomach drop. He was lucky to be in the same bed again as her, and after his awkward pause for the right response, he replied with a flat, "No."

She took a moment to turn on her side toward him; the coils in the mattress creaking as she hooked her arm and stopped, a bit reluctant before curling it over while cuddling into him. David's body stiffened up as he stared at the ceiling, and Emma noticed as she slightly brought her head up. "You are trembling," she pointed out.

He opened his mouth to say something but nothing came out. The dim blue moonlight was streaking through the window across the room to highlight his face as she stared at it. "It's been a long time since you've been in a bed with a woman," she guessed.

There was almost a touch of embarrassed shame within his shaky voice as he mumbled, "Yeah..."

He felt her eyes still laying on him, which made him all the more uncomfortable as she moved a bit closer, nuzzling her nose into his neck. "It's nice to share a bed with someone again," she stated. He didn't reply to that either, and as they continued to lie there in silence, he felt her barely shake and give a sniffle. She kept holding it back — holding it back from coming out of her eyes with tiny little gasps. David swallowed. She reached to her face and wiped her eyes, laying her head back into his shoulder. She tilted her face into his neck and pecked it with a faint kiss, then gave another. She carefully worked her way upward until reaching his lips, connecting them with the warm, deep gratification of contentment.

David savored the occasion but pulled himself away as he got off the bed, running hands through his hair as she sat up with concern. "What's wrong?" she wondered.

"Nothing, I..." he started to say as the words fumbled about in his mouth. "I'm sorry; I can't do this."

"You don't... like it?" she presumed.

"No, I do like it, it's just... I can't."

"Why not?"

"I can't explain it. It just... it can't... happen."

Her shoulders dejectedly sunk with her eyes. "Is it me?"

He sighed, sliding his hand over his face.

"You don't want me?" she rephrased.

"If I could only tell you how much," he mumbled. "But I can't have you."

"I am right here," she told him.

He lied back down in his spot on the floor with his pillow and blanket, tucking himself in as he turned his back to her. "I'm sorry," he permissively added.

And then he was silent. She sat there watching him... confused. Rejected. Unwanted. That time it was his turn to fight back the watery threats of eyes...

The next morning, Emma had gone off to the bakery without much said, as the prior night's occurrence between them had tangled into an obstructed quietude. She was there all day and well into the night while he scoured the outside markets for some food, unable to re-grow his dignity to keeping her company at the bakery like he usually did. But he did intend to go there around closing and walk her home, only he had fallen asleep back at her apartment, eventually woken only by his internal natural clock to look at his watch and realize he had overslept past the point of the bakery's closing time. She surely hadn't returned home yet, and his protective fear took over as to where she could possibly be, so without delay, his steps down the complex's staircase jogged a little faster than they commonly did.

Of course, had he been awake to leave and head down the street to the corner a bit sooner, he would have been there to see the two men arrive through the door. The two men, in their early-thirties, that Emma had at first politely notified the bakery was closed. The two men that, in their drunkenly immature state, went forth further into the bakery without obedience anyway, playfully toying and flirting with her as she cleaned behind the display counters. The two men that continued to harass and persistently stall time from leaving.

The two men that wouldn't leave.

They told her how beautiful she was, and the places they could take her. She told them that David was on his way and would arrive at any moment, but the fear pumping through her eyes showed the slightest bluffing concern about his whereabouts, for he should have been there already. They didn't believe her. She had asked them again to leave or she would alert the authorities, but they merely laughed that notion off as well. She made a break for the backroom, but one of the men swooped around the counter and cut her path off as she turned to retreat in the other direction; his accomplice hopping over the counter and blocking her off there as well.

They were smooth and easy in their approach closing in on her, staring with the ravenous eyes of vultures and the mischievous grin of the devil. They assured her they only wanted to have fun, and it would be more enjoyable if she were cooperative. There was nowhere to escape as they clashed inward, grabbing her flailing arms as she attempted to wildly break free. The rugged and dirty hand of one of the men clamped her mouth closed as she started to scream and call for help. He told his partner to hit the lights, shedding darkness across the bakery as they wrestled to drag her toward the light of the backroom and disappeared within it.

Tears trickled down her cheeks as they strived to pin her on the floor among the storage boxes. They laughed to each other and struck comments on how much more of a woman they would make her feel after getting through with her. She kicked and kneed one in the shin as he grunted and belted her across the face, grabbing her curly hair and slamming her head against the floor as blood trickled from her temple. His friend mentioned how she was feistier than the others, but he retorted with a grin as he looked down and assured her that the ditch she was going to be buried in would cure her of that.

Emma did what any other girl would have done — anything. And that included chomping her teeth into his hand, ripping away some flesh and blood as he threw his head back with a hollering scream. He huffed and held it to his chest, sharpening his jaw in pain as he reached behind his shirt and pulled out a small handgun, loading it and shoving the barrel under her chin to proudly inform her that her body was going to service him just as good dead than alive.

That's when the gunshot rang out.

Except it wasn't from his gun, and the bullet going through his head and into the adjacent wall didn't stop for a brief moment of explanation as his body toppled to the floor. His friend's face dropped as he jerked his body and turned. David took a few steps forward, unloading three more bullets into his chest as he fell against a shelving unit.

Emma's jaw quivered as she looked over to him. Her face shook, juggling tears as she sprang up and ran into him with a colliding hug. He wrapped his arms around her and closed his eyes, embracing the succoring moment. He set the gun aside and pried her a bit forward to inspect her up and down, gently touching the gash on her forehead. "Are you okay? Are you hurt?" he eagerly wondered.

"No," she confirmed. "I'm fine." She rolled her eyes up to his and sniffled. "I didn't know where you were. I didn't want to leave until you had come. I was afraid to walk back by myself."

"I'm sorry. I'm so sorry," he apologized, rocking her within his arms. "I fell asleep. It's okay. You're okay."

He held her a bit longer, grasping all the moments he could. They were fleeting. He knew right away that this was it with her. Just as he had known those times before. Something on the floor next to one of the men caught his eye as he slightly separated himself from her in order to bend down and inspect it. It was the gun. "Walther PPK," he said aloud to himself.

"What?"

"The gun," he noted as he began to inspect the body up and down. He reached into the man's pants pocket and pulled out a wallet, along with a badge, closing his eyes to give a sigh and display it to her. "Gestapo," he sighed.

Realization set into Emma as her mouth cracked open. She began to shake her head. "They — They were trying to hurt me," she started to protest. "They were drunk and they attacked me. You did what you had to!"

"It's not gonna matter," he bluntly affirmed. "They're German secret police. I'm American and I killed them. You've been illegally harboring me."

"We can explain! We've been doing nothing wrong! They will not care about a single American pilot!"

"They're not gonna tolerate it," he remarked. "We have to... leave..."

She stood in place for a moment, watching him, and gave a solid nod. "Then we will leave. We will run away."

"I can't go with you," he sadly added.

"What?" she confusingly asked.

"We have to leave the country but I... can't go with you," he repeated. "I... I can't explain why."

She shook her head and took his hands in hers. "Nonsense," she stingily asserted. "They will not find us. We will be safe."

His eyes swelled up with water, returning to that place he had regretted before. "I can't."

"Why? Tell this to me. Tell me why!"

"I can't tell you why, and I can't go with you," he said, choking up as he wrapped his hands more tightly in hers. "Listen to me, Emma..."

"No. No!"

"You have to leave tonight and never come back to your apartment. If they catch you, what I did will have been for nothing. Do you understand? I promise you — you will be okay as long as you leave," he explained.

"Is it about last night?" she wondered, still fighting for an opposing point. "You won't have to kiss me if you don't want to. Please! I want to stay with you!"

He wiped his eyes, trying to toughen himself up as he reached forward and stroked a bit of hair from her face. "I wish I could tell you everything. I wish I could explain, but... I can't. It's for you. It's all for you, it always is. Maybe there will be a day where you'll know why I have to do this. But until then, you'll be safe."

Her breathing grew short and sporadic as she tried to comprehend something to which she wasn't granted an answer. She muddled through her thoughts and finally conducted to mildly ask, "Will I ever see you again?"

David wasn't sure how to respond to the question. On the technical level, either answer would have been true, but there was still the lengthy percipience behind both, and rationalizing was not a road he was allowed to travel down with her. So he did the only thing his heart wanted at that particular moment by placing his hands on her face and kissing her forehead, resting it against his. He closed his eyes and whispered, "You'll be okay now..."

David had returned to her apartment alone to pick up his sacred journal. The faucet at the kitchen sink dripped. The bed sat cold. And as he stood in the emptiness of the room around him, he stared at an easel holding a painting he wished he could walk into.

*May 28, 2004.*

*I'm afraid to leave you whenever I find you.*

*Our time together is always a ticking clock. I'm uncertain of how long it will be. Uncertain of how well I'll get to know who you've become this time. Will I get to look at your face for three days or three months? The image of your smile in my mind may sustain me during your absence for decades and decades at a time, but it's your eyes that keep me near you once I've found you.*

*Do they look for me in the moments I'm not there? Do they expect me to come around the corner to meet you for our daily visits? Do they see me at all in the way they saw me those so many years ago beneath our oak tree?*

*Do they look for me after I'm gone?*

*I've left you again and again now, and inevitability is all that seems to remain in this routine as once again I must wait for the culminating moment to fulfill my requirement. Will you see it coming? Can I stop it again this time? All I can do is wait by your side. For I am your savior. I am your hero. I am your protector. And when that threatening moment arrives, I will be there at your side as your salvation, for that has been the purpose of my world, no matter how often it has changed around me. Everything changes.*

*Yet you remain the constant.*

David gave a light exhale as he looked up from his journal to the park around him. It was more than a beautiful late spring day, and the city was at its best. There, in Union Square, he sat on one of the infinite benches next to Tanya, who dug her thin hand into her bag again and forcefully decorated the paved walkway with bouncing bird seeds. He closed the journal completely and sat back so he could watch her. She was prompt in her nice buttoned-down shirt and pants, and her golden brown hair was short and bobbed, bringing light to her pretty face. He liked that style on her. And he loved watching her feed the birds, and she loved doing it probably more than anything. An atom bomb could go off in the city and her contentment wouldn't budge a bit, as she would reach back into her bag and flick a fistful of seeds on top of the ones she had just thrown. The pigeons would grow in numbers every now and then, lightly bobbing their heads as they strutted and pecked away at the tiny seeds, which always seemed to excite her even more as she would start to lightly rock back and forth in her seat with her smile getting brighter and wider. When her hand wasn't dipping back into the bag, it was out in front of her, fingers wiggling as if she were playing a piano.

Aside from her usual tendency, David noticed she had done that especially when she got excited, strumming her fingers mid-air, sometimes more slowly and smoothly as if her invisible piano-playing had shifted to the motions of an orchestra conductor. And then there was her smile, using gaping the more excited she had become with her hand affinity. She laughed and plunged her fingers into the bag, sprinkling more on the ground. It was when she reached back in her final time that her smile began to fade. She rocked back and forth just a tad bit faster. "Uh-oh," she stated. "All gone. All gone, David."

"Already, huh?" he asked, cocking his eyes to the empty bag.

"Yeah. Yeah, no more left," she told him. "No more to feed the birds."

He cracked a smile. "I think you put enough down to feed every bird in the *city*," he joked.

"I wanna go to Central Park now," she blurted.

"We won't have time. I have to take you back now," he said with a somewhat sympathetic response. "I'll take you tomorrow night, I promise."

"I like to go the Central Park."

David stood up, winding the string around his journal to secure it. "I know you do. It's very pretty there at night."

"Yeah, very pretty. It's very pretty. You can take me there, David," she repeated. "You can. But tomorrow night."

He stepped toward her, lightly laying a hand on her shoulder and giving a helping gesture for her to get up. "Okay, we gotta go," he gently insisted.

"Okay. Time to go. All done with the birds," she said.

"Bye, birds," David waved as he slipped his hand around hers and she slowly stood to her feet.

"Bye-bye, birds," she quickly called out as well, starting to walk with him. Her free hand continued to sway in the air; fingers dancing. Her eyes dragged along the ground as they walked, and her head slightly swiveled and bobbed, almost like the pigeons.

A short while later, David had returned her to her housing uptown, where he was greeted by Gloria, an African-American woman in her late-thirties. "Hey, guys," she greeted with a smile as she approached them in the hallway. "Did you have fun?"

"We fed the birds," Tanya mentioned with a self-satisfying tone.

"You did? That sounds terrific," Gloria encouraged.

David smirked. "Never a shortage of food for flying rats when Tanya's on the town."

"Not flying rats. They're pigeons, David, they're pigeons," Tanya corrected him as she moved past them and into her open bedroom. "Feed the pigeons."

Gloria crossed her arms and watched. "Tanya? What do you say to David?"

"Thank you, David," she said without turning back.

"You're welcome," he replied.

"David's leaving now," Gloria reminded her. "Don't you wanna say goodbye?"

"Bye, David," she spoke as she stopped and stood in front of a painting on the wall.

"I'll see ya tomorrow, okay?" he added.

"'Kay, see ya on tomorrow," she concluded. She just stood there, slightly rocking in place as she stared at the beautiful painting — a giant oak tree in a field. It was an older painting, but the colors were still bright and full of life.

Gloria watched her, leaning her shoulder against the threshold of the doorway. "She'll stare at it for hours," she said. "She'll come in here and just sit or stand in front of it. For someone who can't even spend two minutes coloring, it sure seems to grab a hold of her. She's really happy you brought it for her."

David was lost in thought as he stared beyond Tanya and into the painting. He could almost feel the warmth of the sun and the passing of the summer breeze as it fluttered through the leaves. Gloria turned more toward him. "You've done wonders with her, David. I've never seen her take to anyone like she has with you. You're the only one she'll let touch her without getting upset."

"Yeah... I, uh... guess we have a good connection," he murmured.

"Well, I don't know what it is, but I'm happy to have you here," she supported. "You know, I'm been meaning to talk to you in regards to that. I was thinking, perhaps, that because of your success with Tanya, you might consider... taking on someone else as well. Nothing too heavy; you would start with maybe one visit a week with them and build upon that, but you seem to have a real knack for this. I'd be interested in seeing how much of your magic you could use on someone else."

David lightly scratched his head, molding an unsure expression. "Yeah... Look, Gloria — I'm really flattered and all, and maybe under different circumstances I could take you up on that offer, but... I think my attention is pretty much dedicated to Tanya and Tanya alone. I'm sorry."

"Oh, don't be sorry," she retorted, waving it off. "Just thought I'd put it out there. But if you ever feel like you want to welcome more onto your plate, I certainly could work it out. It's a pleasure having you here with us."

"Thank you. That means a lot," he nodded. "I should... probably get going now. She was talking about Central Park again; I thought maybe I could take her there tomorrow night."

Gloria smiled. "I think that can be arranged. You have a great day now, David. Thanks again for everything. We'll see you tomorrow."

David nodded and waved, turning to leave as Gloria stepped into the room to talk with Tanya. He wasn't ready to leave yet — it was still far too early in the day, but that was how some days went. Some were shorter than others, and some extended further than planned. But nevertheless, each of those minutes, short or long, were treasured by David. And although for creeping fear of the certain fate that could extend its hand and try to strike her at any moment or place, he left her for the day and could only look forward to the next.

Those seconds between the times he could spend his mornings, afternoons or nights watching her do the simplest things were hard and stretching. To think that he had waited so long to find her once again and be broken apart from her vicinity once he had was atrociously unbearable. He would often spend his nights walking the city or parks, sleepless and relentless, sometimes attending a movie or having a drink at a bar among the faceless patrons of time. He wouldn't converse too often with them, but occasionally there were one or two he would get to know on a small level. And he didn't spend too much time at his apartment, for it was never truly home to him, nor would last that way much longer. It never did. It was merely a place for him to eat, wash up or sleep, when he wasn't lying awake with dreading thought.

And there was the Brooklyn Heights Promenade. He found himself going there in the late hours of night after leaving Tanya. He would sit on one of the benches looking over the waterfront and watch the city and its twinkling lights in its gloriously bold view. For some odd reason he slightly felt more protective there, as if he could overlook the city and Tanya nestled deep within it without actually being there.

Still, the minutes he was back in her beauty made the impatient experience of all of those waiting tactics seem insignificant and passive, because he was reunited with his purpose. She had wandered a few steps away across the path near some bushes and had emerged from the fireflies as if she were one of their own.

He had never seen fireflies like that before. Swarms and bunches of them drifting and dancing, floating with a wisp in the Central Park summer night air. Of course, the park itself was lit with the occasional lamppost here and there, but that particular patch seemed to be a world of its own, illuminated by the illustrious glitter of their mysterious presence and perhaps reminding him of the tiny patterns that lined up the aisles and rows of movie theaters with an ominous guidance. It wasn't all that unusual, and it was May, opening up a nightly invitation to all things warm and limited to the summer.

But there she was, turning the corner of the pathway and breaking through them with her slow and soft steps. Her brown eyes reflected their glow, and he felt as if he had wandered into a mystical fantasy. They were the only two souls there at the time, and for all they knew, the rest of the world had slipped into a hidden retreat away from them. His heart leapt and his stomach dropped as she casually moved in his direction. She didn't say anything or continue her walk, but merely stopped and turned within the sea of blinking lights, captured and mesmerized with their entanglement of beauty as her right hand floated and conducted her usual symphony — this time with the array of a sparkling orchestra.

She was the most beautiful girl he had ever seen. He couldn't possibly rationalize what he was feeling at the mere physical sight of her. He knew that at the base of human anatomy, beauty was a combination of facial tones, skin and random genetic structuring, but she was different. And although her face and genetic make-up had always remained the same from life to life with miniscule differences in each, he would never lose his wonder of attraction. She tilted her head upward and watched, hypnotized with an open smile as bright as their lights.

David's heart skipped beats. His eyes melted with a combination of sympathy, gratitude and devotion that he carried with him back to her housing shortly after. Being a bit later in the evening, not many people were around as he signed them in at the front desk and led her down the hallways to her bedroom door. He opened it and she took no reservation in entering, immediately shuffling across the room to ponder and inquisitively investigate her desk before losing interest and taking a seat in a chair in front of the oak tree painting as if she had never left.

David followed in behind, crouching next to her as his eyes pierced into her with wonder. He studied her face for a long moment, searching before turning his head to glance at the oak tree painting. He looked back at her and shifted himself a bit closer. "You see it, don't you?" he softly whispered. "You remember it."

Tanya sat there, inattentive and oblivious to his presence as her body barely rocked from side to side. David's hand crept over and cautiously enveloped hers, still receiving a non-responsive reaction. He brought his face a little closer to hers and searched deep within her soft brown eyes. "Are you in there?" he wondrously pondered. "Do you know who I am? Are you trying to tell me something?"

Tanya's eyes glazed over to his body and trailed for a moment until finding his face, lighting hers with a smile. He reached his other hand up and froze, thinking twice before laying his fingertips against her cheek. He streamed them along to her chin and released his other hand's grasp of hers to gently brush her short hair. "How can I tell you how much I miss you?" he asked.

He closed his eyes and meticulously crept his face forward, gently laying his lips over hers. He began to delicately kiss her, losing himself in his emotions as she suddenly snapped her head away, quickly shaking it in a fit as she began to rock back and forth, groaning. She threw her arms up, making him spring back as she panicked and threw a fit, loudly moaning and crying out. "I'm sorry, I'm sorry!" David repeated, trying to calm her down with the waving of his hands. "Tanya, I'm sorry! Look, I'm not touching you! See?"

She got up and knocked the chair over, huddling into the corner and making a commotion as Gloria and another man hurried into the room. "What happened?" Gloria wondered as the man stepped over to assist.

"We were just sitting here and... I touched her. And she started..." David blurted, putting his hands on the back of his head.

"It's okay, David. Just give us some room," Gloria assured him as she went over and lightly took Tanya by the shoulders, beginning to lead her out of the corner. She had managed to calm her down pretty quickly, and by her tactics, seemed to be no stranger to the incident. "Come on; you're okay, pretty girl — everything's okay," she would comfort Tanya with, sitting her on the bed.

All David could do was helplessly watch.

It was a little while later that Gloria had made her way down the main hall to surprisingly spot him sitting in one of the lobby chairs, hunched forward as his elbows rested on his knees and his chin rested on his hands. "David?" she curiously said, walking over. "I thought you left a little while ago?"

He looked up at her and rubbed some tiredness from his eyes. "Yeah, I... just felt like I would stay a bit longer. In case she... needs me," he explained. "How is she?"

"She's fine," Gloria told him, sitting more seriously in the neighboring chair. "Listen, David — about what happened earlier — I don't want you to blame yourself. Sometimes we have to understand that people like Tanya are just... different. No matter what we may say, think, do or not do — sometimes we just don't have the control."

"Yeah," David mumbled, keeping his eyes on the floor. "I just wish I could find that control."

Gloria took a deep breath and laid a hand on his shoulder. "She's lucky to have you. Why don't you go home, and we'll try again tomorrow?"

"If it's all right, I'd kinda like to hang around for a bit," he suggested. "I just... wanna make sure she'll be okay. Just be near her, ya know? Sorry, it's... this force of habit of mine."

Gloria flashed her usual warm smile. "You stay as long as you'd like," she welcomed, patting his shoulder as she stood up and walked away.

David sighed and ran a hand through his short hair, left alone in the lobby with his thoughts.

He must've been on his third cup of coffee in the diner a few streets over when he saw the first fire truck roar by. Of course, he didn't really intend to stay that long to begin with; he only wanted to grab a cup to go and return to the lobby, but he ended up sitting at the counter in the diner anyway, and once he had finished that cup and got another to go with the intention of leaving with it again, he only ended up right back at the counter where he started. The other few patrons scattered about the eatery thought nothing of the common second fire truck that honked and blared past the windows, and David would've thought the same if it weren't for that pit in his stomach. Something had told him to leave — to get back to Tanya. And this time, his third cup of coffee sat on the counter as he hurriedly pushed his way out the doors.

He jogged his way through shortcuts to Tanya's housing, which was surrounded by an immensely-growing crowd of police personnel, firefighters and other medics who tended to the smoke and fire-infested building. His eyes flashed wide as he veered his head upward. Smoke came from the various windows illuminated with an uncomfortable red and orange glow. Pushing his way through people, he came across Gloria, who was wrapped in a brown blanket with smoldering black spots charred across her face.

"Gloria! Gloria! Are you okay?!" he eagerly shouted.

"Oh my God, David!" she cried out.

David jerked his head to see various personnel helping people out of the building one by one. "Where's Tanya?" he then quickly asked. "Gloria, where's Tanya?! Is she out?!"

"No! They — They're trying to get to her floor! It's too bad up there!"

David nervously looked around, trying to think on his feet, and before she could say anything further, he had pushed his way past some of the people as he headed for the side alley of the building. "David? David!" Gloria tried to call out.

He had no intention of waiting out there in front of the building while firefighters "tried" to muddle their way into the burning establishment. Perhaps he had already mapped out a direct route to Tanya's floor via the zigzagging fire escape staircase outside or perhaps he was just using his protective instincts to get to her without further delay, but nothing was going to keep him from *doing* nothing. He gripped onto the steel handles and pulled himself up the ladder, reaching the actual platform stair section as he hiked his way up. He stopped in front of a window and kicked at it a few times, finally breaking through as smoke plundered out into the nighttime air. Covering his face with his arm, he ducked inside the empty bedroom and trudged through, exiting out into the hallway. Smoke detector alarms were beeping and blaring as fires burned everywhere around him. A board fell, nearly crushing him as he staggered back. The smoke was so thick he could hardly see, but he made his way down the hall until finally reaching her door.

Charging his shoulder against it, he burst through and into the room, where he briefly froze at the awe-stricken sight of flames everywhere. The red and orange colors danced their threatening dance, and huddled on the bed in the middle of it all was Tanya, crouched in the fetal position and rocking back and forth as her free right hand dangled in the air with fingers wiggling. "Oh, God — Tanya!" was all David could muster as he soared over to her.

He tried to wrap his arms around her, but she merely moaned and cried out, starting to throw a bodily fit. "Come on, we have to leave!" he urged.

"Too hot in here. Too hot," she told him. "No-no. Mama says don't touch the fire. Fire bad."

"I'm gonna get you outta here," he promised, placing a hand on her cheek. "Let me help you."

"Oak tree safe," she blurted, continuing her rocking. "I wanna go to oak tree, David. Oak tree safe."

David's eyes shot to the wall, where the oak tree painting was being consumed by the flames creeping across. A section of her ceiling on the opposite side of the room fell, crashing upon her desk. David reached down to the bed and clawed his hand over one of the blankets, yanking it up from underneath her and wrapping it around her. "Here you go," he said, trying to keep a gentle tone. "We're gonna put your blanket around you. We're gonna keep the bad fire away."

"Keep bad fire away," she repeated, playing her piano in the air. "Too hot."

David eased her to her feet off the bed and started to lead her across the room when a small explosion came from across the hall. She cried out and nervously balled into him, shaking her head. One of her windows blew open, shattering glass as they fell to their knees on the carpet. And that's when David noticed the sudden rage of fire roaring across the ceiling into the room like a wild avalanche. He widened his eyes and pushed her down, throwing the blanket more over as he covered and held her with his body.

It was slow motion to him, like an inescapable dream. The whoosh of flames ripped across the ceiling and through the air as if they were a river, stretching and looming for everything and anything. He held her tightly within the room of devouring flames. It was barely a room anymore. Just a four-sided burning oven sealing them in the center. He turned his head to the painting on the wall and watched as the fire erased the last of the oak tree and its wondrous branches until there was nothing left. Hooking his arms under Tanya's wrapped body, he lifted her in his arms and got to his feet, moving for the door.

His legs were like jelly. He could barely run, and each step he took only amplified the slow motion feeling surrounding him. The smoke was thicker now as he hurried down the hallway. Another section of the ceiling had collapsed just as he passed beneath, crashing right through the floor and down to the next as he nearly lost his footing. He held Tanya close as she burrowed her head into his neck.

David's slow motion moon-walking steps had managed to lead them out the main entrance doors as they emerged outside into safety. Medical personnel immediately took the wrapped Tanya from his arms as he fought to keep her close, trying to follow after them with hesitation from other reaching medic arms pulling him back.

He was later told that the cause of the fire, which spread and slightly damaged the two neighboring buildings, was speculated to be from a janitor who was smoking inside near an open window and didn't properly dispose of his remaining cigarette butt. In the aftermath of the ordeal, David stood with a brown blanket draped around him and watched the medics routinely tend to Tanya in the back of an ambulance. Gloria, after making sure she was fine, strolled over to him and looked back at her. "She's gonna be okay. They're gonna wanna take her and some of the others to the hospital overnight for some testing," she noted. She glanced back to him. "That was very brave, what you did. If it weren't for you, they might not have gotten to her in time. You saved her life, David. And I'm sure she's eternally grateful."

He didn't take his eyes away from Tanya. "I saw her sitting there in her room. Just — sitting there. Like she couldn't move. And she seemed so scared," he softly explained, still in thought. "It was like my whole world was on fire and I couldn't control it. I saw the lights from outside as I got closer to the door and I thought... if I could just take a few more steps... all that mattered was holding her out for someone to take. That's the only control I had..."

Gloria laid her usual comforting trademark hand on his shoulder. "I'll let you know which hospital we're going to as soon as they tell me. Shouldn't be much longer."

"Actually... if I could just have a minute alone with her," he wondered.

She casually nodded and turned away among a group of others as he stepped to the back of the ambulance, where the paramedic assisting her had gone off to momentarily help with someone else. David stared at her for a moment. Her eyes were veered up to the sky and her hand was orchestrating as her calmness suggested that nothing had ever happened.

David began to get choked up. "Um..." he started to say, searching for words. "I have to go away now, Tanya."

She didn't reply nor look at him. His eyes gleamed with tears trying to fight their way back. "God... do you know how beautiful you are?" he then asked her. "All I wanna do is look at you, and... I can't, because you're just too beautiful."

"I'm a pretty girl," she stated, shifting her gazing eyes to one of the lights inside the ambulance.

"That's right, you are," he agreed. He took a step closer to her and lightly placed his hand over her left that rested on her leg. "You keep feeding the birds, alright?"

"'Kay, I'm gonna feed the birds," she confirmed.

David sobbed and sniffled, wiping a teardrop away. "You're gonna live a good life," he mentioned. "You're gonna be okay now."

He turned and started to walk away. "Bye, David," Tanya's voice had called out. He stopped and looked back to her. Her gaze was still lost within a spot in the ambulance as her fingers tapped her leg. "See ya on tomorrow."

"See ya on a tomorrow," he quietly said to himself, breaking out in a quick cry.

He wanted to watch her as he walked away. He wanted to keep his eyes locked on her every bit until she was out of sight, but he knew it would be easier this way...

David swallowed the lump in his throat as he climbed up the side railing of the Brooklyn Bridge. He clutched a cable for balance and took another step to a level higher up. It was colder up there than it was down on the roads below in which the cars still coasted back and forth on, even at that late hour. He peered over the edge to the black water far below; its light waves briefly bouncing the reflections of the surrounding city lights. His jaw jiggled as a border of tears cupped beneath his eyelids. A breeze fluttered through his hair and he took it as an invitation to peaceful tranquility, slightly releasing his grip on the nearest beam that had given him stability.

"Are you sure you want to do that?" a voice had spoken from his side.

He reopened his eyes and turned his head to see the mysterious man standing merely feet away, hands in his long black-jacketed pockets. He had looked the same as he had when David first met him all of those haunting years ago. And it took David a moment or two to conjure up some sort of reactive response to his sudden presence as he peered back down to the water below. "You. You're the whole reason I'm up here," he finally blurted with an accusing tone.

"Am I?" the man wondered. "Or are you?"

"I can't do this anymore," David said as he shook his head. "I'm done."

"Yet you've already come so far," the man flatly spoke.

David gave a heavy, helpless sigh, resting his forehead against the beam. "Do you have any idea of what I've been through?"

"Perhaps. Yet you keep going."

"But *why?!* What is the point?!" David barked.

"I thought you understood it quite well when I explained it," the man said.

"I mean why did you come to me? Who are you? What does this have to do with you?"

"It has nothing to do with me. Only with you," the man plainly answered.

"Ya know, every answer from you is like a goddamn mirrored riddle that doesn't tell me anything," David sourly sneered.

"Then jump," the man suggested, nodding his head to the water.

David's eyes veered back down as the possibility processed once again in his head. The mysterious man took a step forward, raising his height a bit more on another beam. "Or perhaps a part of you wants to continue forward."

"You said that if I killed myself a certain way, I'd have a chance of ending this by changing her fate in future lives," David reminded him.

"Do you believe this is the way?"

"Is it?"

"Perhaps it is and perhaps it isn't," the man simply shrugged. "Perhaps you may find yourself with two possibilities — the first being that you will die and transcend into your next life where you will meet her and live a full life without the experience of her fated death. The second being that you will die and transcend into your next life, where you will meet her and she will die. And if that is the case — our deal will have ended. You'll go on to your next life, you'll eventually meet her again, and she will die. There will be nothing you can do to see it coming or stop it. You will remember nothing of the conversation two individuals held on a bridge and the choice that you presented yourself with. Are you prepared to take that chance?"

David's eyes flooded with water as his jaw jiggled to fight the tears from spewing out. He carefully slunk down and sat, crossing his arms around his knees. "If you could only see the people she's become," David added. "Who she is *now*. *She* doesn't even know who she is now. All because of a mental disability that prohibits her from living a life of control. I look in her eyes and I see who she really is inside. Someone who's trapped... and helpless. And I wanna... stay with her... and help her out of that dark tunnel. I don't want to just save her. I want to give her a place in the world that she's lost in."

"Your job isn't to give her a place in the world," the man firmly told him. "Your job is to ensure that the place she already has continues. You've already been there many times. And the next time you meet her will be no different from the previous — she *will* be someone different. She will have disabilities, or disfigurements. She will have different careers and hobbies. She will love other men, or women. And they will be lives of control that even I cannot alter, no more than I can alter the changing of seasons or the setting of the sun on the horizon."

The tears gently rolled down David's cheeks. "Please... I can't... wait... countless years to find her again and be cursed with a feeling of sympathy to fix her from a life she didn't choose or deserves that I merely prolonged for her."

"Then jump," the man merely gestured with an elegant wave of his black-jacketed arm. "But the only control you have in this world now is the power of choice. The choice to wait with a chance of saving her again — or to jump into the uncertainty of water that could forever wash that power away."

David squeezed his eyes shut tightly, sobbing and pouting as he buried his face into his hands. When he lifted them away, he saw that the mysterious man was gone, leaving him alone so very high up on top of the world. The sounds of the city were his only connection to life then, as he slumped his head back against the beam and veered his glassy eyes up to the ageless starry sky.


*September 17, 2187.*

*So many stars... So many possibilities... I feel so lost yet so found within them all. It's as if I've been endlessly drifting. Waiting. Waiting for you to rescue me this time, so that we may have a chance to float together to a place where we belong. I used to see stars when I kissed you, and now I know why. It's been a long time since you've given my lips life. But that's the price I've paid. The price I'm paying. If you could only know. If I could only tell you. What would you think of me then? Would you ever be able to forgive me? All of those years... all of those lives... all of the things that could have but never happened between us, because I made that fateful decision. That haunting night so very long ago where our paths would only start to cross with the turning of time.*

*Pieces of me regret that night but rejoice in the fact that you woke up the next morning to feel the beauty of being alive. That was, is and has been my only motivation to trek this far... to keep planting my walking stick into the ground so that I may take another step forward down my path and eventually cross you every once in a while. To not know where you're going once I've left you again but to know that you'll get there safely.*

*How I feel no longer seems to be a factor. I'm so empty inside yet I'm so full of love for you. I've met so many people on my journey yet I'm the loneliest person in history. And now every time I find you, I find that my emotions spoil the time I am blessed to spend with you. I dread and fear for that moment of departure from you so much that I miss the ones leading up to it. I ruin them with despair so deep that I fail to cherish who you are... who you've become... And then our time is over again.*

*I've weighed the options of killing myself so many times... so many different ways... Just so I can be with you. Leave behind the knowledge I was blessed and cursed with and start over. I haven't seemed to be able to do it.*

*Would you want me to?*

The infinite stars twinkled within the abyss of the black universe surrounding David's cabin room. He would often get lost in his thoughts staring out at them through his circular window, generally for hours at a time — feeling the light and soft rhythm of some distantly haunting tunes or sounds that really captured the universe's presence. Just like a planetarium. He had been to some numerous times before, but never really imagined it could be this beautiful. Those people at the planetarium got it right with those sounds and images, though. But it was these star-gazing hours in particular that always made him realize that he had all of the hours in the world, even if he was no longer on the world. He had all the hours of time itself, and time for him seemed to expand longer than the furthest regions of space. It was in those hours in that particular time period that he felt the most at home sitting on his bed and writing in the journal that was as worn and tattered as he had become.

David ignored the knock coming from his closed door. He kept writing and scribbling in the journal until the point when it whooshed open into the wall, allowing Bobby Rhodes to step in. He was tall, almost brute with his Italian heritage and black bushy eyebrows that went with his short-cropped black hair and budding five-o'clock-shadow. He stood there in the open threshold for a moment, watching as David kept writing, impervious to his presence. "You didn't hear me knocking?" Rhodes wondered.

"I heard you," David simply answered. "I just chose to ignore it."

"Like you chose to ignore me when I asked you to recharge the oxidation in the coolant tanks over an hour ago?"

"They'll get done," David stated.

Rhodes stood and scratched his head, notably growing annoyed with David's attitude. "Yeah. When we're all incinerating to death in the middle of space, right?"

"It's not my job," David flatly told him.

Rhodes perked an eyebrow, replying with, "Uh, the United Space Federation seems to think it's part of it."

"It's just something to do. Like everything else on this ship. Something to do to pass the time until my *real* job," he explained.

"Which would be...?"

"Something way over your head. Something you wouldn't understand," David mumbled.

Rhodes unbelievably smirked and placed his hands on his hips, shaking his head. "Yeah. But you sure as hell give time and priority to that journal of yours. What do you even write in it? You're not doing anything around here, so what is it you're writing about? "Rhodes is an asshole" or something?"

"No. I wouldn't write that; I would just flat-out tell you that."

"Reality check — This shitty attitude of yours has been getting worse since the second you got out of cryo. You don't listen, you don't follow orders, you don't care about this mission... I don't even know what you did or how the hell you even got *on* this mission, but if things don't change around here, I'm gonna have to put corrective action into effect."

"Corrective action. What are you, gonna ground me? You gonna lock me in containment 'til we get back home? Or you just gonna shove me in the emergency pod and *send* me home?"

"You know what? Fuck you, David. 'Cause there's four other people on this ship that actually give a damn about being here and I will *not* tolerate a shitty mind-blown attitude that'll only jeopardize their safety," he huffed, shaking a stern finger. He took a deep breath, trying to ease the hostility he had built up inside himself. "Look — I wanna help. Too many people have fried their minds out in space and I don't wanna be held responsible for another. So if you've got some stuff to work out, I want you to go to Julie and talk about it. Seems like she's the only one around here you give time to, anyway."

David's eyes veered up from his journal to Rhodes for the first time. "What do you know about time?" he keenly asked. "What do you know about giving it to anyone? You think your sense of time has to do with minutes on a clock? A dial on a cryo-chamber? A punch-audit federation pay-credit for a crewmember? Time is a dream for you that will inevitably end after a series of seconds. Things are invented and broken. Man takes his first step on the moon. Woman takes her first step on Mars. Vehicles get tires on one day and wings on the next. Time graciously gives to so many things around you yet you never truly give back to it. So you can only use what you're given to collect a series of people and call them "life" without ever really managing to know how to equally spread the minutes between them. Tell me what *you* know about giving time, Bobby Rhodes. Because all I see anymore are people who waste it without cherishing those struggling minutes. As for me? I have my own agenda for my minutes. Recharging the oxidation on coolant tanks is just something to do in between them. So how 'bout you let me finish what I'm writing in my journal and get the fuck out of my room — Captain."

Rhodes didn't know what to make of the epilogue. He stood and stared at David for a dragging moment until answering with a simple turn of his back and exit out of the room.

She floated like an angel... gracefully. Back and forth, free as a drifting feather within the free float room — it was an anti-gravity room on the ship specifically designated for those wishing to float about and forget any problems, worries or duties they carried with them in the loneliness of space. Especially on that particular trip aboard the Infinity 9, a routine study of Neptune — so close to home yet so far. David loved to watch her in the free float room, mainly because she loved to go there. And not because she was worried, or was trying to forget problems — because Julie was always at peace. She would carelessly drift and slowly turn about in the air, spreading her arms like wings. When she had reached the opposite end of the room, she would merely plant her feet against the wall and spring herself back out into the open air, crafting that perfect smile over to David when he was there watching. Her golden brown hair would of course be tucked into that ponytail, opening and clearing her face like a budded flower.

He could stay out there in space forever watching her do that. There was no music playing, no one talking, no mechanical noises — just pure peaceful tranquility. And surrounded by the sparkling stars of eternity, David would rather be nowhere else. Perhaps it was there — it was then — that he had felt the most connected to her.

He occasionally would rip his eyes away from her for a few moments here and there so that he could etch something inside his journal, almost as if he were a concentrated painter, meticulously studying his subject for the perfect piece of artwork.

She floated past him as he lightly drifted in the entrance to the room, shooting him a playful smile as she glided on her back. "Hey," she eventually mustered out.

"Hey there," he responded with the safety of a comforting grin.

"How ya doin'?" she wondered.

"Hangin' in there," he said.

She perked her eyebrows. "You wanna hang in here with me?"

"I've never really been good at that anti-gravity stuff. I mean, anyone that can still smack their head against ledges and walls going like one-mile-per-hour can't be destined for space travel."

She giggled and turned again. "You can wear a helmet."

"And be ridiculed by the only four other people three billion miles from Earth?" he chuckled. "No thanks."

"Rhodes said you were having some... issues," she mentioned, crafting her eyes to a more concerned shape. "Anything you wanna talk about?"

David hiked a foot against the threshold. "Nothin' you'd be interested in."

"Try me," she shrugged. "In an official capacity, it's what I'm here for. But in a friend capacity — it's what I'd *like* to be here for."

"If only telling you were that simple," David dejectedly said.

"Well, if you're not gonna tell *me*, I'm glad you're at least writing it down," she said in a somewhat satisfied tone as she nudged her head toward the journal in his hands. She cocked her head and noticed that he was in fact drawing. "Or drawing it."

She playfully lifted the cover back as he unsuccessfully tried to conceal the inside, revealing to her the giant oak tree that took up most of the page. Her mood floated to more serious as she stared at it. "It's beautiful," she softly complimented. "Is it... is it an... oak tree?"

"Yes," he told her.

She gave a wondrous huff, thinking to herself. "That's so strange."

"What is?"

"Nothing," she insisted with a quick smile. "Never mind."

"Tell me," he asked, intrigued.

"It's just... this is going to sound stupid, but... I have this weird dream, every now and then — about an oak tree," she told him, feeling a bit silly. "It's really stupid. I don't know what it means. I wouldn't even call it a dream, really. More like images. Just this giant oak tree in the middle of nowhere on a nice summer day or something. My self-diagnosis is that it's some kind of coping mechanism for home. Like a reminder of something good and wholesome, no matter where I am."

David's eyes were lost within her once again as she floated away across the room. "How secure does *that* make you feel? Having a doctor onboard who dreams of trees?" she asked with another quirky self-mocking smile.

"That sounds like a nice dream to me..." David retorted, letting his sight fall back down to the sketch as he shaded in some more black.

"Guess we all have some symbol like that in our lives. Whatever it is, it makes me feel safe," she continued evaluating, coasting by one of the circular windows. She glanced out and softly touched the tips of her fingers to the glass. "Sometimes... when I'm all the way out here in space... I feel like the stars are my oak tree..."

It wasn't difficult for David to produce tears at that point in his journey. Like an old-time film actor who could cry on cue for a performance, his emotions got the best of him within a split-second as he attempted to casually swipe the lines of water from his eyelids with his finger. Julie had noticed this and pondered a concerned face as she floated backwards. "Hey — you okay?" she comfortingly asked.

He cleared his throat and closed his journal, wrapping the string around to secure it tightly. "Yeah. I just... had something in my eye," he quickly blurted.

She pushed her feet against the wall and started to soar toward him. "Come on. That's the oldest excuse," she muttered.

"I'm gonna get washed up for dinner," he told her, bluntly ending the conversation when he turned and lightly coasted out the opening to the room. She softly floated to a stop, bracing her hands against the threshold as she watched him leave.

When David's feet were back on the floor, literally and emotionally, he had taken a quick shower in the tiny facility next to his room to clear his head. Julie and her professional curiosity, of course, had managed to sneak into his room, where her seeking eyes wandered over the few things lying around that made up what poor-excuse-of-a-homestead he had manifested within the small bunker. Her attention was captured by the bed, and with a simple step, she shifted over toward it and gazed upon the tattered journal sitting on top of the sheets. She cocked her head over her shoulder for a cautious check and began to unwind the thick string, carefully opening the pages as if coming across some ancient historical artifact. She thumbed across the words, gently peeling the next page over. Some of them were loose, barely clinging on for dear life, and she didn't want to obstruct their order among some of the other small things pressed and packed inside. There was a wilted flower, surprisingly in good shape but certainly on its way to decaying into nothingness. And there was an old movie ticket stub, mostly worn out with the words and date faded away. But what really nabbed her nosy perusing was the photo that had dropped to the floor after slipping out among the ones that were stuffed in the rear of the book. She bent down to pick it up and was about to flip it over when she saw David standing in his open doorway, shirtless with only his pants on while his wet-frizzled hair still dripped a few drops of water.

She nervously stuck the photo back into the journal, trying to tidy and close it up. "Oh, uh, um — I'm sorry, I — came in looking for you and... I saw this on your bed..." she blabbered.

David wasn't angry. He didn't shout, or become upset. He merely walked further into the room to take it from her hands as he wrapped the string around it.

"I'm sorry. I didn't mean to pry," she softly pleaded. "It's none of my business."

He swallowed and covered the journal more protectively within his grasp, wanting to say something but holding back.

"I'm just concerned, David. I want to know what's going on in your mind," she stated. "You never seem to want to... talk. About your feelings."

"Look — I appreciate your concern, and I know you're just trying to do your job, but there's things about me that I... just can't tell you. For a million reasons. No matter how much I want to," he finally spoke out with.

"I don't want you to look at it as my job. You're my friend, David. I'm really glad I met you. I'm glad we became friends, and we got the opportunity to work on this mission together," she explained. "I just wanna know you're all right."

"I'm fine. I'm just a little... homesick. Let's just forget it, okay?"

She bobbed her head, laying a hand on his arm. Her touch was soft and delicate to his bare skin, and almost immediately he couldn't handle the preciousness of it, so he turned his body and let her fingers slip off. When he had walked over to his dresser to fish out a shirt, she had curved mysterious eyebrows to the number of round scars on his back and his other arm. Walking over, she squinted her meddlesome eyes and pointed them out. "What are those?" she wondered.

"What are what?"

"These marks on your back and arm."

David cocked his eyes to the spots and casually slipped on his shirt. "Bullet wounds," he said under his breath.

Julie mystifyingly shifted her expression, arching her eyebrows. "What?"

David didn't look at her. He went about picking some clothes up as she crossed her arms. "You said bullet wounds. David, that — that's impossible. How can that be? The last reported gun had to have been over seventy-five years ago," she noted. "How did this happen? Did you... did you do that to yourself?"

"No," he softly responded. "I was helping someone. A long time ago."

She pierced her eyes into him, as if waiting for him to change his answer. He scratched his head and turned to her, keeping his eyes off her as if she produced the bright rays of a blinding sun. "Listen, I... I'm gonna get some sleep," he said.

"Tell me, David," she calmly insisted, re-approaching him more closely. "You don't have to be afraid. You can tell me the truth. What makes you so broken inside?"

"I'll see ya later, okay?" he said, as if politely hinting for her to leave.

"Let me fix you," she suggested. "Let me help."

He shuffled his way to his bed and climbed in, curling his arms around the pillows. "Your role is just — to be. Nothing more, nothing less. Nothing is more important. It's not your job to help," he assured her. "Even if you think it is."

She was at a loss for words, and within moments had left him alone in the room. A bit later, she had eaten dinner in the main dining area with Rhodes and the other two crew members, who retreated off to other parts of the ship for their usual duties. David didn't particularly speak to them often let alone cross their paths. He wasn't even sure he knew their official jobs, as they were always working around the clock. He only cared about Julie and mildly tolerated Rhodes, who of course was sure to jump on Julie about his current status after dinner. She fixed some coffee and handed him a cup, stating, "Well... he's depressed."

"No shit," Rhodes agreed with a cooling blow and a sip.

"He's emotionally deteriorating inside. It's hindering his attitude, his motor functions, his ability to care about anything," Julie further explained. "I can't seem to break through and get to the core of what he's so distraught over, but it is something particular. I'm pretty sure he's been writing about it in his journal."

"Is he dangerous?"

"To others — no. I'm not really getting the sense that he's anywhere in that realm, but to himself? That's another issue," she concluded.

Rhodes cocked a sharp face. "Suicidal?"

Julie lightly sighed, running a hand through her hair as she leaned against a counter. "I don't know," she gently answered. "I noticed these small round scars on his back and arm and when I asked him what they were, he lied and told me they were bullet wounds."

Rhodes froze in bringing his cup back to his mouth. "Bullet — wounds?"

"I know, right? I can't be sure what they're really from and whether or not they were self-inflicted, but however he got them, it's a pretty good bet it has to do with what's going on with him on at least some level. As for predicting his present actions, well... All the analyzing and tests and talking and evaluating in the world can never guarantee what a person is going to do and when, but... with every passing moment, I'm feeling more and more concerned. If he really is jotting down his feelings and thoughts — that little book might be the only thing that's keeping him at bay. I've tried to take a look at it, but... from a moral and legal point of view, I can only go so far over the line without his consent."

Rhodes tossed his free hand. "Great. Terrific. So, what, then? Quarantine?"

"He's not an animal," she huffed.

"He's *sick*, Julie," he sternly reminded her. "You said he doesn't seem to be a threat to anyone else but if he's a possible threat to himself than that means he's a possible threat to the mission."

"Just give me a little more time, Captain," she positively requested. "Please."

Rhodes took an unsure breath. "We're gonna be entering planetary orbit within the hour. I just want him stable to do the things we're here to do."

Julie gave a nod, and he took another sip of his coffee as he walked away. She was left with the thoughts and concerns she had held with her through that trip, and it was more than evident in her brief professional experience that things would only get worse if she didn't break through his walls soon. She was still curious about his journal and its contents, and had even a short while later journeyed back to his room when he was fixing himself something to eat in the kitchen so she could peruse to an emotional solution. She had even considered plainly taking the book and locking herself in her own room to read and look through it, physically giving it back to him afterwards and apologizing for the intrusion on the whim that she felt it was the only way to jumpstart a breakthrough session for the sake of himself and those around him. She was most curious about the picture that had fallen out when she was looking through it before; her tenacious tendencies gnawed away at her curiosity for wondering who or what could be on it.

She didn't receive the chance to swipe the journal, though, for as she was advancing down the hallway toward his room, alarms started blaring and blinking across the ship, catching her perturbed attention as she double-backed to the main bridge. Rhodes was already there, straddled over the control board as he pushed and pulled various buttons and levers. "What's going on?" Julie asked.

"The main power panel is fried!" he angrily barked. "The oxidation in the coolant tanks was never recharged!"

"How can it be fried? Doesn't the computer go to an emergency reserve supply of coolant if that happens?" she wondered.

"Yeah, but when it tried to switch over to the reserve, a modulator short-circuited and blew out access, reverting back to using the old coolant," Rhodes quickly explained. "Goddamn one-in-a-million fucking chance something like that could happen! How we could lose the main power panel over this is beyond my comprehension. I told David forty fucking times to recharge it! Now we've got sensor failures across the board."

Julie tried to look over the controls and assist with what computer and ship knowledge she had. "Can't we get manual control and switch to the reserve coolant ourselves?"

"Getting manual control is the problem," he told her. "I can't access anything. The ship is breaking out of orbit and we're heading into the atmosphere. I'm gonna have to see what I can do in the coolant room. Find Werthers and Marsh and tell them to meet me there."

Rhodes had blasted out of the main bridge and on his way across the ship as David hurried to meet Julie. "What's happening? Are you okay?" he immediately queried.

"We've got coolant failure. The system tried to switch to the reserve but there was a malfunction so it kept using the old. We've lost computer control and we've broken out of orbit," she delineated.

"Jesus," he mumbled. "Without control, this ship will break apart in Neptune's atmosphere. Where's Rhodes?"

"On his way to try and get manual back up. We've gotta hail Werthers and Marsh but the com and sensors are down!" she noted. "I've got their locators showing they're on the west wing."

The alarms continued to blare around them, and as they watched the other two crewmen's locators on the board, the west wing section of the ship started to break apart and explode, blipping their blue electronic dots off the screen as their lives blipped out of existence. "Oh my God," Julie murmured with her mouth hanging open.

Rhodes was next to go, as the coolant room section disengaged from the ship, bursting with various fireballs until it was nothing but excess debris floating into space beside the planet they were descending toward.

David and Julie couldn't believe it. It was happening so quickly, without any type of reasoning. And as David stared blankly ahead, realization sunk into him. "It's my fault," he conjured. "It's all my fault. I put you at risk. I put you in this position."

She turned and grabbed his arm. "David, no — don't think that right now. We need to keep our heads on straight. We can fix this. We just need to think fast. The ship is already closing off the breached hulls from the sections we're losing."

Even then David knew that she was merely reaching for any possible solution, but neither was in any position to stop the chaos that was happening. The ship was already far too gone to salvage, and even if they could, neither were properly qualified to control it back home. So he came up with the simplest solution he could think of — the emergency escape pods. The first was already gone since it was located on the west wing with the ill-fated other two crewmembers, but the other was in reasonable reach. Without argument, Julie had of course agreed to their only resolution, so they began to hurry down the hall when David had skidded to a sharp stop. "What are you doing?" she nervously asked.

"I have to go back and get something," he hesitatingly told her.

"What? No, David — forget it. We have to get to the escape pod! There's no time!" she insisted.

He placed his hands on his shoulders, giving her a firm look. "It's important. I'll meet you there. I promise."

She didn't want to go forth without him, especially since the ship in whole was on the verge of breaking apart at any moment. He could get hurt or even marooned should he be separated by one of the devastating splits. She was tempted to ask him what could be so important to jeopardize their only chance of departure, but only responded with, "Just hurry."

So they went their separate ways, both running and turning corners as lights flashed all around. The ship trembled and shook, nearly making Julie lose her footing as she tripped and planted her hands against the walls, springing herself off and continuing her running escape. David held onto the open door threshold of his room, bracing himself as he was thrown about. He tumbled forth and slapped his hand over his journal, grabbing it off the bed and exiting the room.

It was like an earthquake in space. His feelings that the ship was starting to move were proved correct when he glanced out a window and noticed they were on a slight tilt as Neptune's giant blue gas ball seemed closer than ever. He clenched his teeth and pushed himself off the wall, trying to keep on his feet as he ran down the hall. He had reached the free float room, which he had to cross through in order to get to the escape pod, but since the mainframe computer was down, the anti-gravity was still in effect. Julie waited for him behind the door on the other side, opening it as she floated into the air. David opened his and felt his feet lift off the floor.

The ship rumbled and shook as sparks blew around him. He planted his feet and pushed forward, soaring softly through the air as she did the same. The movement may have been slow in actuality, but to David, he was back in slow motion as they drifted across the room toward each other, both reaching a hand out. Their fingers stretched with the promise of touching salvation until they finally collided; David wrapping an arm around her and guiding her out of the room into the safety of the connecting area. He reached back and closed off the room by punching his fist into a button, and the artificial gravity kicked on to drop them to the floor.

The remainder of the ship back beyond the free float room point had disengaged and broken off, leaving them in their own small private section. They continued forward just a bit further until reaching the escape pod. David opened the door, allowing her to wobble inside as he stalled with a thought. She grasped one of the seats and flashed a crazy look. "David, get in here!" she called out.

"The computer is down. Without power from it, we're not gonna be able to eject ourselves from inside the pod," he perceived. "And Rhodes never regained manual control."

"What does that mean? We can't leave? We *have* to leave! We have to get out of here, David! We're gonna die!" she cried.

David's eyesight caught the old-fashioned manual level on the wall outside of the pod. "No," he disagreed. "At least *you're* not."

She pushed herself back to her feet and stumbled back to the threshold. "What are you talking about?" she ecstatically asked.

"I have to stay behind and pull the manual lever," he informed.

She turned her head to see and began to shake it, looking back at him as tears welled in her eyes. "No. No, no, no, no. There has to be another way! You're not staying behind!"

"Julie," he said, trying to calm her. "Julie! There's no other way! If I don't do it, we both die!"

"I don't want to be alone!" she begged. "Don't leave me alone, David. Please. We can figure something out!"

"There's no time. Get inside. You're the only one that matters."

The tears rolled down her cheeks as she gave breathing sobs. "You matter, too! D-Don't do this, David. Please. I still have to help you. I have to fix you."

"It's not your job to help me," he told her, holding out his journal. "Just take this for me."

She looked down at it and reluctantly took it in her hands. She sobbed and wanted to argue her case further, but in the end, understood that it would have to be only her going into the pod. "You're going to live a good life," he assured, laying a hand on her cheek. "You're going to be okay now."

Her eyes gleamed into his, and she took a step forward to wrap him in a tight hug. He closed his eyes and consumed it, running his hand across her back, feeling all the inches he could. He was comfortable with the warmth of her body. It charged an essence into him that he had been lacking for so long.

She kissed his cheek and stepped back into the pod as he closed the door. She placed her hand flatly on the glass window. He swallowed and did the same, and although there was the thick material of the pod to separate the actual contact, he could feel her, more than he had ever before. He closed his eyes and yanked down the control lever, disengaging the pod from the remainder of the ship as it shot upward and away. And as he watched her, he was overcome by a sense of peace when a notion had crossed his mind. "Self-sacrifice," he said to himself, thinking.

He turned and for a brief moment, could barely make out the image of the mysterious man watching him from behind the window of a connecting room with a contempt and somewhat underlying righteous expression.

David was comfortable then. The gases of Neptune were bold and colorful, streaming rays of blue, green and aqua among the vibrant sparks of the ship falling and breaking apart around him. He felt he could almost reach out and touch them beyond the windows, as if skimming fingers across a divine river of bliss. For whether or not that sacrifice he was making was the correct method the mysterious man had mentioned to curing her repeating ill-fated lives, he was ready to move on. Ready to start over. Because only then he realized it didn't matter. Her destiny wasn't to succumb to her fate, and his destiny wasn't to save her from it. Her destiny was him, and his was her. Their destinies were each other. They could walk toward that moment together, whether they would successfully surpass it this time or not.

David closed his eyes — and the remaining life of the Infinity 9 exploded in a single, massive burst. There were no screams, no cries, no pleas. Just serenity. Serenity among the stars that stretched beyond the threshold of eternity.

David was never really truly immortal.

He had only lived four-hundred eighteen years.

And despite his emotional deterioration, he was always genuine. He was a protector. He was a savior. A constant traveler with a heart too big for his chest. A heart that ceased its beating in the years between the moments he found her. Life was only in motion during those select times, like a wind-up clock or music box that inevitably slowed to a stop until being rekindled with the turn of sentience. He left her that time the same way as all the others, only this time he departed not with a dread of waiting, but with a hope of finding.

And as Julie had found herself coasting across the stars in her small escape pod on an automated return home, she delayed her entrance into the security of a dreamless cryogenic sleep to read through David's journal completely, fingering away the drop of each countless tear before it had fallen to whatever page she was on. She looked again at the worn and tattered Polaroid picture, dated 2004, of a beautiful young woman — a beautiful young woman with a striking resemblance and an innocently tranquil smile as delicate as the day it was taken on. She stayed on the page with the giant oak tree sketch for a bit, sobbing with her shaky breaths while giving it a smooth, feathery touch with her fingertips as if she were brushing through the leaves of time.

She eventually flipped to the next page; the last written...

*If I could tell you how much I love you, I would, but I only have the written words within my years to describe it. I hope you can forgive me for that, and know that my intentions were not for the good or not for the bad, but for you and you alone. There is no world without you continuing forth through it, and that is how I love you across the sea of time. Because love is recurring. Love is endless. Love is forever.*

*I'm never sure when the syndicate of time will collide us together, or where it might be, or what role you will be playing in it, but only one thing within my power is always certain —*

*I will save you.*

*And if there is ever a time when this eternal odyssey of mine comes to an end, I will wait for you beneath the oak tree shade of our amity. Until then, know that if you should ever happen to wake up one morning and feel the beauty of being alive, it's because I love you.*

May Fortune Smile Upon You

It's never easy being the new guy. And although Chase had never been through it before, he was quickly beginning to feel all of the clichés he had seen in movies and on TV. Rural Pennsylvania was a lot different from busy New York City life. Things seemed to be on hold in that new small town, as everyone around took their time. The brown, red and orange leaves of fall were nice though, shedding a crisp and quietly quaint feeling that he welcomed, because that feeling of peace and serenity was all he really had for the time being. He was a normal guy, so even he expected to make friends or fall into a group eventually, but it was the how and when that was going to be the deciding factors. Not to mention that he didn't even have a car, so he'd have to take the *bus* to school everyday. An eighteen-year-old high school senior taking the bus. It was laughable. He would probably be the only one. And riding his bike seemed like an even more immature and pathetic method of transportation, aside from the distance being just a bit too far. Of course to buy a car he would need money, and to get money he would have to get a job, so that was a top priority among settling in. He worked part-time at a corporate electronics store chain back in New York where the customers were plentiful and the extra help was greatly appreciated, so making money or securing a job was never difficult, but now he was in this small town, where every establishment seemed locally-owned in the aspect that one would have to be blood-related to get a job at, so he figured the pickings would be slim until he met some people that could hook him up. Even the local McDonald's would probably urge some sort of generational credentials in the application process.

Besides needing a new car to cruise to school in, there was the financial issue at home. It was just Chase and his mother. His father had left when he was around the age of four, so he didn't remember much of him nor had he ever really seen him since. Money was tight, and he would need a job just to help out with the basics around the house. And then there was college. He was going to need some serious financial loans just to get into a local community school, so he didn't want to be burdening his mother with the need of even more money without a job to help provide it.

On the plus side of things, if he didn't end up making enough friends or the new move turned out more horrible than he expected, he would only have to wait a year to start over at college with a new setting and new faces, so he figured it could've been worse. He could've moved there as a freshman and gone through four torturous years waiting to hit the reboot button on his life. And if he was really feeling homesick, the city was always there for him, granted it would be quite a drive, but it would be worth it to journey there for the weekend or during an extended school break where he could crash with some familiar old friends or family and get away from the lame setting he was unwillingly dragged to.

He did try to keep a positive aspect on the change, and with that fueling his feelings, he grabbed his bike after he had helped his mother and the moving men unpack a great deal of boxes and furniture and ventured off into town to explore or see what jobs were available. There were plenty of "Help Wanted" signs in stores, but most of them seemed out of his league of interest, being arts and crafts, hardware, or other places he had no knowledgeable experience with let alone interest. And most of them seemed closed anyway at that time of the evening, which was no surprise, seeing as how most of them were indeed locally owned and the patrons probably kept a sharp closing time to get home and prepare dinner. There was one store, however, that caught Chase's eye as he approached it on the corner and gazed at the sign with the wiggly letters that read, "The Magic Emporium". There was no apparent sign seeking help, but he was curious anyway and as it was getting later he didn't really have anywhere else to go. Aside from that, his mother's birthday was coming up, and he thought that he could maybe find something interesting for her.

So he hiked his bike up against the side of the building and circled around to enter through the front door as the old-fashioned bells on top jingled his presence. Right away, he was bedazzled at the layout of the small and condensed store and its infinite countless items stacked on shelves, piled on the floor, bundled on spinning racks, or hanging from the ceiling. He stepped further in, glazing his eyes around with wonder at all of the trinkets and gadgets. Then he noticed the giant glass globe near the front by the register counter and slightly dropped his jaw. It was like a snow globe, except without the water and snowflakes, about the size of a large dresser, very complex and delicately crafted with an actual solid glass bubble, unlike the inflatable ones people might find in front yards during the Christmas season. And jam-packed within it was a city, complete with an absurd amount of buildings, skyscrapers, bridges, alleys, parks and streets — a scale model-lover's dream. "Whoa..." was all Chase could end up blurting out as he circled around it.

A girl his age had come up front behind the counter from a backroom and noticed him studying it. She gave a small smirk and crossed her arms. "Tell me about it. It's a good thing it's not filled with water and those sparkly things, or else I'd need to drive a forklift in every time just to shake it," she noted.

He looked over to her. She was really pretty, with soft brown eyes that complicated her wavy brown hair, thin eyebrows, curvy lips and thin figure. Chase smiled at her remark and looked back into the globe. "This is incredible," he added. "You actually have this thing for sale?"

She made her way from behind the counter and over next to him, looking in as well. "Nah. Kinda just for show. My parents buy all sorts of weird crap from around the world and bring it here to sell but always end up taking off the price tag."

"I used just moved here from New York City, actually," Chase said, gesturing to the city within the globe. He streamed his finger along the bubble and squinted his eyes. "Yeah, I lived right about... there."

The girl laughed. "Yeah, you have that new guy vibe about you," she said.

Chase embarrassingly scratched his head. "I really gave that off just by coming through the door, huh?"

She shrugged. "Eh, it's cool. Us small town folk are pretty hospitable when it comes to new faces," she said in a quirky attempt at a southern accent.

"Thanks," he said, bobbing his head as he looked back into the globe. "Something like this would really blow my mom's mind for a birthday present. The detail is amazing. Imagine if you were a tiny person living inside there. You would think you were walking around in a real city."

"So you're looking for something for your mom?" the girl wondered.

Chase shrugged. "Well, I saw the place from outside and figured I'd come in and look around. To tell you the truth, I've never really believed in any of this magic hokey. No offense."

"None taken," she replied. "I kinda side with you on that. Magic is a hard thing to believe in. Everything has to have a logical explanation."

"Yeah, like the invisible new guy act I'm gonna be performing tomorrow at school," he jokingly stated.

She perked inquisitive eyebrows. "You going to Garrington?"

"Yeah."

"Senior?"

"Uh-huh."

"Me, too," she noted, shooting a quick smile. "I'll have to introduce you to some people. Show you around."

"I'm sure I'll already have plenty of junior high pals by the time I get off the bus," he disappointedly added.

She gave a somewhat sympathetic expression. "No car?"

"Not unless you count a bike."

"You can ride in with *me*," she offered in a more upbeat manner. "If you don't mind riding shotgun in a busted Honda with a loud muffler, cassette tape player and no heat."

He grinned. "What can I say? You had me at "cassette tape player"."

She smiled and held out her right hand. "Name's Bridget."

He shook it and gave a nod. "Chase."

She was almost blushing. They were making a real connection. But Bridget followed up the awkward silence by gesturing around her. "Well, uh... I gotta lock up for the night. So... if you're not gonna buy anything... I'm gonna have to boot your ass out of here for loitering. See ya tomorrow morning?"

"Sure thing," he confirmed. "I'm at Twenty-Five Chestnut."

"Great. See ya tomorrow morning," she said, then clumsily catching herself to add, "I already said that, didn't I?"

Chase turned to head for the door, chiming in with, "I'll listen for the loud muffler" as he waved and exited, leaving her to smile to herself as she walked back behind the counter.

Chase was feeling pretty good himself as he hopped onto his bike and peddled home within the dusk of the fading day. Maybe things weren't going to be that bad after all. He had only been there for the bulk of the day and already he seemed to have one friend by his side — a friend with a car, especially. And if even a third of the students at school were anything like her, he was in for quite the ride on Easy Street, something he hadn't expected with his luck.

But luck has a way of changing...


Chase's first couple of weeks were pretty general to him, even though it was already nearly two months into the semester and everybody else already knew each other. He got the occasional "new guy" looks from time to time, but the eyes were never judging or harassing as he feared. His peers may not have been overly friendly to his arrival, but at least they weren't mean-spirited. Plus, he did have Bridget as his personal tour guide and newfound friend, so he was muddling his way successfully through the days and into lunches at the cafeteria, where she had always solely joined him at one of the empty octagon tables with a tray of health-hazardous scholastic toxic waste. She congratulated him on bringing a sub of his own and heeded warnings of what to pick and what not to pick should he ever brave his stomach to the school's cooking. It was usually around that time each day when he noticed the beautiful blonde enter the cafeteria. She was earth-shattering in every way to him, dressed perfectly in jeans and a tank-top and accompanied by two of her lackey gal-pals who although were pretty themselves, held their place rightfully behind her grace.

Bridget would of course stop chewing her food and turn in her seat to see what he was staring at, looking back at Chase and immediately noticing the trance she had put him in. "Oh. And here I thought that someone was choking," she said. "I mean, what else could drive your attention away from Miss Wonderful?"

He would always snap his attention away, as if pretending not to have been looking at her. "Uh... who? What? I don't know who you're talking about."

"Gag me," she murmured. "Who else but the great and all-powerful Lana Lanecaster? Head cheerleader, prom queen, ho-coming queen — I'm sorry — I meant *home*coming queen."

"Quite a repertoire," Chase noted with his eyes still completely frozen and locked back in her direction. "I'll have to introduce myself now that I'm settled in."

"Ha. Be prepared to schedule an appointment," Bridget added. "Miss Universe doesn't bide her time with just anybody. Her looks may set you on fire, but don't expect her to put you out."

"She hasn't seemed serious around anyone. Does she have a boyfriend?"

Bridget gave a barely audible sigh. She knew where this was going, and she didn't need to have special mind-powers to know just exactly what he was thinking. She licked her lips and shifted herself in her seat. "Yeah. Uh, let's see — the football captain, basketball captain, baseball captain, class president, and I think one of the teachers. And that's just *this* school," she explained. "Look, Chase — no offense, but — I'm sure as the new guy here, you can understand that even Garrington has its little groups and cliques, and Lana is the head of one of those groups."

"And what group is that?" he asked.

"The kind that purposely doesn't associate with any of the others," she simply retorted.

He slouched in his seat and defensively held his hands up. "Hey, I just... wanna know who she is, that's all."

"I know what you want," she told him. "I just don't understand why. Beauty is only skin-deep. She doesn't have much to offer beneath those golden locks and bra. Trust me. You seem like a really cool guy. If you're really looking to hook up with someone, there's plenty of other girls here who would value and appreciate you for more than what your social standing is."

Chase crossed his arms. "Oh yeah? Like who?"

Bridget gave a light shrug as her eyes drooped to her tray. "I don't know..." she mumbled. "Maybe you'll get to know some girls better after a little bit of time and see what the real difference in quality is." He only briefly snickered, shaking his head as she more promptly finished with, "Besides — I don't really see you as a fan of blondes. You come off more as a brunette kinda guy."

"Well, you know what they say about blondes," he smiled.

"Yeah, about four thousand different punch-lines," she answered. "Can you honestly sit there knowing what kind of guy you are and what kind of girl she is just by looking at her and tell me that you have the slightest bit of chance in hell?"

He shook his finger at her and rebounded with, "Normally — no. She wouldn't even *accidentally* look at me. You're right. But I have an advantage."

"Yeah? And what's that?"

"She has no idea of who I really am. Therefore, I can *be* anybody. If I can get her to look past the aspect of me simply being "the new guy", the possibilities are limitless. This is a loophole chance not many guys get."

"Whatever," she said, rolling her eyes and tossing her hands. "Don't listen to me. So you go ahead and woo her with whatever fake-guy-personality you plan on presenting. Good luck."

"Thanks," he confidently nodded, standing up.

She arched her head up from her food and gave an unbelievable look. "What? Y-You're going... *now?*"

"No better time than the present."

"This should be good for a laugh," she slyly remarked. "Don't say I didn't warn you."

He took a quick, readying breath, and surged forward across the cafeteria, snaking around the tables and through passing students as his eyes zeroed in on what Bridget had dubbed as the "popularity patrol". His palms began to sweat. His heart thumped. Back at the table, Bridget poked at her food and pretended not to care, but couldn't help turn her head back as she rested her chin on her shoulder and watched; her expression quickly shifting to one of slight gloom.

Lana talked with her friends as Chase approached, crossing through the open mid-section of the cafeteria. But unbeknownst to him in his travels, a girl at another table nearby accidentally knocked her carton of milk onto the floor as the fluid spilled out and streamed forward across his path. With his eyes plastered onto Lana, he began to transform his mouth into a smile when his right foot hit the spill, causing him to slip back and bat a tray of food out of the hands out of a student walking past as it flung everywhere. Chase continued to lose his balance, then wobbled against a stack of empty trays on the return counter and crashing them down as he fell to the floor. An uproar of cheering and clapping came from nearly the entire cafeteria. Lana tried to hide her laughing by casually covering her mouth.

Chase embarrassingly smiled and quickly sprung up, giving them all a brief wave before hurrying out of the nearest exit.

Later that night, Bridget chuckled as she bobbed her head while she stacked items onto the shelves behind the counter at The Magic Emporium. "Well... I think it was two souls destined to meet. Love at first sight," she said to Chase, who was leaning on the other side of the counter toying with some trinket.

"Hardy har," he sarcastically huffed. "No thanks to that, now I'll forever be known as the guy who slipped in the cafeteria and made an ass of himself in front of everyone."

"If it makes you feel any better, *I* wasn't laughing," she tried to comfort him. A smile crept across her face. "At least not out loud."

"Gee, thanks."

"Oh, come on — by tomorrow, nobody's gonna even remember it happened. Teenagers have a memory span of like five minutes," she assured. "It would've never happened if you had listened to me in the first place. As your first official friend in town, I was only trying to uphold my duty of looking out for your well-being."

"And on *that* note, I propose we go out somewhere tonight that's very dark and willing to conceal the discomposure of my identity — like a movie theater," he suggested. "What time you getting out of here?"

She glanced to a nearby clock. "If you wanna hang out for another fifteen or twenty minutes, I should be able to close up and we can head out then."

He nodded and drummed his hands on the counter. "Cool," he conformed, starting to look and play with more items. Bridget pulled a pair of slinky-eyed glasses from a box and put them on, proudly displaying them to him as he smiled and noted, "Has anybody ever told you that you have incredibly sexy eyes?"

She giggled and took them off, tossing them back into the box. She bent down and dug through it more, until the sound of her voice saying, "Whoa! Check it out!" diverted his attention back to behind the counter. She stood back upright and opened a small velvet box containing a ring inside.

"Hey! Oh my God! Cool!" Chase exclaimed. "It's a — ring."

"Not just any ring. It's a ring of fate."

"A what?" he wondered.

She leaned over the counter as she pulled it free of the box, holding it out between her index finger and thumb for him to see. "A ring of fate. It's supposed to grant whoever owns it five wishes. Haven't seen one of these in a while." She pulled out the small folded piece of paper from the box and continued by reading off it — "Wishes bold and true, this ring grants five, on quick and swift wings, they shall arrive. Choose wisely, and they will do you great, what you wish is what you get, with your ring of fate."

Chase took it from her and held it up, letting the red and green amber inside the brass shell gleam against the light. "A ring that grants wishes, huh? Sounds like quite a seller. How much these things go for?"

She curved a strange face as she bent back down and rustled through the box. "I don't know. We've never sold them before. It was the only one that was in here. It's not on the shipping invoice, either. Kinda weird. Maybe the factory or distribution center accidentally put it in with this stuff."

"Well, I'm no jeweler, but this thing sure doesn't look like it belongs in the bargain bin," Chase noted, inspecting it more closely.

Bridget smirked and raised an eyebrow. "Hey, now you have a legit way of winning over your beauty queen. And it's not even your basic run-of-the-mill three crappy wishes, either. Imagine what you could do to her with *five!*"

Chase beamed a smile, tossing it in his hand. "And it beats having to deal with an annoying blue cartoon genie voiced by Robin Williams." She laughed. "If anything, it looks cool. Maybe my mom would like it as a birthday gift. How much you want for it?"

Bridget shrugged and tossed a careless hand. "Take it. It's yours."

"Really? No. Come on. I couldn't do that. Your parents are trying to feed you with this place; I couldn't just take it," he urged.

"Seriously, Chase — it's not a big deal. Like I said — it's not even on the invoice, so it won't be missed. Anyway, I wouldn't even know what to price it as," she told him. "Consider it a welcome to the neighborhood gift, only... a little late."

"Thanks!" he gratefully said as he went back to inspecting it closely, but Bridget was instead looking at him; her eyes lost for a dragging moment before snapping herself out of her trance.

"Well, uh... If we're gonna catch a movie at a decent time, I better finish this stuff up so we can get outta here, unless you wanna use your first wish to help out in that department," she blurted.

Chase chuckled and circled around the counter to help her lift the box into the back room.

Hoping that the next day would be a bit less embarrassing than the previous, Chase got into Bridget's car the next morning and ventured off to school. He had casually gotten to know a few more people here and there a little better throughout his classes, and was quite surprised when not one of them mentioned his little cafeteria catastrophe. Maybe this wasn't the type of town to hold something against someone. Maybe they really were going to give him a chance. And that gave him a boost of confidence, especially to make another attempt at talking with Lana as he stared at her from behind his book during study hall in the library later in the day. She was at the table behind his, quietly conversing with the same two friends who were at her lunch table. Chase heard every word they were saying as he pretended to read his book, which, at one particular point, he noticed was upside down and had to correct his unskillful endeavor of secretly eavesdropping. They talked about girl things — their hair, the latest clothes they bought, actors who had just entered rehab, and somewhere in the mix the topic of cars had come up. More specifically — convertibles. "Oh my God. I'd love one in red. I swear, if Justin had a red convertible... it would be such a major turn-on. Cruising around at top speeds with the top down..." Lana had described with a dreamy gaze.

"Don't you mean with *your* top down?" one of the friends joked.

After Lana had argued that her personality was nothing short of angelic, the other friend laughed and added, "Don't even try. You are such a major slut and you know it."

Chase, who had been leaning back in his chair listening, arched a bit too far and toppled back against their table, knocking some books off as he scrambled to his feet and tried to clean up as they strangely watched. "Oh — uh — I — I'm sorry," he murmured with a dopey smirk.

One of the girls narrowed her eyes and studied him. "Aren't you that guy that slipped during lunch yesterday?"

Lana and the other friend lightly giggled. Chase casually laughed back, grumbling under his breath, "Five minutes my ass."

"What?" Lana confusingly asked.

"Nothing," he answered, waving it off. "My name's Chase. I'm new here."

"No shit," one of the friends said.

"Where ya from?" Lana wondered.

"New York," he answered, bobbing his head. "City, that is. In case you thought I was talking about the state. Most people automatically assume when you say "New York" that you mean the city when you really mean the state, but in my case it... is... the city."

The three girls weirdly darted their eyes to each other. Lana tried her best to prevent another laugh from breaking out. "Oh. That's... cool."

Chase knew he was derailing. He wasn't an idiot. But on the other hand, he was establishing first direct contact. That was the hardest part. He was there, talking to the hottest, most popular girl in school. So it could only get better, that is, if he thought quickly and came up with something less dorky to say. But unfortunately before he had the chance, three tall, muscular, better-looking guys in blue sports letter jackets came to the table, each protectively curling an arm around their rightful property. "'Sup, ladies?" the one who sat with Lana greeted.

The bell rang, signaling the end of the class period, and not a moment too soon. It was Chase's cue, so he flashed a quick smile and waved, saying, "I gotta jet. Nice to meet you." He grabbed his books and made his way toward the door before he figured one of the muscle-heads would have the chance to flatten him by turning him into a book*mark*.

"Who was that?" the one jock asked Lana.

One of her friends leaned forward. "Some new dork from New York." A few of them snickered in response.

All Chase could do on his way down the hall was shake his head in disappointment to himself. "Great first impression," he unbelievably noted as he stopped at his locker and spun the combination lock. He opened the door and put some of the books away, then began to empty some of his pockets when he came across the brass ring. Looking it over, he smiled to himself and huffed a quick laugh, trying it on one of his fingers. He turned and rubbed it a little, thinking. Then, looking back at it, he promptly said, "I wish I had a brand new red convertible with a bottomless gas tank."

He sighed and closed the locker door, turning and making his way down the hall with the plethora of other students trying to make a break for their freedom.

After he had met up with Bridget at her locker and she had given him a ride home, he arrived to see a vehicle parked in the driveway covered with a tarp. Upon asking his mother who it belonged to, she answered with a simple, "You." At first he surprisingly thought she had sprung a few bucks to buy him a clunker now that they were in the sticks and he didn't have a subway or cab to take around, but after she had led him outside and unveiled the car, his jaw nearly dropped to the driveway.

It was a red convertible. Brand new. Brand *sparkling* new.

She explained that it had been delivered right before he had arrived home, and that he had won it through a local drawing, showing him all the proper paperwork that proved his lucky ownership. "Not such a bad idea to move out here after all, eh?" she cunningly said before leaving him alone out there to marvel at the sleek ride.

Chase must have walked and circled around it a dozen times, streaming his fingers along the smooth red coating. He couldn't believe it. He didn't know how to react. A thousand thoughts drove through his mind, but only one kept hitting the brakes as he slowly brought his hand up in front of his face. The amber inside the brass ring gleamed within the sunlight. He glazed his eyes back to the car, softly saying, "No way."

But it had happened. It was there, sitting in front of him in his driveway, still within the hour he had wished it. He tried to rationalize possibilities of some sort of prank, but no one had heard him wish it, and he certainly didn't have the time let alone notion to tell anyone. It was his. It was true. And it had *worked.*

He looked back at the ring and gave a much brighter smile. He decided his first initial action was to drive it over to Bridget's and tell her what had happened, but upon checking the gas tank level, he noticed it to be empty. So borrowing his mother's car, he hurried out to the nearest gas station in town and filled a good-sized gas can to bring back to it, only once he was back home and emptying it into the convertible for a good minute or two, he noticed the long gushing river of gasoline coming from beneath the car and trailing down the driveway and into the storm drain in the street. "What the hell?" he outlandishly babbled, pulling the can's nozzle out of the car.

Chase got to his stomach and investigated beneath the belly of the vehicle, seeing that the gas tank in fact had no bottom to it, and all of the gas he had been pouring in only went straight through to the pavement below. It was then he realized what exactly he had said in his wish — "A brand new red convertible with a bottomless gas tank". *Bottomless.* Of course, when he said it, "bottomless" was referring to a tank he could continually and infinitely re-fill without paying for, but it seemed the ring had taken it a bit too literally. He was only saying the first thing that came to his mind, not taking the time to analyze the correct way in both acquiring a car at no cost *and* driving it at no cost. But there the car sat, every inch of it his and his alone, so laughing his poor choice of words off, he figured all he'd have to do was buy a new gas tank. A small price for a *free* brand new convertible that he was more than willing to pay. So he wasted no time calling up a few auto shops to find one that had a new sizeable tank ready for pick-up, and once he did and successfully acquired it at an appropriate price, decided to use his personal auto-fixing expertise to install it himself.

Only the same thing happened.

He had been pouring gas into the tank again when he noticed it coming out from under the car, and checking beneath it, his eyes popped out of his head to see the bottom of the tank completely missing. He was sure it was one hundred percent new, and had even checked it when he picked it up, eliminating any chance of accidentally being given back the one he was handing in. He even thought of calling the auto shop to double check, but he knew deep down that it was no use. He could put a thousand different gas tanks underneath the vehicle and the same thing would happen every time, because he got exactly what he wished for.

That didn't stop Bridget from laughing once she had driven over to be told and shown the big news. "A bottomless gas tank. I'm sorry; that's just too funny," she said.

"Not to the guy whose only use for it is as a driveway decoration," he huffed.

"Do you really expect me to believe this? That you overheard Lana's biggest turn-on is a red convertible and you wished on the ring to have one and it was magically waiting for you after I dropped you off earlier?" she noted, crossing her arms.

"Do you really think I'd be bumming rides off of your Honda to school if I had something like this sitting around?"

"Gee, thanks," she blabbered, rolling her eyes. "Besides — I don't know *what* to think. For all I know, it could've been in the shop, or storage, and you were just waiting for it to get here, and thought you'd have a little fun at my expense, starting off by sneaking a ring into that shipping box back at the store."

"I didn't put the ring in the shipping box!" he insisted. "Look — all I can tell you is that this thing works. We're not dealing with something out of a Cracker Jack box."

"Okay, then," she said, starting to nod as she zeroed her playfully suspicious eyes into his. "Prove it. Make another wish. Wish for something right now."

"And waste my second wish on something stupid trying to prove a point? Forget it," he shrugged her off.

"How convenient," she grinned.

"All right, then — fine," he bluntly stated. "Tell me what to wish for. That way I'll have no chance to prepare it, and you'll see I'm not lying. Just wish for something... good."

Bridget licked her lips and arched her eyes upward, thinking for a moment as she tapped a foot. "Okay... then how about... a convertible for *me?* Brand new. Blue. And a gas tank with an actual bottom."

"Another car?" Chase almost outrageously asked. "And for *you?*"

"Hey! Remember who *gave* you that ring — for *free*."

Chase sighed, as she did have a point. So rubbing the ring with his fingers, he promptly said, "I wish... Bridget would immediately be given a brand new blue convertible in perfect working condition. There. Good enough?"

Bridget looked around her, as if expecting the car to magically appear in a poof of smoke. But it was nowhere to be seen. She perked her eyebrows to him. "It would be, if the absence of this sleek mechanical chariot of awesomeness didn't prove you were full of it."

Chase was about to open his mouth to say something, although he wasn't quite sure how he was going to argue against her accusations since he did technically use the word "immediately" within the wish — but then her cell phone rang in her pocket. She dug her hand in and pulled it out, putting it to her ear. "Hello?" she greeted. She listened a little and took a few pacing steps around the trail of gasoline on the driveway. "No. I'm over at that new guy's house. Chase." She listened more and looked at her old rusted Honda sitting at the end of the driveway. "Yeah, how do you think I got here?" She listened again, this time for a bit longer and more intensely as she froze in her tracks. "W-What...?" she softly asked, veering her eyes over to Chase. "Mom, this isn't funny. Are you like, bugging my conversations or something? Are you in on this?" She listened. "What color is it?" she then wondered. The answer made her face drop. "No, no. I'm coming." She hung the phone up and stared at Chase.

"What's up?" he wondered with a straight expression.

She attempted to crack a smile. "You're screwing with me, aren't you? She's gotta be listening. You've gotta have your cell on or something so she could hear me. That's the only way she could know what I just made you wish for."

"What are you talking about?" he asked with an innocent shrug.

"The car. The blue convertible. That was my mom. She just told me that a couple weeks ago she and my dad found some old lost stock bonds my grandfather bought, and cashed them in to buy me a new car. A new *convertible*. A new *blue* convertible," she explained. "I don't know how you did it, but she gave both you and herself up with that call and line of crap, because if you really knew my parents, and they really *did* discover some stock bonds that were worth dozens of thousands of dollars, you'd know they certainly wouldn't use it to buy me a super-fancy car when I have that old hand-me-down Honda to chauffer my embarrassed ass from place to place."

"Look, I already told you I'm not playing a prank on you," he tried to convince her. "You can strip-search me for wires, check my cell call history, search the front lawn for tiny microphones — whatever. But I guarantee when you go home you're probably gonna start clearing your things out of that Honda, because I sure as hell didn't have *this* convertible in my back pocket before today."

"Sure thing," she sarcastically remarked with a smile and a circled "okay" gesture with her fingers as she started to back up toward her car. "So I'll see you at the usual time tomorrow morning? In my usual Honda?"

He grinned and looked away as she got into the car and drove off. He turned his attention back to his red convertible in the driveway.

Bridget did pick up Chase at the usual time the next morning, although she didn't pick him up in her usual Honda. And when she had pulled the new blue-gleaming convertible into an open space in the high school's parking lot, she got out with a bright smile. "I still can't believe this is happening! I mean, this stuff doesn't happen in real life. And especially not to *me*," she said.

Chase didn't seem as enthusiastic as he slung his book bag over both shoulders while they headed for the school across the giant lawn littered with other students hanging around. "Hey, at least you can actually drive yours," he sourly murmured.

Bridget snickered and playfully nudged his arm. "Oh, come on — don't be so negative. Now if you really wanna impress Lana, all you'll have to do is hook up a movie projector and point it toward your garage and you can take her to the drive-in!"

That made Chase smile, and he nearly even laughed. "Oh, sooo funny. How about you let me take that Honda off your hands if you're so comfy with your new perfect ride?"

"I would, but it has sentimental value," she told him. "Maybe you should word your wishes more carefully next time. Speaking of which — what's gonna be our third wish? I've been thinking of some stuff and thought maybe we could hook up at lunch and start making a list. I mean, we're really gonna wanna think this out long and hard before jumping to desires. I've got this huge buzz just thinking of all the possibilities!"

Chase's steps slowed to a stop as his face altered to one of confusion. "Um... *our*... wishes?"

She stopped as well and bent her eyebrows. "Yeah."

He cracked a pretend smile and scratched his head as if searching for the best way to break his feelings about the subject to her. "It's just — I mean — *I'm* wearing the ring and all... You did give it to *me*..."

She cocked a more serious stare at him, immediately knowing the direction he was going with the topic. "Yeah, that's right. *I* gave it to you. So, what? I can't stake a claim in this? It was partly my doing, you know."

"Yeah, yeah, I know, but..."

"But you can't share them with me?"

"Well, I don't want it to sound like *that*, but... come on. I gave you a wish. And my first one blew up in my face. Now I've only got three left," he explained.

"Then what the hell are you gonna use them on?" she blurted, almost to the point of being upset.

He gave a simple shrug. "I haven't really thought about it. Look, I can give you the ring when I'm done, and you can have five of your own all to yourself. What's the big deal?"

"Well... what if you wish for more wishes?"

A mischievously realizing look sprawled onto his face. "You think that would work?"

She gave a huff, stiffening her stance as he laughed and laid a hand on her shoulder. "Hey, hey, come on — I'm only kidding. I wouldn't do anything like that to you. I swear. Just let me have these last three wishes and you can have the ring."

Bridget took a deep breath and seemed to calm down pretty quickly. "Okay. Deal," she agreed. "So what are you gonna wish for next, then?"

Chase's attention was diverted to Lana as she got out of a nice looking Mercedes Benz nearby with her usual attachment of friends. Bridget noticed her as well and looked back at Chase. "Oh, you've gotta be kidding me," she mumbled. "So on whose bed and in what positions?"

"Although I can't deny your assumption of the general male desire, I was hoping you'd give me the benefit of the doubt for thinking of something a little less monumental... like a date."

Bridget held back a chuckle. "A date. That's... what you'd use your third of five wishes on. To get a date."

"Why not?"

"I dunno. You've only been drooling over her since the moment you walked into school. I only figured with the perfect chance you'd go for the gold," she speculated.

He thought for a moment and bobbed his head in agreement. "You know something? You're right. Why settle on a date or a flimsy one-night-stand, when I could win her over completely."

"What do you mean?"

"That's what I'm gonna do. I'll gonna use my next one to make her fall in love with me," he determinedly confirmed as he started advancing forward.

She quickly scurried to keep up, grabbing his arm in attempt to halt him. "Whoa, whoa, wait! You're what? You can't do that!"

"Why not? It was *your* idea."

"I — I didn't mean it like that," she tried to refute, but she had indeed fallen into a trap she had constructed. "Seriously, Chase? You're not gonna do that, are you? You can't do that. This is somebody's life we're talking about."

"So?"

"So it's not fair to them! You're making someone feel a way they might not want to feel against their will, without them even knowing! It's sick. Love doesn't work that way, Chase. It's unnatural. It isn't real. It isn't true," she disputed.

Chase gave her a sarcastically shocked expression as he responded with, "Oh, look who thinks the prom queen has moral rights all of the sudden."

"This has nothing to do with my personal opinions," she snipped back. "You're talking about a human being with freedoms and rights. Wish for a million dollars or something. Why can't you just... have your way with her for a night and get it out of your system?"

"Maybe I want something more meaningful than that."

"So let someone fall in love with you because they want to," she suggested. Her eyes lightly sank to the ground. "You should give that notion a chance. Maybe there's already plenty of girls here or somewhere else that are getting to know you that might fall for you eventually someday... the right way. If you just wait and see."

"Gimme a break," he groaned. "Maybe waiting at that rate I'll meet somebody in a retirement home. Girls don't fall for guys like me. Not in this day and age. For some crazy reason, girls don't like guys who are already nice. Girls like jerks and try to turn them *into* nice guys. This is the only chance someone like me is gonna truly have with someone like Lana Lanecaster. I'm doing this for all the guys who were ever turned down by all the Lana Lanecasters for being themselves."

"Is that what this is? Getting back at a girl like Lana Lanecaster? Or do you want something just because you can't have it? You know what? Go ahead and wish it. See if I care. Because either reason seems pretty pathetic to me," she snapped, turning to walk away by herself.

Chase watched and sighed, hanging his head. He glanced at the ring on his left hand and looked back to Bridget as she disappeared within the sea of students heading into the school. He sharpened his mood and placed his other index finger and thumb around the ring, giving it a firm rub. "I wish Lana Lanecaster would fall in love with me," he proclaimed.

He didn't care what Bridget had said. He didn't care about the moral implications behind doing so. He didn't even presently care about his remaining two wishes. He just knew what he wanted right then and there, as long as he spoke the words.

And he knew he was going to get it.

It took a few classes and some eager anticipation for Chase to finally spot Lana in the hallway. He had gone to his locker to grab some books within the rush hour of students passing through when he saw her coming in his direction. She had her eyes locked directly onto him, as if being guided by some invisible tractor beam force. A small lingering smile was hitched to the corners of her mouth as she cutely held her books up to her chest. "Hi, Chase," she said in a dreamy tone as she leaned her right shoulder against the neighboring locker.

Chase immediately knew in his gut that it had worked, but it still seemed a bit surreal. He was still a tiny bit wary of his luck, and it showed in his voice when he answered with a simple, "Lana — hey."

"I've been looking for you all day," she told him, slowing her words.

"Well, uh... you found me," he assured, shimmering a quirky smile as he tossed his shoulders.

Her eyes were dead-panned into his as she playfully reached out and thumbed the collar of his shirt. "I love this shirt on you," she complimented. "Then again, anything looks good on you."

"Thanks," he responded, then shooting her a somewhat concerned face. "Are you, uh, feeling okay today, Lana?"

"Oh, never better," she sweetly answered. "If only all these classes weren't getting in the way of me seeing you. Knowing sometimes that you're in the room next door — just drives me crazy. My heart pounds so hard I feel like I could just burst my way through the wall — just crash it down so there's no barrier between us." She inched closer to him, seductively streaming her finger down his chest as he grew a little uncomfortable. "Last class I just daydreamed the entire time of being with you. Fantasizing that you would come through the door and rescue me. You'd take me by the hand and we'd run out of school. We'd just run away somewhere together, to some place romantic, like a beautiful deserted beach. Wouldn't that be so romantic?"

Chase squirmed a bit and lightly cleared his throat, looking around. "Uhh — uh — y-yeah. Yeah, it — it sure would."

The sound of the bell ringing through the halls made the students start to disburse to their classes. "Ugh. Another whole forty minutes without you," she groaned with the roll of her eyes. A smile sparked onto her face as she lovingly wrapped her arms around his neck and nuzzled her nose against his. "But I'll see you at lunch, where I get to spend forty minutes *with* you." She laid a long, passionate kiss onto his lips. "Bye, cutie."

She turned and hurried in the opposite direction, leaving Chase standing at his locker as the bodies in the hall thinned. He was dazed. He was star-struck. He wanted to physically touch his lips with his fingers, but he felt that would take away from the lasting feeling of warmth still pulsating on them within the aftermath. A small smile crawled onto his face.

And that's when he knew it was real. It was *actually* happening.

Sure, Lana strangely seemed a bit... robotic. But the more he thought about it through his next class, the more he convinced himself that he was reading too much into it. It was a big deal. The prom queen — the head cheerleader — the most beautiful and popular girl herself — had *kissed* him in front of everyone! And not a friendly kiss-on-the-cheek, either. It was full-on lip-to-lip contact, and she had a whole lotta lip to her. So even with the extremity that he had made it happen by wishing it, he didn't blame himself for feeling a bit insecure that it was true. "Romantic this", "taking him away" that — Chase could fully understand how it felt to have an incredible infatuation with someone, and how that might cause someone to sound a bit more loopy and befuddled than usual. So he had no issue arriving in the cafeteria for lunch a short time later and excitingly waiting for her at an empty table.

She emerged out of the serving room line onto the main floor, holding her tray as she scanned her eyes across the endless landscape of teenagers. Her usual two friends sat at their table and waved to her, but she completely ignored them at the sight of Chase on the far left, which sprang a bright smile to her already-beautiful face. She steered herself in his direction, leaving her friends to awkwardly look at each other and watch as if she had gone crazy. She disregarded every single seat around the table until planting herself directly next to him, even shuffling it a bit closer. "Hi," she sweetly said with her accompanying smile.

"Hey, there," he greeted back.

"I missed you," she then added. "Crawling through math waiting to get here to you was like crawling through hell."

"Well — even in hell you'd still be an angel," he told her, although in the rear of his mind, his intelligent side was laughing at him for such a corny remark.

Her face melted weakly. "Oh my God. That is sooooo sweet," she moaned. He gave a smile. Corny, but it worked. She continued with, "So I was thinking about us going out tonight. Maybe a little dinner, a moonlight stroll, and then something more stationary, if you know what I mean."

Chase began to blush, and then he remembered the specifics behind his original first wish. "That sounds really great and all, but actually, Lana — my car — well, it's kinda temporarily indisposed at the moment sitting in my driveway. I mean, I could hook up a movie projector and point it at the garage and take you to the drive-in."

She threw her head back and let out a laugh, hitting his shoulder. "That is *so* funny! You are *so* funny, Chase! That's what I love about you! Don't worry, silly — we can take *my* car." As Chase opened his small milk carton and drank a little, she looked around and asked, "You don't know where the nearest janitor's closet is, do you?"

"No, why?"

She bit her lower lip and hiked up her eyebrows. "Because I want somewhere to make-out with you so bad right now."

Chase choked up the next sip of milk he was drinking, spitting some forward as he coughed. Lana grew more concerned, patting his back. "You okay?"

He nodded as he wiped his face with a napkin. "Yeah. Wrong pipe," he told her.

"Stay here; I'll get you some more, okay?" she told him, but before he had the chance to answer, she had leaned over and given his cheek a quick kiss before trotting off back to the serving room.

Bridget was watching the entire scene from not too far away as she stood and held her tray. She snapped herself out of her unbelievable gaze and made her way over to Chase, firmly setting her tray on the table as she leaned forward with a stern expression. "Tell me you didn't," she flatly blurted.

Chase finished wiping off his shirt and table and looked in the direction of the serving line, then back at Bridget to give her a careless shrug. "So what if I did?"

"Did you not listen to a single word I was saying this morning?" she scolded.

"Oh, yeah. I heard it all. Thanks."

Bridget shook her head and sat back, tossing a hand up. "I can't believe you. I can't believe you did it. You actually had the balls to screw up someone's life."

"Hey," he insistently shot back, bending his eyebrows down. "Nobody seems screwed up around here to *me*. Everything's just fine, by the way. You don't have to be so damn jealous about it."

"Oh, yeah — I'm jealous. I'm jealous over a blonde air-headed pom-pommer who shops for her tee-shirts at Baby Gap. Yeah, you've really got it all, Chase. Please, stop and share the wealth. I want — no — I *need* a piece of that," she sarcastically snapped.

Chase poked at his food. "Considering how you're just about my only friend around here so far, maybe you could try being happy for me? Just a thought."

Bridget gave a barely audible sigh, letting her small guilt get to her. "So, you two gonna live happily ever after now?" she mumbled, dragging her eyes away.

"It's lookin' like that," he noted. "By the way — you think I could maybe... borrow your convertible tonight?"

The question immediately veered her attention back to him. "Why? She's already head-over-heels for you; it's not like you need to impress her or anything."

"I know, but... I'd feel more proper if I had a nice ride to pick her up in."

"I can let you borrow the Honda," she suggested.

Chase gave her an irritated look. She gave a whining groan. "Fine. Whatever. Don't say I never did anything for you in your quest for a perfect life with the perfect girl."

"Thank you," he solidly said, eating some of the food.

It was at that point when Lana had returned to the table with a new carton of milk as she set it in front of Chase and flashed heedful eyes in Bridget's direction. "Here you go, handsome," she said, curling up closer to him and hooking an arm under his. She turned her head back to Bridget and spoke out with, "I don't believe we've met."

Bridget swallowed some milk and cut her food with a fork, refusing to bring her eyes up to the blonde beauty. "We've been going here four years together. You just haven't graced the lower class side of the cafeteria with your presence yet."

"Hey," Chase sharply warned.

"It's okay," Lana assured him as she curled some fingers through the back of his hair. "She's just being protective of a friend. I know how that is. I can't stand when any other girls look at you. You're just so gorgeous and perfect in every way. How can any other girl *not* want to steal you away for themselves?"

She dipped her head in and gave his cheek and neck tiny butterfly kisses. Bridget tried not to watch, softly stabbing her corn with her fork. Justin, the guy from the library who seemed to claim physical ownership of her, had marched over in his sports jacket. "Lana? What the hell are you doing?" he demandingly asked.

She stopped and gave a weird look. "Kissing my boyfriend."

"Your boy — what? What are you talking about?" he wondered, looking back and forth between them. "What is this, some kinda joke?"

It must have been the proud and invincible feeling Chase felt he was charged with from Lana that made him slightly arch a smile to her. "Why don't you show him how serious you are — honey."

Lana grinned back and more promptly wrapped her arms around him. "With absolute pleasure," she welcomed, landing back on his lips as her tongue snaked around inside his mouth.

Bridget's waiting eyes darted from the affectionate couple to Justin, and the longer they had kissed, the more his expression morphed into outrage as he reached forward and grabbed her arm, attempting to yank her away. "All right, this isn't funny anymore, Lana! Quit messin' around with this dink and come back to our table!" he ordered.

Lana smacked his hand away. "Get lost, asshole. We're through. I'm with a real man, now. A man who knows how to properly treat a lady like a lady. Maybe you should drop by make-out point later tonight with a pen and pad of paper so you can take notes on how it's done. That is, if coach has taught you how to write yet."

Justin's teeth grinded so hard it was a surprise that he had any left. He stiffened his index finger and gave Chase a threatening point. "You're dead," he merely announced before turning and striding off.

Lana rolled her eyes and skimmed a finger across Chase's cheek. "You know what they say — "Attitude reflects the size for some guys"."

Chase didn't respond as she fluttered him with more kisses. And just when he thought he had entered the lunch period with a sense of exhilaration, he was now going to leave it with a lingering dread.


Of course, that didn't stop him from capitalizing on his newly-acquired prize by taking Lana out to dinner, a movie, a walk through town and lastly a parked spot on the dubbed "make-out point" among the hills the town was nestled within — all provided no doubt on the wheels of Bridget's sharp blue convertible.

And lucky for them, they were the only souls in sight. It had been an all-too-perfect night for Chase, so it was only fitting. He couldn't believe he was there. The make-out point surely wasn't just for kissing and other assortments of sexual activity, but also a hot-spot for underage teen drinking, hanging out, or simple star-gazing when the time of year was appropriate. But there he was, behind the wheel of the convertible with Lana sitting next to him and the radio softly playing the latest grooves.

Make-out point with Lana Lanecaster.

He wanted to jump out of the car and use the location to shout it at the top of his lungs so that the entire world could hear — and from that height, they most definitely would. But being in the moment was always better than analyzing the moment, so Chase quickly forgot about *thinking* how good it was when Lana had leaned over and started kissing him. Her motions and rhythms were slow and steady, starting off with his neck and working her way up to his chin and cheek before finally journeying to his lips. It wasn't long after things had gotten hot and heavy that Chase heard the knocking from his fogged window. Managing to pry Lana away, he recaptured his breath. "It's probably just a cop with nothing better to do," he calmly assured her.

So he rolled down his window, expecting to be spoon-fed a mouthful of curfew or private property muck when the fist came flying into his face, practically knocking him over in his seat. His door immediately opened after that, and the fist had extended to two arms that reached in and grabbed his jacket, pulling and dragging him completely out of the car and onto the rough grassy gravel below. Still a bit dazed, he managed to bring his eyes up to notice Justin in his sports jacket standing above him before he was clocked across the face with another right hook. "Hiya, dink!" Justin had proclaimed, snagging him by the jacket and pulling him up to his feet. "How ya doin'? Havin' a good time?"

At that point, Lana had scrambled out of the car and circled around the front, yelling, "Justin, stop! Leave him alone!"

But the first of his three teammate friends had blocked her path, preventing her from advancing any closer. Justin ignored her similarly following pleas and spun Chase, shoving him away and into the arms of the other two. "Ya know, earlier at lunch, I thought maybe she was playing some kinda joke on me, or she had PMS and was pissed for some reason. So I figured I'd take a ride up here and see for sure," he explained, taking a few steps closer as his friends unfairly held Chase. "Now, I don't know what the hell she's doing with you, or what you think you've got going on with her, but you're gonna pay."

He gave Chase a sharp sucker-punch in the face and then rammed his fist into his stomach, making him huff out a cough as he dropped to his knees. "Chase!" Lana screamed, trying to break through Justin's friend. Justin kicked him in the stomach, flipping him over as he curled up on the ground with a groan.

Justin chuckled, savoring the easy victory as he trailed over to his car and opened the door, reaching inside. Chase spit out a glob of blood and said, "Forget it, asshole — no matter what you do or say, she's gonna be with *me* now. Always. She's done with douche bags like you. Consider it a loss on your otherwise perfect sports record." Justin pulled out a heavy brick from his car, causing Chase to let out a quick chuckle. "Are you serious? What's the brick for? You gonna smash my windshield and threaten me more? Steroids make you deaf? I just told you that she's never coming back to you. Trust me on this one."

"No, no — the brick is for the gas pedal," Justin alerted him, stepping past him and over to the convertible. "The windshield will smash when it hits the bottom of the cliff."

Chase quickly attempted to get on his feet in an effort to stop him, but his two friends were there again to strongly hold him back. "Wait, wait — no! Don't! Please! This isn't my car!"

"Seems like you're in possession of a lot of things that aren't yours tonight," Justin simply retorted without care as he slightly sat inside and shifted the car into "drive" and laid the brick onto the gas pedal, getting out and closing the door as it surged forward. Chase helplessly sank his shoulders as the convertible broke through the weak guardrail and sailed off the edge of the cliff. Justin had peeked over and watched, giving a rousing applause for the destruction that was only the sound of anguish to Chase.

He turned and fixed his sports jacket, rubbing his hands as he gave a nod to his crew. "All right, boys — we're outta here. Lana — let's go," he ordered as they all started heading for his car.

Lana hurried over to Chase and took him in her arms. "I'm not going with you," she stated. "I'm in love with Chase now. Now and forever!"

Justin paused in opening the driver's door and looked back at her. "I'm not gonna ask you again," he barked with authority.

"You can go to hell!" she snapped, then looked down at Chase to rub his cheek.

"Whatever," Justin mumbled, shrugging his shoulders and waving her off. "Screw you, bitch. You'll get bored and come crawling back eventually. You always do."

With that, he got into the car and drove off, kicking up a cloud of dust and dirt that Lana protectively shielded Chase from. She looked back down to him and tipped his chin up. "Forget about him. Nothing is gonna keep us apart. I'm gonna love you until the end of time. Forever," she assured him.

Chase cleared his throat and cocked his head to look at the fading red taillights down the road.

"You've gotta be shitting me!" Bridget unbelievably bellowed as she paced in Chase's bedroom.

"I said I was sorry," he tried to offer again with his sympathy as he held the paper towels to his nose. He dabbed them and pulled them away, assuming that the blood had stopped. "Jeez — it was a car. How about a "Chase, are you okay? Maybe we should get you checked out for internal bleeding"."

"Maybe I could do a whole lot worse to you than some meager wussy quarterback ass-kicking!" she threatened. "That was *my* car! And now it's completely totaled! It's more useless than the one you have on your driveway! You wanna know why? Because my parents didn't file any of the insurance paperwork on it yet!"

"Oh, like that's my fault," Chase grumbled. He got to his feet and threw his arms in the air, chucking the paper towels into his trash bin. "What are you getting so damn worked up about? The car was free! And besides that, you can just wish for another one once I give you the ring."

"I don't wanna use a wish for it," she insisted.

"God, fine! Then I'll use another one of mine to get it for you again if that makes you happy," he growled.

She stepped closer to him, piercing serious eyes. "No, you're not listening to me. I don't wanna use *anybody's* wishes for it. I don't want the ring anymore. I don't even want *you* using it again!"

He conjured a crazy face. "What?" he strangely asked.

"Don't you see what's happening? Every wish that's been made has been ending up in disaster. Your "bottomless tank" convertible, my convertible at the bottom of a cliff, and now Lana and her psychotic jock terminator boyfriend."

"Ex-boyfriend," he corrected her. "And like that wouldn't be the case if what Lana and I had was legit."

She crossed her arms. "So now you admit that it's fake."

He stopped and thought it through, knowing he had fallen into a trap of misused words. "No — I — that's not what I meant. I meant legit as if it happened without me using a wish to make it happen."

Bridget grabbed his arms and tried to be a copasetic as possible. "Chase," she sternly began, "Lana does *not* love you. You *made* her love you."

He pulled away from her and shook his head. "What does it matter how it happened? She loves me. *Loves*, present tense. And I'm pretty satisfied with that."

"Justin's gonna be hunting you down everywhere you go. Has it really been worth all this trouble so far?"

"It's not like he's gonna be after me forever," he assured her. "He'll give up. He'll stop caring eventually."

She cocked an intriguing eye to him. "And how about that Stepford Wives Nineteen-Fifties act she's been doing? Telling you she loves you every five minutes, staring at you like she's some *Night of the*

*Living Dead* zombie — you can't stand there and tell me to my face that it's not unnaturally creepy?"

He gave a light shrug. "Maybe I like it. Maybe I never get tired of hearing that every five minutes."

"I'd bet my five wishes any day of the week that you're gonna get sick of it; that you're not gonna be able to take any more of her awkwardly absurd peppiness," she slyly noted. "Please, Chase. I'm begging you. Use your next wish to end it and then throw that damn ring down a well or something."

Chase plopped himself on his bed and grabbed a magazine, starting to flip through the pages. "I knew it. I knew you were jealous. You can't stand the fact that I'm happy with something I got despite how you observe it from your perspective. And as for your paranoid theory on the wishes coming back around to slap their owner in the face — I admit that the first was my fault due to poor wording, the second was just an unfortunate casualty of circumstance, and the third, well — despite the slight temporary hitch-of-a-muscle-headed-asshole problem, and despite an over-analyzed case of lovey-doveyness, seems to be going very smoothly."

Bridget gave a nod and headed for his door, saying, "I hope you're right." She stopped in the threshold and turned back to look at him. "Just remember you've got two wishes left. I hope they make you just as happy."

She left, leaving him to pretend to graze through the magazine. After a moment, he sighed and closed it, tossing it aside.

Bridget was right.

Well, in a way, she was right. Because despite Lana's increasingly perturbing personality, Chase still loved every aspect of being with her. He loved that they walked down the halls together, arm-in-arm, while all of the other students watched with their jaws dropped to the floor. When they were in study hall, they only studied each other. In lunch, every meal was like a romantic picnic in the cafeteria. Bridget, of course, would watch from another table, as she veered from sitting anywhere near the flirting couple in the following two weeks. They didn't talk much then, and it wasn't because Chase was mad. He really wasn't. All of his time was just consumed with Lana, whether it was watching her at cheerleading practice after school, or making-out in Lana's car in some secluded park or woods. His reputation didn't seem to rise. Hers seemed to decline, as being deemed "the most popular girl in the county" was a title of the past. She didn't hang out with her old snobbish clique of friends anymore, and

Chase certainly didn't grasp the experience of meeting new ones beyond his already-small casual handful of acquaintances. He did, however, try to keep clear of Justin, who still spouted his verbal threats and evil glances, but nothing ever seemed to escalate past the point of some shoving while passing in the halls. It was as if he had given up and finally realized that Lana's feelings for Chase were more than accurate. No one could explain it, and not for lack of trying, they constantly asked her motives behind choosing such an... "ordinary guy". Her face would simply melt like chocolate into her dream-like gaze as she reflected upon her catch of such a perfectly-mannered and good-looking bachelor. That in turn did make Chase more noticeable to other girls, as the most popular of them dating him had to mean there was something worthwhile. He never took advantage of his new status, and even if he wanted to, Lana was right there to steer them off and continue claiming him as her own forever and until the end of time.

Still, there was that lingering feeling in the back of Chase's soul. The one that, regardless of how much fun he was positively having, persisted on keeping him up at night a little later than he wanted. He loved that she was around him all day and all night, constantly hounding him with affectionate kisses and phrases of her feelings, but the more he had thought and evaluated it all, the more he was becoming bothered by it. Perhaps if she had said one less passionate compliment in a conversation, it might've kept his ignition going. It's not like he wanted an argument out of her like any other normal couple, but it seemed like an inviting change of pace, because some level of argument or disagreement is generally healthy in relationships. He tried to persuade himself that he was starting to think too deeply into it, but that bothered him even more.

Then it reached the point one day in lunch where he actually tried to pick an argument with her, just to test her responsive feelings. The harder he pushed, the more closer she had seemed to feel it was bringing them together. He even went as far as raising his voice to her one night and leaving her in an annoyance to go home, but she only followed with her countless phone calls and pleading voicemails on his cell until he finally turned it off. She called his house phone, but he had to take it off the hook. "Are you okay?" "Are you mad at me?" "I'm sorry." "Do you still love me?" "Do you still want to be with me?" "Please call me." "Please come over." "Do you want me to come over?" The pleading made him want to tear his hair out. He never thought he would reach the irrational point of *trying* not to be with her; trying to avoid her. But the harder and further he strayed, the stronger she had gotten in her persistence to ensuring their survival as a couple. He could not escape her. And as he lied in bed that night, staring up at the ceiling, he glanced at the ring on his left hand and came to the realization he had been deluding himself from all along.

Bridget was right.

He got his wish.

Lana had fallen in love with him.

Only it didn't turn out the way he wanted. A small part of him clawed for the opportunity to stay optimistic and use his fourth wish to maybe slightly amend the situation by making her a little less clingy and needy. That way, he wouldn't have to lose her. He could draw out specifics by molding and shaping her the exact way he wanted. Not too caring, not too distant. A kiss and a compliment here, an argument and a face-slap there, just like any other relationship. But that wouldn't have done it. Maybe he was just tired of it all. Maybe it was just time to end it and move on. At least that way he could look back and think to himself that he had her — that if he got to kiss the most popular girl in school whenever he wanted, and she constantly had her eyes only on him and him alone — he could move on with the positive notion that anything in the world was possible.

So taking a deep, ready breath, he began to rub the ring on his finger as he spoke out with, "I wish Lana Lanecaster would fall out of love with me."

He didn't feel *completely* better, but he sure went to sleep a lot easier that night.

The next day at school, he was fully prepared to put the wish to the test. She didn't pick him up that morning, which was the first signal toward it being true, but he still wanted some sort of face-to-face confirmation. So between classes, he roamed his eyes through the halls searching for her, but it seemed there was no sign of her presence anywhere. At first, he thought it was possible that she wasn't even there, and was at home sick, or something else had occurred that kept her from getting there. But when he had reached the lunch period, he finally spotted her sitting back at her old table with her uptight female friends. And as he began trotting over in that direction, his determination was subsided by the sight of Justin walking over and slinging an arm around her as he sat in the neighboring seat. She smiled and pecked his nose with a kiss, holding his arm tightly.

Chase resumed his venture and stopped when he had reached the table, waiting for their talking and laughing to halt. Justin gave a firm nod to him, blurting out, "Yeah? What the hell you want?"

"Uh," Chase fumbled, forgetting what he was going to say. He gave a light gesture toward Lana. "I just wanna ask her something."

"Yeah? Sure," Justin obliged, bobbing his head. "You can ask her how many seconds you have left to live before I punch your face through your head if you don't vacate my line of sight immediately."

"I don't want any trouble," Chase calmly assured, looking at Lana. "I just wanna know if it's... over between us. That's all."

Lana gave him a weird look. "What are you talking about?"

Justin pulled his arm off of her and cracked his knuckles, itching to pounce. "The only thing that's gonna be over is your life if you don't start walking, dweeb."

"So it's over? We're done? You mean you don't love me anymore?" Chase interrogated.

Lana sourly scrunched her face, looking him up and down. "Look — I don't know what kinda sick fantasies you're having, but I think you'd better hit your alarm clock so you can wake up from your dream."

"Do you even remember *anything?*" Chase then queried.

Justin stood up, slightly slamming his chair as he huffed, "All right, that's it."

But Lana quickly interjected by rising to her feet and holding him back. "No, wait, wait, honey — let me handle this," she insisted. She grabbed her carton of milk and circled around him, stopping in front of Chase to stare him in the eyes. He wasn't quite sure what to do or say in the following moments of silence, until she opened the carton up and completely emptied it over his head. She shook the last remaining drops out and aggressively threw it to the floor, sharply raising her voice to say, "Let me make this *clear!*"

The talking of the students sitting around fell to a hush, and the domino-effect of silence spread throughout the whole cafeteria when Lana continued with, "I will *never* go out with you! No matter what you think you can do or say to try and win me over, I will never give you the time of day! What, you think that just because I'm beautiful and popular you can take that as an invite to come over to me and try to get into my pants whenever you want?! The closest someone like you will ever get to someone like me is a yearbook photo, so give it up and *stop trying!* Read my lips, loser — Get — a — life!"

She turned and went to sit back down as an uproar of laughter and clapping blared through the cafeteria, plaguing Chase with total and utter embarrassment as he made a sudden break for the doors and ran out. Justin laughed as Lana sat back down and unbelievably shook her head.

Bridget was the only one not partaking in the ridiculing.

And maybe that's why Chase ended up at The Magic Emporium later that night, so he could be around someone who would never judge him for anything. He pushed his way through the door and past a leaving customer as the bell jingled. She was behind the counter, jotting something down on paper when she looked up and noticed him. He slowly dipped his hands into his brown suede jacket pockets and didn't make any immediate attempt at saying the first word, so she intervened by finally saying, "I saw what happened at lunch."

He looked at her but didn't say anything.

She took a light breath and tapped a hand on the counter. "I'm guessing you made your fourth wish."

"What gave you that impression?" he sarcastically grumbled.

"I'm sorry it didn't work out for you," she said, trying to be a good friend. "But you made the right decision. It was for the best. I know you know that."

"Really? Do you? Thanks for that."

"Hey, don't make me the enemy," she softly insisted. "I told you well ahead of time where it was going."

"Yeah, it's so easy for you to stand there and say that," he murmured. "But you weren't the one covered in a carton of milk who got embarrassed in front of everyone."

She briefly rolled her eyes and shrugged. "Who gives a shit what they think? Really, Chase. Screw 'em all. That's your problem — you worry too much about what everyone thinks and you don't stop to listen to the people who actually try to help."

"It's just bullshit. It's all bullshit. I mean, was it too much to ask for a beautiful girl to fall in love with me and maybe live happily ever after? Apparently it was, because even with the magic of a ring, true life always ends up blowing anyway!"

He turned and headed for the door as she hurried around the counter and chased him outside to the curb. "You still don't get it, do you?" she stressed. "You can't get what you want from some stupid ring. You have to go out and get it yourself. You think that you can just pick a face out of a crowd and make them fall in love with you? You think you can turn some snob like Lana Lanecaster into someone you want her to be? It doesn't work that way, even with magic."

"Let me tell you a little something... being me — sucks," he flatly told her. "This was my chance to change it. It was never about Lana. It was about being the one nobody in history who could take something like a daydream and shape it into reality. To be the one loser in history who got to have the popular girl. To change all the clichés for once."

"You're a great guy, Chase," she responded. "If only you could see the things that were in front of you, because any girl in the world would be so lucky to have you if you only gave her a chance. She may not have Lana Lanecaster's popularity, but she would give one hundred and ten percent of herself to you in every way, because she knows the real you. She can see it inside you, and knows what kind of genuine person you are. You don't need any wishes for that. There's nothing in this world that fifth and final wish can give you that you can't go out and get yourself."

"Yeah, I'm sure this town is just pouring with those girls," he remarked. "I'm really glad I don't need a stupid wishing ring for that." He turned to walk away but stopped, noticing the ring on his finger. Sliding it off, he re-faced Bridget and shook it between his fingers. "You know what I wish for? I wish I was living in New York City and everybody here would all just leave me the hell alone!"

He grinded his teeth and frustratingly threw the ring to the road as it bounced and rolled against the curb, eventually falling into the oblivion of a storm drain as he paraded away. Bridget wanted to run after him. She wanted to yell out to him. She wanted to do a lot of things.

But all she ended up doing was standing there in silence on the curb outside of the store with a sorrowfully drooping face of failed effort.


Chase had woken up on a sidewalk bench as he slowly leaned forward and rubbed the sleep from his eyes. He was feeling a bit groggy and out of it, and the inside of his head swiveled. But it didn't take long for him to fully become alert as he wiped his nose and looked around him. He was indeed on a city street, confusingly trying to make sense of how he had gotten there and what he was doing on a bench. He stood up and began to walk, looking at the surrounding buildings and arching his head up to the towering skyscrapers. It was when he noticed the Empire State Building in the distance that he realized where exactly he was — New York City.

But something was off. There was no one around. He was completely alone. And that sent him into a frantic whirl as he raced over to buildings and tried to enter inside, but all of the doors seemed tightly locked — no — *sealed* shut. The parked cars sitting in the streets were inaccessible. He started to jog. He jogged up and down streets and through back alleys as he jerked his head everywhere, screaming for somebody. Anybody. But no one answered. There was something just too strange about the city, and the soundless air, and how the sunlight pouring from the sky all around refused to reflect or gleam off any of the skyscraper windows.

Making his way down a center street, he smacked his head as he walked forward into clear glass, causing him to slightly stagger back and give a strange look as he reached out and touched it. It seemed to stretch forever in both directions, and higher than his touch could reach.

Realization hit. And he abruptly remembered something he had said to Bridget once before — "Imagine if you were a tiny person living inside there. You would think you were walking around in a real city."

His eyes grew wide as his mouth softly dropped. His heart pounded hard within his chest as he flatly placed his hands on the glass in front of him, turning to horrifyingly gaze at the massive city around him.

# DOUBLE BACK

Ashleen was always the bad sister. Well, maybe "bad" was a bad word to use. More like troublesome. Black sheep. Misguided, misunderstood. Whatever it was, that's generally how Shayna and anyone else used to associate her before she left home at the age of eighteen. Of course, Shayna had left home also, but she had left to actually do something with her life — college, for starters, that eventually landed her into the position of a human resources manager in retail sales. Ashleen was... well, Shayna really had no clue what Ashleen was doing. Nor did she even care. She was just returning the same favor Ashleen had showed toward her for the past seven years.

And now there they were, riding in the same car together through a seemingly infinite desert. They were forced to interact, although there wasn't much interacting between the two. Shayna glanced over from resting her head against the window to Ashleen behind the wheel. She relaxingly held onto the steering wheel with her left hand while her right arm casually rode her side with a tilted body; her black-haired bangs slightly drifting over her eyesight. Who drove like that, anyway? Only guys wanting to be thuggish in their ridiculously tricked-out cars looking for attention.

Shayna would try to guess what was going on in that head of hers, but the sky was the limit, and it was a big sky. She probably didn't even care that their mother was lying in a hospital bed dying. When Shayna had finally managed to track down a working cell phone number for her and discovered that she was actually on the west coast, she could sense that tone of dread and reluctance in Ashleen's voice upon the proposed idea of them driving together to see her that possible one last time. After all, she had probably talked to their mother even less than she had talked with Shayna those past seven years. But for whatever reason Ashleen had finally decided to give a damn, she was there, driving her own car and her slightly younger sister to Tucson, Arizona.

It was one thing to have a distantly difficult relationship with your family, but it was another to not see the light of losing them and being faced with the possible regret of how things may have been different. Shayna doubted that's why Ashleen was going. She probably wasn't looking for any closure or redemption. She was probably going to merely satisfy her own twisted and barely breathing conscience with the notion that she wasn't inhumane and would at least do this one last thing so everyone could shut up and finally leave her alone. Shayna couldn't even see how they were related. For one thing, they didn't even look alike. They were half-sisters, and Ashleen's biological father had ditched their mother practically right out of the maternity ward at the hospital the night of her tainted birth. Then their mother shortly remarried and thus came along Shayna, and everything seemed kosher for a while until father number two had bailed and Ashleen grew a pair of breasts and an attitude. "It's her Portuguese side" their mother would always say of her physical and emotional inheritance from her father. She was just a tad bit darker-skinned than Shayna, but the boys always seemed to like that ethnic trait over Shayna's natural American girl-next-door presentation. Not that they ever had any kind of competition over the opposite sex, but it would've been nice to at least have something to bring them together, even in a conflicting way. What they had, if anything, was nothing short of casual friendship in and out of the house, instead of sisterly ties that bonded them together with all-night chats in their bedrooms.

Shayna couldn't identify with her anymore. It was way too late for that. But perhaps it was that small good-natured piece of her that clung onto some kind of newly-rejuvenated hope for them to bond together on that road trip. Fat chance. Even when Shayna attempted to initiate any topic of conversation, Ashleen immediately derailed it with flat and quick answers, and she sure wouldn't try to start up any chit-chat on her part. So at that point, Shayna started to turn toward the back seat to retrieve her only option left with her iPod when she was reminded with all of Ashleen's own bags and suitcases crowding up the car, forcing Shayna's few to be inaccessibly stuffed in the trunk. She turned back forward and barely managed a sigh. It would have even been worth a tuneless ride if Ashleen had spoken about where she was moving herself to and why. But the most in depth she had gotten with the subject was with a simple, "Visiting mom and moving on."

Shayna reached forward and turned the radio on, tuning through the fizzled crackling of the stations in search of anything to fill their uncomfortable silence. "You're not gonna get anything out here," Ashleen had mentioned. Holy shit! Did words just come out of her mouth?!

Shayna ignored her regardless, fiddling with the buttons until landing on a news radio station. Ashleen gave a quick grumble and continued with, "Except for boring-ass talking."

"Some people like to talk," Shayna murmured, tuning the station in better. "You should try it some time."

"Overrated," Ashleen merely opinionated.

Shayna glanced out her window to stare at the desert surroundings as the newscaster went on with, "And police have confirmed there is still no sign of the wanted bank robber out of Prescott from late yesterday afternoon. There has been no accurate description of the male suspect since he was wearing a ski mask during the robbery, but he is believed to be heading south alone after a bloody massacre that had him killing his own three accomplices and four officers at the scene. A civilian is reported to have been killed as well during the incident along with more injured but details remain unclear at this time."

The newscaster babbled on with more details as Ashleen shot a quick smirk to the radio. "Now stuff like *that* is worth listening to."

Shayna unbelievably narrowed her eyes at her. "How can you even say that? Innocent people were getting killed and hurt and you think that's entertainment?"

Ashleen shrugged. "Just the way the world works. More blood, more bullets, more chaos. It's not my fault if as a society we're subjected to be hooked up to an I.V. tube of violence." Shayna gave a huff and shook her head, looking back out her window. Ashleen shunned a smirk. "Hey — if hearing stuff like that makes you quiver, then maybe you should stay indoors rather than venturing out into the real world for some fun."

"What is that supposed to mean?" Shayna sourly wondered.

"It means even though I haven't seen you in seven years, I can already tell you're the same person — afraid of change," Ashleen stated. "It's simple, really. What did you have on your bed when you were a teenager? Stuffed animals. You know what *I* had on my bed when I was a teenager? Boys."

"And just look how far it got you in life," Shayna mumbled. "You know, I was just as overly-thrilled as you when I got the call from mom with the wonderfully-crafted idea to get us together to come and see her on her deathbed, but you know something? I gave it a chance. I thought that maybe it might ring an echoing bell in that vast egotistical head of yours that getting us together might be one of her last requests, but you don't even care, do you? It's just a chore for you between whatever monumentally important things you have going on right now."

Ashleen drove a bit in sharp silence, perhaps a bit bewildered inside from the truth that had been hashed in front of her. She stiffened her jaw and conjured up some sort of comeback that bluntly consisted of, "Look — I'm not happy that she's dying. It sucks, all right? And it's not like I don't wanna see her. I just never had that nineteen-fifties mother-daughter relationship with her that you were privileged to grace, so how do you expect me to feel? One last visit isn't gonna wipe the slate clean. It isn't gonna give me some Ebenezer Scrooge epiphany, because this is real life, not some dramatic tear-jerking movie. So how 'bout you just get off my fucking case and let me deal with it my own way, huh?"

Shayna didn't bother to retaliate with any kind of verbal lectures. She just veered her attention back out the window to the nothingness around them. It was better than looking at *her*, at least. And after a minute or two had passed by and the steam between their ears had settled, Ashleen took an exhaling breath and reached out to the radio, fiddling with the station knobs. "Well — this is what I call true sisterly bonding," she merely said.

It wasn't much longer when they had noticed the car and individual sitting on the side of the road up ahead as Ashleen began to slow down. "What do ya know? A sign of life," she mentioned in an almost upbeat and positive tone. As they got closer, she continued her assessment by adding, "And it appears to be of the broken-down-and-stranded-cute-guy persuasion."

She coasted the car to a steady stop as the guy, appearing to be in his mid-to-late-twenties, approached her window and bent down. She unrolled it as he gave a nice smile and perked his eyebrows. "Afternoon, ladies," he charmingly greeted.

"Hey, yourself," Ashleen flirted. "Having some car trouble, are we?"

"Thing just quit on me," he shrugged, gesturing toward the steaming and hissing engine of his dusty and dirty car. "I'd call for a tow truck but I don't have a cell."

"Would be pointless, anyway. Can't get reception for shit out here. And believe me, for in-car conversation-sake, I've been trying," Ashleen noted, and to which Shayna sniveled at. "Hop on in. We'll give ya a lift to the next town."

"Great," he said, tapping his hand on her window ledge. "Just lemme grab my bags."

As he turned to head back to his car, Ashleen reached below and pulled the trunk open, yelling out to him, "Just toss 'em in the trunk."

Shayna stared at her without approval. "We're just gonna pick him up? Just like that?"

Ashleen gave a weird shrug. "His car is busted."

"We don't know that. There's people out there that stage stuff like this so they can hitch rides and steal from the people that pick them up. He could be anybody," Shayna tried to convince her.

Ashleen smiled and eerily wiggled her fingers. "Ooh, maybe he's the Prescott bank robber," she said and then began laughing. "Gimme a break. Look at him — he's too cute to be dangerous."

"Oh, I'm sorry; I didn't realize there was a physical etiquette to being dangerous," Shayna shot back. "Didn't you ever see what happened to Thelma and Louise after they picked up Brad Pitt?"

"Thelma and Louise..." Ashleen repeated, thinking to herself. "Are those the chicks that worked in the factory and put that glove on the bottle on the conveyer belt so it looked like it was waving?"

"No. That was Laverne and Shirley."

"Well, excuse me, all closeted lesbians," Ashleen arrogantly mumbled with the roll of her eyes. "This is exactly what I was talking about before when I said you're afraid of change. I'm sorry, but — I'm gonna have to throw your little cozy and safe speculation of our awesomely-kick-ass car ride out the window by adding in a wild card. My car, my rules."

At that point, the individual had tossed his two bags into the trunk and closed it, circling around to get into the back seat as Ashleen arched her eyes to the rear view mirror and smirked. "Good to go, cowboy?" she asked.

"Definitely," he answered.

Ashleen rolled the car forward, putting them back on their way down the dusty road. "So what's your name?" she then asked him.

"Xavier," he said.

"I'm Ashleen. That's my sister, Shayna," she introduced. "So where were you headed?"

"Mexico," he answered.

"Mexico," she repeated. "Why Mexico?"

He thought for a moment and answered with, "I guess I like tacos."

Shayna's uncomfortable level was rising by the second. There was something about the guy she didn't like. Maybe it was just the fact that she wasn't into picking up hitchhikers for safety reasons, but she really didn't want to be in that car. She began kicking herself for not taking the opportunity when the trunk was open to grab her iPod, for that would have at least partially gotten her mind off it. As Xavier pulled out a pack of cigarettes, he continued with, "Actually, a friend of mine is getting married. I'm going down for the wedding. Hey — you mind if I smoke?"

"Nah, it's cool," Ashleen allowed. "Long as you give *me* one of those bad boys."

"Got a light? Left mine in my car," Xavier said as he patted himself down and handed her one.

"Coming right up," she noted, pushing the cigarette lighter down. "It's a damn shame they don't put these things into too many cars these days."

"Tell me about it," he agreed with a quick chuckle. "Before we know it, we won't even be allowed to smoke outside."

Shayna slightly turned in her seat to Ashleen. "Actually, *I* mind," she made apparent with a somewhat displeased tone. She twisted more to look back at Xavier. "Our mom's dying of lung cancer."

"Jesus Christ; pack yourself inside a plastic bubble if you're so concerned about your health," Ashleen snapped. "My car, my rules — so open up your window and stop bitching or get the fuck out."

Shayna stared at her for a moment and then sat back forward, reluctantly rolling down her window and crossing her arms in a silent pout. Nobody would have been smoking if they had been riding in *her* car. In fact, the proposition of smoking would never have even emerged because she would have never have picked up Xavier in the first place. Xavier tried to lighten the mood between the two by then saying, "You know why Mexicans aren't allowed to play the game Uno?"

Ashleen looked at Shayna and then shrugged. "I don't know. Why?"

"Because they always steal the green card," he said with a smile.

Ashleen laughed and gave Shayna a small nudge. "I like this guy. He's funny."

Shayna was hardly amused as the cigarette lighter suddenly popped up with a spring-loaded force that sent it flying into Ashleen's lap as she yelped and jerked her body back, giving the car a quick swerve as Shayna held onto the dashboard. Xavier was lightly tossed in the backseat as Ashleen sat up and tried to shake it loose. "Ah! Shit! Goddamn it!" she cursed, finally grabbing a hold of it and shoving it back into the socket. She took a deep breath and ran a hand through her hair, regaining control of the vehicle. "I've been meaning to get that fixed," she embarrassingly noted.

"Maybe that's one of the many reasons they're not being installed into cars anymore," Shayna mumbled with a smug I-told-you-so face.

Ashleen clenched her jaw and reached back down, grabbing the lighter and plunging it against the cigarette dangling from her mouth. She gave a long, soothing puff as she blew some of the smoke and looked over to Shayna while handing it back to Xavier.

Not too much further down the road, they had come to an old rundown gas station and mini-mart, and it couldn't have come too soon. Shayna needed to get out of that car and away from Ashleen, even if for the briefest of minutes. She had actually even considered staying and making it worthwhile to wait for the next car and hitch a ride to the next town where she could take a bus or some sort of taxi the rest of the way. Did she really expect things to be any different on the way back? Just the thought of repeating the whole journey in reverse was dreadful enough, but she had remembered Ashleen mentioning something about not going back in that direction as per her "moving" plans. No matter; it would work better that way for both of them. Besides, Shayna was going to their mother's to temporarily stay, not visit. The most she expected out of Ashleen was probably a wave, some lunch, some kicked-around poor excuse of a final goodbye, and then her departure.

Ashleen pulled the car up to one of the pumps and shut it off. "Can you pop the trunk?" Shayna asked. She did so and got out of the car, followed by Xavier, who let them know he was going to the bathroom. On her way back to the rear of the car, Shayna noticed Ashleen flick her cigarette butt away and immediately head for the mini-mart. "It's okay — I'll pump the gas. Don't worry about it," Shayna grumbled with a wave. She shook her head and headed for the back trunk, where she leaned over and started to shuffle through all of the bags. She unzipped one of hers and dug inside, grabbing her iPod and twirling the headphone cord around it. She froze as Xavier's bags caught her eyes, and slipped the iPod into her pocket.

*Just a quick look.*

Something had compelled her curiosity. She pinched the zipper and slowly began to pull it over the first bag, peeling the sides open to reveal stacks and stacks of neatly-bundled green dollar bills — one hundred dollar bills, to be exact, filled to the brim. She tried to catch her breath as her eyes grew wide. She quickly unzipped the other bag to see it similarly filled with thousands upon thousands of dollars.

It was true. She couldn't believe it. When Ashleen had joked about him being the Prescott bank robber, even a part of Shayna wanted to laugh inside. But now there she was, snooping through his only two bags — his bags filled solely with stolen money. And then a horrible thought crossed her mind — he wasn't just a bank robber.

He was a murderer.

A murderer who had killed his own three partners just to ensure his getaway. And now he was there with Shayna and her sister, accompanied only with his two bags of money. It was all he brought with him, and to Shayna, a man whose only possessive concern while hitching a ride was money made him a very dangerous individual. She had to tell Ashleen. She had to tell the *police*. So she zipped the bags closed and reached up, closing the trunk only to jump back in startled surprise at the sight of Xavier standing beside the car staring at her. At first, she didn't know how to react. So she managed a shaky smile as she reached into her pocket and pulled out her iPod, wiggling it. "Had to get my iPod," she flatly told him.

"Take the money and run?" he asked, slightly raising his eyebrows as his stony face didn't change.

Shayna lowered the portable player and took a wary step back. "Excuse me?"

"Take the Money and Run, by the Steve Miller Band," he stated, gesturing toward it. "You got it on there?"

Shayna looked down to the iPod and gave a relaxing smile to realize what he was talking about. "Oh. Um... I... no. I don't."

"Good band. You should get some of their albums."

"Yeah. I'll... have to do that," she nodded. She then thumbed back toward the mini-mart. "I'm gonna... go grab something inside."

He didn't reply, nor give a nod or any kind of bodily motion. He just stared as she turned and shuffled her way toward the shop, barely managing to look over her shoulder as he prepared to have another cigarette. She pushed her way in through the doors. The interior was much more contemporary than the outside, filled the same way as just about any other corner gas station in the country. Shayna quickly shot her head around until finding Ashleen browsing through the magazine stand. She stepped over and grabbed her by the arm, wasting no time in nervously saying, "It's him. He *is* the bank robber. We have to call the police."

Ashleen shoved her arm away and gave a weird look. "What? What the hell are you talking about?"

"Xavier! He's the Prescott bank robber!" Shayna stressed. "When I was grabbing my iPod from the trunk, I looked in his bags. They were filled with money! And I'm not talking about some little piggy-bank withdrawal. I'm talking thousands! Maybe a million!"

"Get bent," Ashleen sneered with an unbelievable smirk. "If you're attempting some kind of twisted joke as a method of bonding, it's really lame."

"I'm serious! I'd tell you to go look for yourself but he's out there! We have to call the police!"

"Sure," Ashleen said. "So when he comes in here and wonders why the hell we're not ready to go, we can just tell him that we found the money in his bags and we're waiting for the cops on a suspicion that we think he's a bank robber. Right."

"Well, we can tell him something! Anything! We can tell him we can't take him any further!" Shayna pleaded. "He's a murderer, Ash! He'll kill us the first chance he gets!"

Ashleen asked, "Did you pump the gas yet?"

"What? No."

"Well, then — we're not gonna get very far from Mr. Scary Bank Robber if we run out of gas down the road," she said, slapping the magazine she was reading against Shayna's chest. "Way to make yourself fucking useful."

She trotted out the door, leaving Shayna feeling helpless. She noticed the cashier behind the counter — big, old and gruff, dressed in dirty overalls and probably doubling as the establishment's mechanic — and trudged over to the checkout counter as he read a magazine, oblivious to her presence. "Excuse me — do you have a phone I can use?" she asked.

He slightly lowered his magazine and peeked his eyes over to her, sizing her up. "No," he ended up gruffly snorting.

It was obvious he was lying as his expression beamed with the classic untrusting shopkeeper routine. Shayna gave a quick huff and furrowed her eyebrows. "No you don't have a phone I can use or no you do but you won't let me use it?" she curiously put him on the spot.

"What's the matter? Run outta minutes on your fancy little pink city cell phone?" he shot back.

"The reception's for shit out here," she told him. "Look — I need to call the police. There's a guy outside that my sister and I picked up after his car broke down and I think he's that wanted bank robber. The one up in Prescott that killed his partners and all those people."

The mechanic didn't jump to action; he instead lazily drifted his eyes toward the windows, as if to get some sort of glance of the mentioned individual, but when he couldn't spot him, uncaringly sighed and blurted, "Whatever. Payphone's in the back corner."

Dumb desert redneck. Shayna figured she'd have a much easier time trying to convince Ashleen than she would of a fat counter jockey, so she quickly hurried down the aisles and found the payphone on the wall, lifting and placing the phone to her ear as she dialed 9-1-1. It rang two or three times, and a man answered with the standard, "Nine-One-One, please state your emergency."

Shayna turned and muffled the phone closer to her mouth as if to conceal her dialogue, fearfully saying, "Hi, my sister and I are at this gas station and I think we picked up the Prescott bank robber."

"Okay, ma'am. Can you tell me if you're in any immediate danger?" he then asked.

"No, no — he's outside. I found the money in his bags in our trunk and my sister won't believe me and I don't know what to do to stall or not bring any attention to him."

"All right, ma'am — can you tell me where you are?"

"No — I don't know. A gas station. I don't know where. I wasn't driving," she said. "Can't you just trace this call or something?"

He started to answer with something, but Shayna didn't quite fully have her attention on the call as she heard the footsteps slowly approaching. As she slowly turned, her eyes stared unblinking at the sight of Xavier stopping before her. He kept his eyes on her as he opened one of the cooler doors and pulled out a can of Pepsi. The phone slowly slid from her ear as the operator could be heard saying, "Ma'am? Ma'am, are you there? Can you hear me? Please respond."

"Girls and their phones," Xavier finally blurted. "But I don't think you can text on that."

Shayna nervously swallowed the lump in her throat and carefully hung the phone up. "I was just... checking my messages," she lied.

Xavier licked his lips. "Your sister told me a funny joke out there. And here I thought that *I* was gonna be the top comedian during our road trip." He began to take a few small steps toward her as she cowered back. "She told me you seem to think that I'm that bank robber. The one up in Prescott."

Shayna stepped back until the sound of potato chip bags rustling signaled her boundaries. "Where'd you get all that money?" she managed to ask.

"What were you gonna do? Leave me here? Ask me to go back inside and grab a map while you two kicked up dust down the road? Tell the mechanic to give the car a tune-up while you waited for the cops to come?"

"No. No," she said, quickly shaking her head. "Look, please — just take the car and go. You don't need us. You'll be long-gone before the police could get all the way out here, anyway."

"You think I would drive in that piece of shit with the license plates glowing for every cop from here to Mexico to see? Don't worry; I've taken the liberty of removing my property from your car. My plans have changed — I'll be taking the mechanic's now."

As Shayna slowly shifted to her left, she looked straight down the aisle to the check-out counter and noticed the mechanic slouched back in his seat — throat slit and his front side completely covered in drained red blood. She turned her head back to Xavier, who loomed toward her with his evil indication, and then took off running for the doors. She plowed through and stopped, noticing the line of fire streaming its way along the ground toward the car which Ashleen sat in. "Ashleen!" Shayna shouted.

Ashleen looked over to her, but before she could properly react, the car exploded in a large fiery blast, immediately catching onto the gas pumps as they in turn blew up and added to the catastrophic eruptions. Shayna was slightly thrown back inside by the force as the windows around shattered. Debris flew as the ball of smoke soared high into the blue sky. After it had settled, Shayna coughed and groaned as she pushed herself to her feet, but Xavier grabbed her neck and yanked her toward him. "You're right — cigarettes can kill. Especially at a gas station," he told her.

She stiffly elbowed him in his stomach as he grunted and toppled back against a shelf, knocking many of the items off. She took off running and he pulled a handgun from the back of his pants, firing toward her and missing as the bullet blasted into a big bag of popcorn. He shot again and she ducked. As she ran past the cooler on the back wall, he emptied the rest of the gun, shattering the glass around her as she hunched her back and made her way to a door in the corner by the payphone. At that point, the power in the store had gone out, with only the light from outside beaming in. Xavier emptied the shells from his gun and dug into his pocket, grabbing more bullets as he made his way toward the back. Shayna pushed her way through the door and slammed it shut behind her, locking it. She was at the top of a small fleet of stairs leading down to a storage basement, barely illuminated by the small rectangular windows on top of the concrete walls lining the ground level.

Xavier finished loading his gun and grinded his teeth, beginning to throw his shoulder against the door. Shayna jumped at the threatening sounds and fumbled down the stairs, worryingly looking for any way out, but she was trapped. She searched for some kind of defense, but only found a lead pipe. So gripping it tightly, she began to back up as she stared at the door.

A lead pipe versus a gun. Who was she kidding? There wasn't even a place to hide and buy her time to race back up the stairs if he had been down there searching. She curled her hands around the pipe and slowly stepped back toward a generator, awaiting her fate. And once the back of her heel had thumped against the machine, she slightly lost her footing and accidentally swung the pipe against it, roaring it to life as it shook and trembled. The lights in the basement started to flicker on as the noise grew louder and louder. Sparks flew and small bolts of electricity wrapped their way around the generator like Christmas gift paper.

Xavier finally kicked his way through the door. Shayna gasped and spun her head to look up as he came down the stairs, but the surge of electricity around the generator had grown too immensely powerful and zapped Shayna like a wrapped mummy, blasting her into a burst of nothingness.

It was like a bolt of lightning. There was a quick flash, and Shayna was sitting back in the shotgun seat of Ashleen's car as she drove along with Xavier in the back seat. Ashleen didn't seem to notice as she looked at Xavier in the rear view mirror.

"Mexico," she said. "Why Mexico?"

He thought for a moment and answered with, "I guess I like tacos."

Shayna held her head. She was feeling a bit dizzy as she squinted and rubbed her eyes, glancing around the car. As Xavier pulled out a pack of cigarettes, he continued with, "Actually, a friend of mine is getting married. I'm going down for the wedding. Hey — you mind if I smoke?"

"Nah, it's cool," Ashleen allowed. "Long as you give *me* one of those bad boys."

"Got a light? Left mine in my car," Xavier said as he patted himself down and handed her one.

"Coming right up," she noted, pushing the cigarette lighter down. "It's a damn shame they don't put these things into too many cars these days."

"Tell me about it," he agreed with a quick chuckle. "Before we know it, we won't even be allowed to smoke outside."

Shayna weirdly looked back and forth between them. Ashleen turned her head to her and noticed her awkward state. "What's up with *you?*" she asked.

"Huh?" Shayna mumbled, taking another look around the car.

"You look like you're tripped out of your mind or something," Ashleen suggested.

"Oh. I... I don't know... I... just feel kinda... weird," she slurred. "Was I just sleeping?"

"Uh, not that I noticed," Ashleen said, trying to hold back a smile.

"I have the weirdest déjà vu right now," Shayna mentioned.

This time, Ashleen did smile as she put the cigarette into her mouth. "Then maybe you're gonna know that I'm about to tell you to roll down your window," she said. She looked back to Xavier and added, "I'm surprised she hasn't jumped at the opportunity to give us a lecture on smoking. Or fill you in with full detail on how our mother's dying of lung cancer."

Shayna rubbed her eyes again.

Xavier then spoke out with, "You know why Mexicans aren't allowed to play the game Uno?"

Ashleen looked at Shayna and then shrugged. "I don't know. Why?"

"Because they always steal the green card," he said with a smile.

Ashleen laughed and gave Shayna a small nudge. "I like this guy. He's funny."

Shayna looked back to Xavier as the cigarette lighter suddenly popped up with a spring-loaded force that sent it flying into Ashleen's lap as she yelped and jerked her body back, giving the car a quick swerve. Xavier was lightly tossed in the backseat as Ashleen sat up and tried to shake it loose. "Ah! Shit! Goddamn it!" she cursed, finally grabbing a hold of it and shoving it back into the socket. She took a deep breath and ran a hand through her hair, regaining control of the vehicle. "I've been meaning to get that fixed," she embarrassingly noted.

Shayna just sat and stared at Ashleen as she reached back down, grabbing the lighter and plunging it against the cigarette dangling from her mouth. She gave a long, soothing puff as she blew some of the smoke and handed the lighter back to Xavier.

When they had arrived at the gas station, Ashleen and Xavier began to exit the car as Shayna quickly stopped her by saying, "Pop the trunk." Ashleen pulled the latch and continued getting out, heading for the mini-mart as Xavier mentioned his detour to the restroom. Shayna got out and headed for the rear of the car, stopping and staring at Xavier's two bags as they sat among the others. She took a deep breath and grabbed the zipper to one, closing her eyes. "Please don't let there be money inside. Please don't let there be money inside," she quietly repeated to herself.

She unzipped the bag and reopened her eyes to see the stacks of green bills that dropped her jaw as she staggered back, beginning to almost hyperventilate in a state of nervous fear. She gasped and took off toward the store, thrusting her way inside to see Ashleen by the magazine stand. She hurried over and grabbed her arm, almost out of breath. "Ashleen — it's him — oh my God — it's happening again," she spoke.

Ashleen tugged her arm free from her grip and gave a strange look. "What?"

Shayna attempted to calm her breath and quickly think of the right words to say. "Okay — I know this is gonna sound crazy, but you have to believe me. Xavier is the bank robber from Prescott. I looked in his bags in the trunk and found only money inside. But — this happened before. I tried to tell you, just like this, when you were in here reading the magazines, but you didn't believe me, so you went back to the car. I called the police but then he came in and killed the cashier."

"What the fuck are you talking about?" Ashleen then asked in a crazier tone.

"I don't know if I dreamt it, or had some kind of, I dunno, premonition — but this all happened before. The line of crap he was saying in the car about the wedding, the Mexican joke, the lighter popping up and hitting you, everything — it all happened before!" she insisted.

Ashleen slapped the magazine against Shayna's chest and held her hands up. "Look, I don't understand a single word you're saying right now, but you're sounding like a complete psycho. Get a cold drink and get a grip, for Christ's sake."

She pushed her way past her and out the door as Shayna called out, "Ashleen, wait!" but Ashleen ignored her and kept walking. Shayna looked over to the cashier and ran up to him, firmly planting her hands on the countertop. "Do you have a gun here?"

He looked up from his magazine and strangely bent his eyebrows. "What?"

"A gun! Do you have a gun behind the counter? Like for robberies?"

"Why?"

"Because that guy out there is a killer! And a whole lotta shit is about to hit the fan!" Shayna barked.

The cashier sat up a little, trying to get a look out the window. Shayna smacked her hand onto the countertop, trying to retrieve his attention. "The gun! Do you have one or not?!" she stressed.

"Yeah, I got one!" he huffed back, trying to match her tone. "If this is some sorta prank..."

"I swear, it's not a joke," she assured him. "Listen, he probably knows that *I* know right about now! You have to call the police and tell them to get here right away!"

"Well, what are *you* gonna do?" he wondered.

"I have to get back to the car before it —" she said as a sudden thought of realization flashed through her head. "Oh my God."

She turned and blasted her way through the door, stopping in her tracks to see the gas line of fire surging toward the parked car. "Ashleen!" she yelled, running forward.

Ashleen looked up as Shayna circled around the front of the car and yanked the driver's door open, reaching inside to grab and forcefully pull her out. "What the fuck?!" Ashleen bellowed as Shayna continued to push and pull her aside. "What the hell is wrong with you?!" As they got to the safety of the small scrap yard beside the mini-mart, the car violently exploded, followed by the chain reaction of the pumps beside it.

The girls fell to the ground, watching in petrified astonishment. Ashleen's jaw nearly dropped to the dirt. The smoke ball rose to the sky as bits of debris rained everywhere. Shayna pushed herself to her feet and grabbed Ashleen's arm, trying to pull her up. "Come on! We've gotta go! Now!" she urged.

Ashleen wrestled away from her, tossing her hands up in a fit of stress. "What the hell just happened? What is going on, goddamn it?!" she blurted.

"Ashleen, listen — we've gotta move! We've gotta get somewhere safe!"

"I'm not going anywhere until you tell me what the fuck you're talking about!" Ashleen told her. And then the bullets pumped into her — one, two, three! Her body fell to the ground as Shayna turned her body to see Xavier near the car wreckage pointing his gun.

The cashier blasted out the door, shotgun ready in his hands. But Xavier merely turned and shot him twice, sending him stumbling back against the building as he slid down and keeled over. Shayna turned and entered the scrap yard as he sent his last bullet her way, bouncing off some rusted metal as it barely missed. He emptied the chamber and reached into his pocket, pulling out more bullets to reload as he calmly headed in her direction. He snapped the gun shut and held it at the ready, entering the maze-like scrap yard. She was nowhere to be found as he slowly stepped forward, glazing his eyes around. "Oh, Shayna — come out, come out, wherever you are," he said in a somewhat clichéd manner.

She hid behind a stack of tires, listening to his footsteps as he got closer. "Hey, I didn't wanna shoot your sister. I mean, she was pretty hot. She could've been a barrelful of motel fun. But I can't have witnesses alerting the cops when I'm so close to the border," he explained.

Shayna quietly twirled her body around the tire stack and shuffled her way behind an old shell to a jeep as he turned the corner, finger itching around the trigger. "Tell you what — to show you just what a nice guy I really am, I'm not gonna kill you if you make it easy and give yourself up now. One less person to worry about on my conscience. You could come with me. We've got enough money. I could use a little senorita down there."

He prepared himself beside the jeep shell and spun around the back, aiming his gun to find no one there. Shayna, of course, had already taken off running toward the mini-mart as he hurried after. She skidded to a stop at the sight of the shotgun nestled between the dead fingers of the cashier and bent down to snag it, but Xavier's bullet ricocheting off it made her jump back and leave it behind, pushing her way through the entrance door as its glass shattered with the next missed hit. The power had already gone out within the store as she blazed her way down the aisle toward the back, stopping with a thought as he entered inside. She grunted and threw herself into a shelving unit, pushing it over as it collapsed on him in the aisle. She turned and continued her way to the basement door, yanking it open and hopping through as she slammed it shut and locked it behind her. She stampeded her way down the steps and found the lead pipe lying where it had been before, grabbing it and looking at the generator.

Wrapping her palms around it, she lifted it and took a heavy swing down, smacking the machine. But instead of whirling to life, the unit just sat there with a brand new dent. She gave a questionable gasp and swung again, smashing its side. Still, there was no effect. She heard Xavier slam against the door upstairs and grew even more ecstatic. "Come on!" she ordered, giving the machine another hit. She smacked it again and again. At that rate, she would probably end up destroying it. "*Come on!*" she wildly screamed even louder.

She clenched her teeth and gave it her hardest hit yet, and this time, the machine birthed to life, shaking and starting up as sparks and electric bolts zapped, accumulating to a powerful surge. The door upstairs was kicked open as Xavier took his first step down. Shayna shot her head back to the machine as the electricity engulfed her and blinked her out of existence.

With a short white burst of light, Shayna was sitting back in the shotgun seat next to Ashleen in the car. She glanced around, getting a grasp on where she was. Ashleen looked at Xavier in the rear view mirror. "Mexico," she said. "Why Mexico?"

He thought for a moment and answered with, "I guess I like tacos."

Shayna was back. She had actually done it again. And this time, she knew she wasn't dreaming, and she knew she didn't just have some sort of strange déjà vu premonition. She was *actually* traveling through time. "I'm back," she mumbled to herself in realization. "I did it. I came back again."

Ashleen gave her a weird look. "What?"

"That's it," Shayna said to herself. "That's what it does. It sends me back in time."

Ashleen gave a short, strange chuckle, shaping confused eyes toward her. "What the hell are you talking about?"

Shayna glanced at her, and then back at Xavier. "Why don't you tell us why you're *really* heading to Mexico?"

Xavier pulled out a pack of cigarettes and curled a sly grin. "A friend of mine is getting married. I'm going down for the wedding."

"Sure you are," Shayna somewhat sarcastically murmured.

Xavier plucked the cigarette from his mouth and shook it at Ashleen. "Hey — you mind if I smoke?"

"Nah, it's cool," Ashleen allowed. "Long as you give *me* one of those bad boys."

"Got a light? Left mine in my car," Xavier said as he patted himself down and handed her one.

"Coming right up," she noted, pushing the cigarette lighter down.

Shayna dropped her eyes to it. "It's broken," she told her. "It's gonna pop out and land in your lap."

Ashleen gave another weird look as Shayna had a thought. She knew where this was all going, but if she could somehow manage to stop it before they reached the gas station, she could save her this time. If she could only get Ashleen to stop the car and they could somehow get Xavier out of it, they could merely just drive away and leave him in the dust. She glanced at the lighter again as an idea sprang into her head, causing her to unroll her window as she waited.

"It's a damn shame they don't put these things into too many cars these days," Ashleen noted of the lighter.

"Tell me about it," Xavier agreed with a quick chuckle. "Before we know it, we won't even be allowed to smoke outside." He then tried to lighten the mood by saying, "You know why Mexicans aren't allowed to play the game Uno?"

Shayna blew a quick breath and jumped in by answering with, "Because they always steal the green card."

Xavier was somewhat shocked that she had stolen the punch-line so easily but nevertheless gave a congratulating smile. "Well, damn — somebody knows their jokes."

The cigarette lighter suddenly popped up with a spring-loaded force as Shayna reached out with a cat-like reflex and snagged it in the air, immediately tossing it out her window. "Hey! What the fuck did you do *that* for?!" Ashleen upsettingly asked.

Shayna gave a simple shrug. "It was gonna hit you. Burning cigarette lighters and drivers behind the wheel aren't a good match. Sorry. Guess we're just gonna have to stop so we can go back and get it."

"How 'bout you're gonna buy me a new lighter when we get to that gas station I saw a sign for a while back?" Ashleen suggested.

"But what about your car? It's gonna be missing the cigarette lighter," Shayna kept trying to persuade her.

"Then you can buy me another one of those, too," Ashleen informed her. "I'm not gonna waste an hour getting sand up my ass-crack searching for a tiny piece of plastic and metal."

Shayna gave a somewhat disappointed sigh, sinking in her seat. There was no way they were going to stop then. But perhaps it was better that way, for now that they were going to be stopping shortly at the gas station, Shayna would have a much easier chance of making a getaway with her when Xavier had gone to the restroom.

And that's exactly how it went. Ashleen pulled the car up to the pumps and shut it off as she got out with Xavier, who mentioned his departure to the restroom like clockwork. Shayna got out and watched as he walked away, then quickly hurried over to the driver's side. The keys were still in the ignition. She looked to Ashleen walking toward the mini-mart and called out, "Ashleen, wait!"

Ashleen stopped and gave a shrug to her following silence. No more games. Shayna knew it would be impossible and eat up way too much time trying to tell her the truth about everything, so she did the most simple thing she could think — "Um... there's something wrong with your car. It's... really weird. You gotta come see it."

Ashleen looked to the mini-mart and gave a reluctant sigh, heading back to the car. "What is it?" she wondered.

"You have to get in to see," Shayna urged, dipping herself into the driver's side as she closed the door and started it up.

Ashleen walked up to the passenger side and opened the door, looking inside. "What?"

Shayna gave a pressuring wave. "Just — get in. You have to be inside to see it. Trust me. You're gonna wanna see it."

So Ashleen got in, hanging her right leg out the door and awaiting Shayna's explanation. "No, no — you have to get *all* the way in," Shayna insisted. "And close the door. It only happens when the door's closed."

Ashleen grumbled and moved her body fully inside, reaching out and pulling the door shut. "All right, now what the hell is so —"

Shayna slammed her foot on the gas, ripping the car forward as Ashleen held on for dear life. "Jesus Christ!" she shouted. "What are you doing?!"

"Trust me! Just hang on!" Shayna assured her as the car bounced back onto the road in a heap of dust and dirt.

Xavier ran out of the bathroom to see their escape, sharpening his jaw.

"Are you out of your fucking mind?!" Ashleen continued her rant.

"Listen to me — I know you're not gonna believe me. I swear; I'm getting sick of saying that to you, but our lives depend on it," she began to explain. "Xavier is the Prescott bank robber. He's got a gun on him."

Ashleen turned her head to look back. "What?"

"His two bags in the trunk are filled with money. I can pull over and prove it to you but I have to get us to a safe place far enough away from him."

"Unless he's the fucking Flash, I don't think he'll be catching up to us any time soon," Ashleen had reminded her. "This isn't funny, goddamn it."

"I'm not laughing," Shayna retorted.

"Probably because you're out of your damn mind! Would you slow down before you get us killed?!" Ashleen demanded.

"*Me* get us killed?! If you only knew!" Shayna barked back. "I already told you; I have to make sure we're in the clear!" She glanced in the rear view mirror, and that's when her expression dropped. "Oh, shit..."

Ashleen turned her body in her seat to look behind them. "What?"

The mechanic's car had caught up to them, and behind its steering wheel was Xavier — determined and vengeful. Shayna tightened her grip around her own steering wheel and pushed the speed a bit faster. "It's him. He must've taken the mechanic's car," she said.

Xavier sped up and bumped into their rear, causing them to slightly be rocked forward in their seats. Shayna veered a quick, stern glance over to Ashleen. "You see?!" she said.

Ashleen looked back and held onto her seat, bracing herself as Xavier nudged them again. He came up to the side and gave them a little hit. Shayna was no race car driver, so she did the first thing that came to her mind and yelled, "Hold on!" as she spun the wheel to the left.

The car screeched and skidded, completely spinning in the opposite direction as Shayna hit the gas and took off back to the station. Xavier hit his brakes, turning the car around and chasing after with a large buffer zone between them. Shayna wasn't sure what to do. She knew the mechanic's car was faster, and with Xavier behind the wheel, he'd be back on their rear end in no time. Perhaps if Shayna could get them back to the gas station fast enough, they could grab the cashier's shotgun. But as they approached the station on the left, one of their front tires abruptly blew out with a loud burst as she tried to keep control of the car. "Oh, shit! Shit!" Shayna hollered, swerving everywhere.

Ashleen screamed as they hit a ditch before the station, and at their speed, the car flipped and tumbled over a few times before finally crashing upright against the side of the building. Shayna, dazed with blood trickling from her forehead, lifted her face from the blaring horn and came to her senses, looking over to Ashleen.

Ashleen's bloody and bruised face was lying against the dashboard, eyes open without an ounce of life to them. Shayna tried shaking her just to make sure, but it was no use. She could hear the sound of Xavier roaring down the road toward them and quickly pushed her door open as it fell off its hinges. She slumped to the dirt, groaning and shutting her eyes in response to the pain searing through her body, but pushed herself up and stumbled across the ground as the cashier hurried out the door. "What's going on out here?" he cried out. "Oh, lord, girl — you all right?"

She pushed past him as the mechanic's car swerved to a sharp halt in front of him. He pointed a proclaiming finger at Xavier as he got out. "Hey! That's my car!" he declared.

Xavier lifted his gun and shot him, continuing into the mini-mart, where Shayna was circling the counter. He aimed the gun and fired a few times, stopping her personal attempt at grabbing the shotgun as she ran for the basement door. The bullets followed, crashing the glass cooler windows as liquids splurged out onto the floor. She opened the door and spun in, closing it behind as Xavier walked and reloaded.

Trotting down the stairs, Shayna once again lifted the same lead pipe and began to whack the generator over and over, nearly matching the hits that Xavier was delivering to the door at the top of the steps. "Come on, you fucker!" she ordered, giving her bloody face a quick wipe and hitting it again.

The machine bellowed to life, charging up the sparks as the electric stream-lines danced and waved, wrapping around her and zapping her away as Xavier kicked through the door above.

With a sharp snap of white light, Shayna was back in the car minus her bloody injuries, riding with Ashleen and Xavier. Ashleen looked at him through the rear view mirror. "Mexico," she said. "Why Mexico?"

He thought for a moment and answered with, "I guess I like tacos."

"He's going to a wedding — supposedly," Shayna corrected as she noticed him stick a cigarette into his mouth from his pack. "And she doesn't mind if you smoke, just as long as you give *her* one," she added, unbuckling her seat belt and leaning back to pull a cigarette from the pack. She handed it to Ashleen, who was a bit bewildered by her odd behavior.

Shayna pushed the cigarette lighter down. "And since you left your lighter in your car, let me start this one up for ya. Ya know, it's a damn shame they don't put these things into too many cars these days. But before we know it, we won't even be allowed to smoke outside."

"You feelin' okay?" Ashleen then managed to ask as she gave her a slight study while carefully putting the cigarette into her mouth.

Shayna tossed her hands up and gave a fake, peppy smile. "Oh, never better. Never goddamn better. The only thing that could make this trip complete is a damn good joke. Anybody know any?"

Xavier spoke up with, "You know why Mexicans —"

Shayna turned back to him. "Because they always steal the green card!" she immediately answered. "Boy, is he funny! Now that lighter should be defectively popping up any second now."

The car lighter shot up from the socket as she caught it in the air, immediately jumping over the seat and plunging it into Xavier's neck as he let out a crying scream. Ashleen's face dropped as she looked back at the wrestling escapade that ensued. "What the hell are you doing?!" she shouted to Shayna.

Shayna kicked her feet, knocking over some of Ashleen's baggage and burning Xavier in more spots as he tossed and turned, trying to throw her off. "You like that?! Huh?! You like that?!" she yelled. "You're not gonna fucking do it again, you hear me?!"

Her shoes nearly nailed Ashleen in the face as she waved her arm to push them away, keeping control of the swerving car. "Stop it! What the fuck is going on?!" she stressfully hollered.

Shayna reached for the door handle. Her fingertips skimmed it as Xavier curled over her. She finally clutched hold of it, pulling it and giving it a slight push as it cracked open. She tried to dig her free hand behind Xavier. "I'm not going back anymore! This is ending!" she insisted.

She pried it free from his pants as he jointly gripped it. They wrestled with it. A shot rang out, blasting through the front passenger side window as Ashleen shrieked and ducked. Another went out the back windshield, and another went through the roof. Shayna finally seemed to get the upper-hand, ripping it away from his grip as she leaned back against her door and clenched her teeth, hiking her foot back. "Find another fucking ride, asshole!" she barked, strongly kicking her foot forward into his chest and sending him through his door and out of the car to hit the pavement hard.

Ashleen shot her eyes to the rear view mirror and twisted her head back to look at the tumbling Xavier behind them, jerking the wheel and keeping control of the car as Shayna reached over and closed the door. "Holy shit!" Ashleen asserted with widened eyes as she started to slow down. "What the hell did you just do?! You just — You just kicked him out of the goddamn car!"

"Keep driving!" Shayna ordered, crawling back up into the front passenger seat as she demandingly grabbed the steering wheel. She gave a tired sigh and slumped her head back against the seat. "And don't stop until we're far enough away from him."

Ashleen gripped the wheel tightly, darting her eyes back to her rear and side view mirrors. "What — the *fuck* — just happened?" she unthinkably asked.

Shayna didn't answer; she instead continued to work on reclaiming her breath. Ashleen wanted to say something else but didn't, instead keeping her tensed vibe as she concentrated on driving. And after a short time later, when Shayna had felt they were safely enough away from Xavier, she asked her to pull the car over.

Ashleen opened her door and got out, looking over the damage to the car. Shayna crawled out as well, running a hand through her hair as she looked over to her. "Pop the trunk," she requested.

Ashleen walked over to the driver's side and leaned in, pulling the latch that popped open the back trunk. She returned to the rear of the car and watched as Shayna unzipped Xavier's two bags and blatantly pulled them open to display the countless amount of money inside. "You wanna know what just happened? I'll show you." Ashleen's face started to drop at the sight of the fortune as Shayna continued with, "The next time you feel the urge to be a bitch by insisting on picking up a cute, psychopathic, murderous, bank robbing sociopath dickhead from Prescott, just do the world and I a huge favor — *don't*."

160

Ashleen stepped closer and reached for the bags, flipping through some of the stacks of bills. She couldn't believe what she was seeing. She opened her mouth to say something, but nothing came out. "Wha...? How... How did you know?" she eventually managed to mutter out. "What the hell is going on, Shay?"

"I'd tell you but you wouldn't believe me," Shayna simply answered, waving off the notion as she slapped the gun into her hand.

Ashleen slid her fingers across the chamber. She looked back to the trunk and thumbed through all of the bills. "Jesus... I was only joking when I said that's who he could be," she said. "He could've killed us!"

Shayna rolled her eyes with a sarcastic smirk. "Yeah. Can't imagine what *that* would've been like."

"Look at this... there must be... hundreds of thousands here," Ashleen noted about the money. Shayna squinted as she looked back down the road. The heat created rippling waves in the distance. Ashleen licked her lips and straightened her posture, as if having an ingenious thought. "Ya know... no one saw us pick him up," she craftily said.

Shayna arched an eyebrow. "So?"

"Sooo..." Ashleen continued, swirling her tongue in her mouth. "There's no proof we ever met him, and it's not like he knows who we are or where and how to find us. I mean, he's all the way back there... and we're here... and this money is sorta just... up for grabs... So, hypothetically..."

Shayna was beginning to catch her drift as she looked back down the road and then back to Ashleen. "No one would know if we took it," she finished the analysis.

"Actually..." Ashleen began to say, swaying a seductive hand across the bags. "No one would know if *I* took it."

The expression on Shayna's face began to drop as she sharpened confusion in Ashleen's direction. "What?" she unsurely mumbled, not sure whether to smile or be serious.

"I mean... it *was* me who wanted to pick him up in the first place. So that kinda gives me first rights."

"First rights?" Shayna strangely quoted. "Ash — you're not serious. If we're really gonna take it, then we're gonna split it."

"Dancers do splits. I don't," Ashleen confirmed.

"Oh my God; you've gotta be shitting me," Shayna unbelievably exclaimed. "Tell me you're just fucking around and you're not that selfish. I'm your sister, for God's sake."

"Well, you're half right," Ashleen corrected as she reached back into the trunk and pulled out Shayna's bags, tossing them to the road. "My car, my rules — remember?"

Shayna's mouth slightly hung as she unbelievably watched. "What are you doing?"

"You can find another ride. I'm not going in your direction anymore."

"What? What about Mom?"

"What *about* Mom?"

"I thought we were going to see her together?! And now suddenly with some cash in your pocket you don't give a shit anymore?! She could use some of that money! That money could help her get better!" Shayna pleaded.

"Mom is fucked, Shay. You don't waste money on dead people," Ashleen blurted.

Shayna stared at her with distraught eyes, slowly shaking her head. "How can you say that? How can you *do* this? You're just gonna leave me out here in the middle of the desert?! What if he catches up to me?"

Ashleen grabbed Xavier's bags and closed the trunk as she started to circle back around the car toward the driver's side. Shayna followed. "You seemed to be handling him pretty well before."

"Don't do this, Ashleen! You can't leave me out here! Forget the money; you can have the money! I don't care! Just drive me to Mom's! Just drive me to the next *town* at least!" Ashleen ignored her and opened her door, tossing the bags onto the shotgun seat as she dipped inside the car. Shayna was steaming. "I cannot believe you! After all I went through for you! For *you*, to save you over and over! I went back for you!"

"Yeah, well, whatever *that* means," Ashleen retorted, shunning her off. She reached into one of the bags and pulled out a stack of bills, tossing them out the window as they plopped into the dirt below. "There ya go. Buy her another carton of cigarettes and tell her I said that life sucks."

She started the car up and drove off, leaving Shayna watching and filled with an immense betrayal. Before long, the car was a speck in the distance. Shayna kicked at the dirt and cursed, placing her hands on her hips. She turned her head all around — especially down the road behind her. There was no one in sight, but that didn't mean that no one was coming, so she performed the only option she had — she started to walk.

And she walked for miles. Miles under a blazing sun that glistened a slab of sweat across her forehead and that nearly soaked her shirt in a pool of perspiration. It was a long, hot walk. Every now and then she would cock her head back over her shoulder — a portion of her fearing to see a figure in the distance, or an approaching vehicle that may contain that figure who would suggest for the driver to pull over and give her a "friendly" helping hand.

But the further she walked, and the hotter it got, she didn't care. She stopped looking. Her blistered feet within her worn shoes kept hitting the pavement in determination with every advancing step forward. Now she was on a mission. And nothing would stop her from getting to that gas station.

When she had finally arrived, she hiked past the unused pumps and headed straight for the entrance door, pushing her way inside. She strolled right past the mechanic sitting behind the counter, oblivious to her presence as he read his magazine, and proceeded down the back aisle to the cooler wall, where she slid one of the doors open and grabbed a bottled water. She unscrewed the cap, letting it bounce to the floor as she chugged the entire contents. When she was finished, she wiped her mouth and gave a natural, thirst-relinquished sigh, carelessly dropping the empty bottle and walking to the basement door. She entered inside and closed it shut behind her.

The mechanic, of course, kept reading his magazine, unaware of her intentions until the lights in the store began to flicker with a power surge.

With a quick flash of white light, Shayna was sitting back in the shotgun seat while Ashleen drove and glanced to Xavier in her rear view mirror. "Mexico," she said. "Why Mexico?"

He thought for a moment and answered with, "I guess I like tacos."

Shayna just sat staring forward — expressionless. As Xavier pulled out a pack of cigarettes, he continued with, "Actually, a friend of mine is getting married. I'm going down for the wedding. Hey — you mind if I smoke?"

"Nah, it's cool," Ashleen allowed. "Long as you give *me* one of those bad boys."

"Got a light? Left mine in my car," Xavier said as he patted himself down and handed her one.

"Coming right up," she noted, pushing the cigarette lighter down. "It's a damn shame they don't put these things into too many cars these days."

"Tell me about it," he agreed with a quick chuckle. "Before we know it, we won't even be allowed to smoke outside."

Ashleen looked over to Shayna and noticed her estranged state. "What's up *your* ass?" she wondered.

Shayna didn't reply. She didn't even glance in her direction. She just kept staring forward. Ashleen shook her head, mumbling, "Whatever."

A short while later, Ashleen coasted the car up to the pumps at the gas station as she got out with Xavier, who mentioned his side-trip to the restroom. Shayna still sat in the car, watching him as he rounded the corner of the mini-mart. After Ashleen had entered inside, she finally exited the car and closed the door, walking in Xavier's direction. She rounded the corner and turned her head all around at the edge of the scrap yard, finding a solid crowbar among some rusted metal. She grabbed it and squeezed her palm around the handle, stiffening her jaw as she headed for the restroom door. She stopped before it and knocked. Xavier opened it as she perked her eyebrows and asked, "Room for two in there?"

He developed a sly smile and leaned against the threshold. "We can find out."

She lifted the crowbar and cracked him upside the head, knocking him cold as he fumbled back into the room and toppled over. "Aspirin is in aisle three," she mentioned as she stepped in and pulled his gun out of the back of his pants. She pulled the door shut and swung the crowbar down again, breaking the outer handle off. She tested the door. It was definitely stuck. She turned and tossed the crowbar aside, dumping the gun into a nearby fire barrel as she headed back to the car and popped the trunk. She pulled her and Xavier's bags out, tossing them aside as Ashleen exited the mini-mart. "We ready to roll? Did you pump yet?" she wondered.

"Pump your own goddamn gas," Shayna snapped back. "I'm going in a different direction than you."

Confusion crawled onto Ashleen's face as she thinned her eyes toward her sister. "What? What the hell are you talking about?" she asked.

"I knew you really didn't care. I knew it. And I went against my instincts by thinking that her dying might have some kind of emotional effect on you, but you know what, Ash? People like you don't have emotion, because people like you don't care about anyone other than themselves," Shayna explained. "You have no appreciation for your life. You take it for granted, and you're ungrateful for it."

"What the fuck are you babbling about? Are you really gonna start up this conversation again?"

"Just go," Shayna simply stated.

"Where's Xavier?" she wondered, looking around.

"He doesn't wanna go with you, either," Shayna answered. "He's gonna be in the bathroom a while with a headache."

Shayna sniveled and unacceptably waved her hand, heading for the car. "Stop being a bitch and just get in the damn car," she told her.

"I already told you I'm not going," she repeated. "I don't care what you're doing with your life, or where you're going, or why, but just leave Mom and I alone. It's what you want, isn't it? Just admit it. I thought maybe you had changed in seven years, but I was wrong. Anything outside your self-indulgent existence is a burden to you. So just get in your car, drive off, and get the hell out of my life. I don't ever wanna see you again."

Ashleen stopped at the driver's door and stared at her for a moment, as if waiting for her to change her mind or make the next move. She almost opened her mouth to say something in her defense, but held back. She turned her head for any sign of Xavier, but when it was apparent he wasn't coming any time soon, she tongued the inside of her cheek and tapped her foot. "Fine," she eventually blurted with a sour tone. "Whatever. Fuck you."

She opened her door and ducked inside, starting the car up and wasting no time in driving away from the gas station. Shayna watched and took a deep breath, then turned and headed for the mini-mart. The mechanic sat behind the counter, reading his magazine as she approached him. "That P.O.S. Chevy out there," she began to say, nodding her head toward the windowed wall. "That's your car, right?"

He brought his eyes up from the magazine to her and peered out the window, warily returning them in her direction. "Yeah. Why?"

Shayna set two bundled stacks of crisp, green dollar bills onto the counter and answered with, "Because I'd like to buy it from you."

# NIGHTLIFE

The night is mine.

For me, there's no better time to do anything in this great span of twenty-four hours we officially refer to as a complete day. When I think about it, there's really no true reason as to why this feeling occurs to any of us who choose the path of the night owl. For some of us, there is no choice. We take the jobs we can get, and if that means pulling night shifts and sleeping during daylight, so be it. Me, well... I choose it with an admiration and excitement that only begins to boil and crackle when I see those golden rays flood across the horizon of a setting sun. A sun that holds a certain jealousy for a silver shining moon that gets to come out and play. My mission is complete, the sun might think. I've done my part and shed light across this world. I've helped the people and economy do their thang. I've given energy and warmth to all things chemical, organic and electronic. Now it's time for me to rest and turn the earthly duties over to the moon. But... what does this moon do? What does this ageless understudy get to see that I can never?

It gets to have fun.

And when it comes to the night, fun is an endless possibility of epic proportions on every scale imaginable. Maybe it's because those of us who bask in its darkness know that pretty much the remaining other half of the world is currently asleep, dreaming those dreams of the approaching daylight's possibilities for their lives. The world is a stupid place for me, filled with stupid people. But when night comes, and I'm surrounded by the shadowy presence of others like me, I feel that low intelligence level curb sharply. I suppose that aspect is simple logic, really. Sure, we might get drunk more at night and wrap ourselves around telephone polls, or fall asleep behind the wheel and pulverize Bambi going sixty because of an absence of guiding sunlight that allows us to see everything and anything, but those like me who really grab the night by the balls tend to have a different mindset on things.

Hell, maybe it's just because half of the fucking world shuts up for a good eight or nine hours and allows us to sit back with some peace and quiet and think about the place we live in. Every now and then, weather permitting, I like to go to my apartment's rooftop and slouch in a nice comfy lawn chair, cracking open a few beers and watching the city and stars. But that's the calmer and more happy-go-lucky aspect of my nightlife, and that's not what I'm here to discuss.

The night has plenty of evil. Across and under these city streets lies a layer of tattered scum and worthless cockroaches, all doing their own bidding. Here's the part where you think I'm probably gonna tell you I'm some secret masked superhero avenger, patrolling the rooftops and alleys with a good-doing vengeance protecting all of those innocent civilians wrapped so snuggly and tight in their bed sheets and blankets. Fuck that. Tights and a cape aren't my thing, although I can assure you there are plenty of other people out there who make a habit of dressing up in different clothes when the sun goes down.

So just who am I then? I'm just like you. But maybe not. Maybe I'm just like you in the sense that I'm only trying to scratch my way through life, night by night, day by day, only I'm different because I'm breaking some rules here and there along the way. After all, what better time for rules to be broken than at night, when no one can see you? When the world is asleep. When you're totally invincible. I've always been a night person. As a little kid, I could never sleep. I never wanted to go to bed early on a school night. Always wanted to play with my toys, or video games, or watch late night TV. Once I got older, through my teen years and college years, I could get away with it more easily. I'd stay up all night, and sleep through the day. I'd go to some parties, hang out with friends, go on the internet, watch movies, whatever. As long as it was at night, it was more than suitable for my tastes.

Going past my mid-twenties now, I've realized that it's much easier to keep people at a distance. That having a circle of regular friends doesn't really fit into my... lifestyle. So what do I do? I do a lot of things. For a while I worked at a loading dock down at the bay. But that got boring fast. I even dabbled in the art of night security at some shithead corporation building downtown. But like I mentioned — I'm a rule breaker, not an enforcer. So I met a guy, who in turn introduced me to another guy, who then introduced me to another guy. That's the way things always seem to start rolling, right? And by rolling, I mean wheels. Car wheels. Stolen car wheels. Stolen car wheels on a stolen car. A stolen car which I bring to a pre-arranged location by an anonymous individual for a pre-arranged reason. I never know the reasons. I don't care. And although I may know most of the time who I'm stealing them for, I tend to keep a knowledgeable distance from their personalities. It's a rush, really, stealing a car. Plenty of people steal cars, plenty of ways. Even in bright daylight. Fuck, even in a jam-packed Wal-Mart parking lot with Mrs. Brown and little Sally Shit-Pants in the stroller walking right by. But you've never really stolen a car until you've stolen it at night. Some people may think it's a bigger rush stealing it under pressure with others around to watch you perform every move, but me — I like the idea of a vacant street at night, maybe three in the morning. When the only sound around comes from the fluttering of the sports section down the sidewalk in the breeze. Knowing that anybody — people like me — night people — could be watching and lurking. And that's why I do it.

It's not like the money's all that great. It's a lot, and it sure as hell could buy me a much bigger place than my apartment, but one thing I've learned in this line of work is that everything in life is temporary. Everything is subject to change at any moment. No sense in settling down in a nice, spiffy brick-laid Colonial house out of the city. Besides, I think an apartment compliments a good nightlife well. It's not like it's a piece of crap or anything. Plenty of space, brand new, good furniture, good noise consolidation. It's simple.

And I know what you might be thinking now that you're getting an idea of things I do for money. I'm not a douche bag. I try not to treat people like shit unless they ask for it. Is it my fault people don't get better alarm systems for their cars? Is it my fault they barf up the extra thousands for that Mercedes Benz rather than for a garage to actually keep a damn car safely in? It's not like I'm a drug dealer or anything. It's not like I sell kiddy porn. I just get told what the car is, where the car is, where to bring the car, and who to bring the car to. Beyond that, it's not my problem. So if Mr. Nine-to-Five wants to complain to somebody about his shitty luck, he should try looking past me to the person or people who actually do something with the car. In fact, I shouldn't even consider myself a car thief, an expert in nocturnal grand theft auto. All I do is move the fucking thing. After that is when it's really stolen. When the motivations and intentions for it become painstakingly clear.

Of course, what's a little grand theft auto without a little luck? I don't consider myself to be that much of a superstitious person, but every thief or criminal has their own thing to get them motivated; their own piece or venue of higher power that seems to save their ass every time. For me, it was my grandfather's pendant necklace. It wasn't anything fancy or expensive, in fact, his grandfather that gave it to him before had noted that he only bought it at some Indian reservation when he was young. Funny, it didn't look Native American, not that I was all that much of an expert on their language or symbols, but the strange markings on the old tainted and smoothed flat circular brown rock pendant portion had to mean something in someone's language. I had asked around here and there over the years but no one could really help. Egyptian, Mayan, Martian — who the hell really cared? I don't think my grandfather really knew, either. He had always simply told me that it meant "good luck" and nothing more. So I used it as a plug-in to charge every job I did, giving it a little foolish rub with my thumb and index finger right beforehand. Not that it had some kind of magic over my success each time. That explanation lied within the simple boundaries of pure skill, because I was good at what I did.

So that's what I do, and what I've been doing. I won't really go into depth about the details behind each job. Just think about the stuff you saw in that shitty *Gone in 60 Seconds* movie. Except it's not that elaborate. And I don't get to bang Angelina Jolie in a stolen car. Only jerk off while thinking about her in a stolen car.

Each night for me is different, but that doesn't make any single one more or less exciting or eventful than another. Shit happens. Jobs get done, or nothing comes up for a while. The night can be a comforting friend who actually returns your damn borrowed movies and CDs or the night can bring you a whole other set of endless wonder and possibilities.

Like the night she moved into the apartment at the end of the hall.

I didn't really actually see her all that much during my endeavors in and out throughout the night. I only know she was moving into that apartment at the end of the hallway that had stood vacant for quite some time. The only apartment on the entire floor in fact that was located at the end of a hallway, rather than spaced evenly out on the sides like all the others. That closed door, always looming with an empty essence and never any tenants. Of course, it's not like I knew anyone's habits on my floor, or knew anyone period, for that matter. Christ, I don't think I've ever actually met my neighbor in the couple years I've been here. An occasional head-nod, maybe a "hello" to one or two people here and there in the hall or on the elevator, but everyone in those apartments had something going for them that disallowed any true type of established connection to the surrounding others. Works for me, anyway.

So you might say my interest for this particular new arrival was a little more than sparked for a change, considering the utter weirdness behind her late-night commotion. Who the hell moves in at night? She didn't seem to have much, as from what I figured the movers were in and out with stuff probably within an hour or two tops. I overheard some people in the lobby the next day bitterly complaining about the noise and the absurdity of a complex allowing such an entrance to be performed that late. Someone had dropped a hint bomb through unsubstantiated gossiped rumors that the landlord had been paid off a good deal of ass-wiping money by this tenant to pretend there was a mix-up in the moving time, or bullshit some bullshit reason that maybe medically or physically she could only move in at night. Frankly, as much as the interest gnawed at my innards, I lost the ability of giving a damn pretty quickly in the matter and went on with my own nightly cares. Occasionally she would happen to be coming or going the same times that I was, always at night. At first I wanted to take her as one of those club girls, using those flashy eyes and fuck-me-smile to dance her way through life with all expenses paid by whatever for-the-moment-fool was dragging his tongue across the floor for her that night. She didn't dress like a club girl, though, with those loose front side glitter shirts tied around a bare backside neck that screamed out dancing gutter slut, which is what propelled that theory out of my head so quickly. Her wardrobe was casually cool, never overdoing or underdoing any attire whatsoever. I guessed she was about my age, if anything maybe a shred bit younger, with the presence and walk of someone much more older and mature. One of those closet headstrong up-and-doers. Someone who could playfully flirt with footsies under the table one second and then bend you over and fuck you up the ass with an intelligent conversation the next.

The thing that struck me most was her looks. This wasn't the type of girl you called beautiful, or pretty, or gorgeous. This was the type of girl you called "hot". As in, fiery hot coals of hell, the way that the word "hot" was originally meant and conjured up in reference for use toward female appearance. As in, fire in my loins hot. This girl was fucking hot.

Usually I've always been pretty good at keeping my cool around the hottest of hottie hunnies, but I always found myself dropping my keys when locking my door on the way out to see her going into her apartment; barely giving her sexy eyes a glance over her right shoulder. Or I'd be carrying a few brown paper bags of groceries and fumble a box of those white powdered donuts out onto the carpet. She would pass them and pick them up, stuffing them back in the bag to my aid while murmuring the words, "My favorite kind" and continuing her way to the elevators while leaving me to stand like a speechless moron.

Most guys might say that the greatest thing about the female gender is the mystery. The complete and full-throttle turn-on of either pursuing the truth in her or stretching out the enigma to fortify a barrier that prevents any sort of permanent commitment. Me, well, I'm always up for getting to the tight perfectly-crafted-by-God-Levi-jeans-ass-bottom of a good mystery, especially if it lies within the realm of my nightly world.

I could have left this alone. But then maybe it didn't matter what I did. Even if we try to leave things alone, maybe certain things are bound to come back for us anyway.


"You don't give powdered donuts to the girl you wanna fuck," Shelly so wryly told me. Wry and bold. That was Shelly. My sister. Must run in the family. All except the troublemaking part. She always seemed to counteract that part of me with her good conscience. Like the angel on my right shoulder. A Jiminy Cricket... but with breasts.

"It's a good way to break the ice. Kinda like... an apartment-warming gift. She said they're her favorite," I replied, shoveling some of my afternoon breakfast cereal into my mouth as I leaned against the kitchen counter. "And I never said I wanted to fuck her."

Shelly grinned, perking her eyebrows. "Please," she slyly murmured. "Like you really wanna start daily donut-eating dates, Adam."

"Okay. Yeah? So? A nice little bonus," I shrugged. "But there's something about this chick. Something I can't put my finger on."

"Or in," she smirked.

"I'm serious, Shelly. She moved in during the middle of the night. Who the hell does that?"

Shelly started to prep a small bowl of cereal for herself. "Maybe she's an insomniac. You two would get along well."

"But what kinda apartment complex allows that?"

"One that graciously accepts stacks of fifties and hundreds from its rich-daddy's-girl tenants," Shelly answered. "Jeez. You never get this ga-ga over any girl. She must be a real scorcher. What do you care, anyway? She's here, isn't she? Shouldn't you be more focused on how to get her rather than how she got here?"

"Good point," I declared with a light nod.

Shelly cringed as she gave a tight chew to her cereal, scooping out the rest into the sink. "This cereal is stale," she mentioned. "You know, there *is* a thing called an expiration date. When you reach that, it's time to go out to get more. In supermarkets. There *are* some open overnight, made especially for people like you."

"Who needs expiration dates when I have you to spout life's little reminding anecdotes?" I casually joked.

"How's work going? Steal anything good lately?" she coyly muttered.

"You make it sound so... dishonorable... when you put it that way," I said.

She lightly rolled her eyes, wiping her hands with a dishtowel. "I'm not gonna stand here and give you another lecture on how to drive your life. But when you're doing in it stolen cars, the gage needle is gonna hit empty sooner or later."

Oh God. How the metaphors and analogies poured from her mouth like roaring waterfalls. Maybe it was the older brother syndrome in me, but sometimes I just wanted to cram all that psychobabble bullshit right back down her throat, and other times I actually did want to consider slamming my foot on the brake pedal of a stolen car and pull over to say to myself aloud, "What am I doing?"

The rush was really too good to pass up. Plenty of other things could probably match the intensity of a good grand theft auto boost. Maybe even legal things. But that's what I did. I didn't picture myself doing it forever, but for the moment, it was me. It was what I did. And I could have told her to just shut up, but I didn't. I didn't retort with anything that would start another long argument. She said it herself — she didn't want to stand there and lecture me.

Maybe she should have.

Anyway, Shelly had left soon after that, off to a late class or another good worldly deed she would undeniably rub in my face later on, but I had an agenda of my own to attend. And I didn't even know her name. So despite Shelly's feminine perspective on the art of donut-giving to a girl you wanna get to know, I found myself standing in front of her closed apartment door at the end of the hall later that day with a brand new box of mini powdered sugar donuts in my hand. Even before I knocked, embarrassment rattled through me like an eighth grader about to give a carnation to the most popular girl in school he knew wouldn't give two shits about him. And I had donuts. Fucking donuts. On the other hand, more positively, I thought it would be a great opportunity to use one of my few charm cards, even though it really wasn't my style. Maybe she'd had a sense of humor. She'd invite me in, I'd remind her of our prior little donut connection, I'd give them to her as a welcome gift, and we'd start head-first into the usual getting-to-know-each-other conversations that would eventually evolve into regular visits and outings, and not long after that — an interesting story to tell the grandkids. I won your grandmother over with a box of donuts.

Although there was also the inevitable topic of my nightly outings. Sure, tell her that I'm between jobs at the moment but I boost cars for other people to make ends meet. That I've done things I'm not proud of. That the night brings out a different side of me. "There's the door" she would probably say with her eyes as they signaled over to it. But then it occurred to me that I didn't know a damn thing about this chick or what she had in store for me. She could be just as reckless and shady as me. She could be a damn thief herself. She could be someone on the run from something or someone, looking to start new, looking to start different. It could be a major turn-on for her. She could be my Angelina Jolie.

So as these thoughts collided in a rush hour of exciting uncertainty within my head, I balled my hand and gave her door a light knock, exerting a tiny breath. I gave it a long minute and figured maybe I didn't knock hard enough. So I gave it another go, boasting up the intensity with my knuckles and clearing my throat.

She never answered.

As I turned to sheepishly make the short hike back down to my own door, infinite possibilities sprang to subdue my disappointment. She could've just been out. Or working. It was only nearly five, after all. Or maybe she did in fact work nights, and she was still sleeping. Maybe she was merely on her bed reading a magazine with some headphones on. Or maybe she did quietly approach the door and caught a glimpse of me through the peephole, wondering why the hell the weird guy down the hall was standing outside with a box of donuts.

Nevertheless, I figured to catch her around eventually, probably in the later hours. I figured the more I obsessed over waiting to catch her, the better chance I had of mucking up that eventual first conversation and destroying any chance I hoped I had. But as that day turned to the next, and that turned to a week, I grew a little annoyed at our missed timing. Where the hell was she? I found myself using any opportunity to exit my apartment and building on a nightly basis in hopes of catching her. The odds were in my favor, but I never saw her. Perhaps she was on a business trip, or a vacation. Something still bothered me about not seeing her, though. It was almost as if I had this sense of feeling that she *was* behind her door. That she *was* around, and I was just barely missing her. A week really is nothing on the grander scale of things. But when you revolve your curiosity around seeing someone, it can feel like a year. Of course, I tried to fill my time in the usual ways, taking jobs, going out for drinks or dinner, and when I was least expecting it, we would bump into each other. Isn't that the way it always seems to work? The second you stop thinking about something, it comes to find you.

That exact point was validated one particular night when I was having drinks at this bar down the street. A nice, decent place, not too loud, never too over-crowded. I wasn't meeting anyone in particular, nor did I usually intend to ever blatantly look for someone to bring home. I was just there for the drinks and atmosphere. One of my favorite leisurely night activities. Just simply watching the nightlife at its finest. No interaction necessary. So as I strolled through the patrons tipping my bottle of Bud into my mouth, I noticed her sitting at the bar counter across the room, nearly blending right into the surrounding youth of America. At first I didn't know what my next move was going to be. Just the fact that she was sitting there, in the same bar I was, after I had been so anxiously waiting to catch her — it nearly threw me off my feet. But I told you that's how it worked. When you least expected it. I considered myself lucky, seeing as how my elaborately unstable donut plan was no longer needed. And that made me feel a little better. A little more confident. I couldn't ask for a better situation. It was a bar, for Christ's sake. A place where people go to mingle and talk. And now I had her here. In my grasp. Before I moved forward, something had caught me a bit off-guard.

She had noticed me. And I don't mean casually, drifting her eyes across the room in search of what able bodies were present. She looked *right at me. Directly at me.* Taking a sip of her drink, her eyes seemed to vibrate a sexy glare, and I could've sworn that the corners of her mouth had barely curled to conjure a hardly noticeable sly grin. My stomach had dropped to my feet. I scratched my head, attempting to do a quick evaluation of those around me in the event that this unforeseen gesture was directed toward someone else, but all those around me seemed to be engaged in their own conversations with others, never returning a look back to her. When I had returned my attention to her direction, not even a moment or two later — she was gone. Her seat was empty. I tried to scan the faces of those around to see if she had just gotten up. After all, even in a small crowd here it was fairly easy to lose someone. But then it became apparent that she was nowhere to be found. I had figured she went to the bathroom or something, maybe even possibly stepping outside for some air or a smoke, but she never returned after minutes and minutes of waiting and searching. Finally, I scrounged up the ability in annoyance to march over to where she was sitting and tapped the shoulder of the guy who was sitting next to her. "Hey," I muttered, raising my voice a bit over the noise. "Do you know the girl who was sitting here?"

"Nah. Sorry, man," he simply replied, going back to a conversation with his buddy.

I let out an agitated sigh and turned my head in circles around the bar, giving her another short chance to return. So I tapped him again. "You happen to see where she went?" I asked this time.

He turned around, a bit peeved but trying to hold it back. "Dude — just chalk it up as a loss. You gotta learn to get on that hot piece before it leaves with someone else."

He returned to his conversation, and I didn't bother investigating any more. I had thought about getting another beer and waiting — hoping — she came back from wherever she left to, but she didn't. I might as well have gotten another drink with the amount of time I spent debating to. But she didn't come back, so I ditched the bar in hopes of maybe catching her going back to the apartment. Which of course, I didn't. Of course. My fucking luck. She looked at me. I think she smiled at me. I hated games. Hated the girls that played them, even innocently. But this one was different. There was something different in those eyes, something in that microscopic smile that made me want to play. Made me want to find out more.

There were moments over the course of the next few days that made me wonder if I was losing my mind. I would think I saw her in a supermarket late at night, and after turning down the aisle she would disappear in, she would be gone. I would think I saw her walking the street and entering our apartment complex, but after quickening my pace and bursting inside the lobby, she would be gone again.

It was on the night of my Porsche job that things took a turn for the interesting. The job was at one of those fancy small window dealerships downtown. You know, one of those corner places completely walled by only windows with only ten cars on display, all priced at "You-Wish-You-Had-the-Dough-to-Afford-Me-Ninety-Nine". I normally didn't do jobs like this; the cars I boosted were generally already privately-owned or not company-affiliated. But a job was a job, and this was a cash crop that was gonna set me for a while and then some. A smash and grab job. Get inside, get the car, get it out, and park it in a pre-arranged spot. But that's all I knew. All I cared to know.

So there I was, walking down the city streets that night toward my mark. Considering the time, not many people if any were out and about, not that I was ever really too concerned about witnessing bystanders. I was quick and simple, and only someone good at what they do will know to only do it when the timing is perfect. To the world that night, I was an Average Joe, walking down the city streets with his hands in his jacket pockets, off to do whatever it was he was doing. That's another thing I liked about being out in the night. The ability of wonder. Wonder as to the agenda and adventures of any single individual that shared the limitless darkness with me. A woman hurrying to catch a bus might have been trying to get home in time to her husband after a brief lustful affair with an inner-city colleague. A man constantly scratching and rubbing his nose might have been on his way to his latest score. Anyway, I'm getting off-topic here. I wasn't far from the dealership when I got that paranoid feeling that someone was following me. Despite my constant head-turns over my shoulder, no one was visible from what I could tell. Not a soul was in sight. So putting these grand delusions to test, I decided to pop into the nearest alley and hid behind a box within the deep blackness. Completely stupid, I know. But when you know the night like I do, you leave nothing to chance. Especially when you've got an important agenda.

I waited a minute or so as the approaching sound of light footsteps came closer. I was right. Someone was following me. When the individual had finally passed the opening of the alley, my heart jumped.

It was her.

There was an essence of slow motion for me as she made those few steps past the opening for those few seconds; her hair very lightly fluttering in the vague breeze as her solid eyes stared intently ahead.

This girl was following me.

This girl was *actually fucking following me.*

Within an instant, she was gone from my eyesight, having already walked past the alley and continuing her way down the street. I didn't move for a minute or two as my mind still processed the unprecedented surprise. My over-analyzing began to kick into full-drive. Coincidence was not an option. There was something deeper going on here, and only then was I beginning to piece together the sections of a puzzle that still had no end. I thought of the night that I saw her in the bar. And then all of the instances lately where I had thought I was seeing her everywhere I was going at night. Had she really been following me all this time? She sure as shit was good at keeping a low profile for it. So after I had come to this conclusion pretty convincingly, I began to run through the why's of the matter. What could this girl possibly want with a schmuck like me? It had to be job-related. Maybe some kind of FBI or police issue, tracking and watching me pull all these jobs.

Come on. Seriously. My crimes were pretty damn petty compared to most of the world's problems, especially not enough to involve some kind of elaborate law enforcement scheme to bring me down. If it really were job-related, they obviously knew where I lived. Wouldn't they have just kicked down my door and cuffed me by now? I've pulled enough jobs lately to give them reason and proof. Maybe it was something bigger. Maybe I was pulling a job that was connected to a mob or something. Maybe there was something in the trunk of the Porsche. Something that was the real reason for me boosting and bringing it to my appointed destination tonight. Shit. Moments like these make me want to rethink my whole "don't ask, don't tell" policy to know what my ass is getting into, in hopes that the information could be used to get me the hell out of it if it came to that. No. Knowing too much is never a good thing. Even if it could help me within some kinda mob testifying predicament.

So after spending a good few minutes flossing my ass with strings of paranoia and possibilities, I decided to get the hell out of there. She had obviously not seen me turn down the alley, or she would've come back by now. Still, I didn't want to re-emerge the way I came, so I turned and headed down the opposite end of the alley to take a different route to the dealership. That's right. Fuck it. I was doing it anyway. Maybe she was some kind of inside snitch, or maybe it really was pure fucking unbelievable insane coincidence that she was walking in the same direction of the city in the same area around the same time as me, but if there was one thing I was still sure of, one thing I knew I still had on my side — was the night.

Catch me if you can. If I'm screwed, I'm screwed. If they had already known about me, and my past, and my current intentions, then there really was nothing to lose. Sure, I could have quit right then and there, just to be safe, and to not dig myself in any deeper, but then that's not living, is it? So I say buckle up. Enjoy the ride.

It took me twenty additional minutes to finally reach the dealership since I had hoofed a different route. I flipped my caution switch on and looked around. No one. No stores open. Hardly any lights on in the surrounding buildings, and if there were, they were covered by curtains, and if someone were peeking out, then how much could they possibly use to identify me with from their standpoint? The lights that glimmered from within the dealership were purple and neon-affiliated, like something out of the '80s. As I mentioned before, there were only a handful of cars on display, parked within the two-story structure. From outside, I couldn't really locate the exact model Porsche I needed, so I would have to be quick once I got in. In this area of the city, I had two, maybe three minutes tops to break in, find the car, jack the car, and drive it a safe distance away before the boys in blue showed up. I gave one final look around as I reached the main entrance doors and pulled the small crowbar from my jacket. I tossed it up and caught it, tightening my grip around the handle. Go time.

Gritting my teeth, I swung it forward as hard as I could, shattering the glass door as the wild alarms immediately whirled and shrieked in banshee mode. I tucked the crowbar back into my jacket and ran in, jerking my head to each car. Nope. Nope. No. Not that one. Shit. My nerves squeezed and my stomach twisted as I realized the Porsche wasn't there. And precious seconds were clocking away. Realization set in as I tilted my head upward. I jolted up the spiraling staircase to the second floor showcase, where among a couple other shiny vehicular treasures sat the black topless Porsche I needed.

On the goddamn second floor.

"You've gotta be shittin' me," I blurted out loud.

First, I thought I made a mistake. Thought I fingered the wrong car, and it was back down on the ground floor where I was too nervous to really realize. I mean, holy hell, what kind of a dumbass sets up a job to steal a car in a dealership that's on the second floor? How the hell do they even get these things up and in here? No ramps. No cool sliding walls that revealed secret roads to my knowledge. In the split second of that thought, I spotted the ledge outside. That's how. They probably crane it up or something from outside and just drive it right in. Maybe the Porsche was on the ground floor until this morning and got moved up. Regardless, the revealing tricks of the trade for multi-floor dealership car placements wasn't gonna help me then. I still had this moment of crossroads to run my ass out of there while I still had the chance, or find a way to get this damn car down within the next two minutes. Fortunately and unfortunately, I decided to go with the latter. I jumped into the driver's seat and began my finger twiddling hotwire work, which really was the easy part of any car theft. Within seconds, the Porsche roared and hummed to life in all of its sleek horsepower glory. I hopped behind the wheel and closed the door, buckling up to wrap my hands around the steering wheel as I stared forward to the glass panel wall in my path. Rationality raced through my head, and of course a moment like this should call for my usual idiotic pendant luck. I reached into my shirt, pulling it out and giving it a quick rub. "Fuck it," I said.

I gripped the gear shifter and hit the gas hard, squealing the tires in place. Kicking the Porsche forward, I shifted the gear and blasted ahead, being tightened against my seat. With a sharp rev, I ripped through the glass like it were paper and soared off the ledge, roaring through the air and landing with a hard thud on the street below. There was no apparent immediate damage, so I wasted no time in taking off down the road.

For a split spine-jolting second, I thought the car speeding up behind me was a cop without the sirens on, but it wasn't. It shifted and sped up beside my left side, making me turn my head to see her hair blowing in the wind as she sat navigating behind the wheel of the convertible. She looked at me with her cool following eyes. She didn't try to stop me, or yell something to me, or warn me, or even run me off the road. She just went faster. She went faster and looked at me, barely curving that hardly noticeable grin. I didn't know what to think. I didn't know what to do, or how to react. I sure didn't slow down any more.

The cop pulling out behind us broke me out of my trance. I looked into my rearview and then over my shoulder for a more in-depth glance to its wailing and flashing sirens. My mysterious neighbor didn't even bother looking. Not even in her rearview, for all I could tell. She just revved her convertible and sped up past me, flying down the road as I fought to both keep up with her and lose the cop. She could sure as hell drive. That was a given. She maneuvered through the traffic with the ease of a snake through blades of grass. I nearly rear-ended and side-swiped a car or two just trying to keep up with her lead. She got bolder, taking on the incoming traffic as each vehicle laid the horn to her swerving misses. The cop was still stuck to my ass as I saw the traffic light to the intersection ahead flick from green to yellow, and finally to blazing and burning red. Guess she didn't really adhere to traffic laws. She ripped through the intersection as another car swerved to avoid a collision, skidding sideways to a stop. Taking a deep breath, I shook my head and floored it completely. The speedometer needle seemed to be off the gage. I hiked up a small bump across the intersection, gaining a cushion of air and landing with a thud of yellow sparks that I saw trickle across the road behind me through my side-view mirror. The cop wasn't so lucky, as it got T-boned by a crossing truck that thus started a domino effect of collisions from everyone around.

Seemingly in the clear, I coasted alongside the convertible and looked back over to her. She didn't appear to be rattled one bit, like she was on some kind of leisurely Sunday drive. Resting her left arm on the side as her right hand guided the steering wheel, she slyly admired her attention back to me. I could only watch with my jaw hanging slightly askew as she sped out in front of me again; her taillights beaming like bold red eyes. She took a sharp veer left when we got to a fork and had me watching as the space grew between us until her convertible was too small to see behind the army of skyscrapers and buildings.

When I was out of the city and safe, I coasted to a stop in a parking lot along the river and sat with the engine running, panting out of unbelievable breath. Speechless. Thoughtless.

I didn't get back to my apartment until at least after nine the following night. I guess you could say the events that occurred in the city the prior night had me a bit spooked. Well, I wouldn't say "spooked". More like "cautious". I really wasn't eager to show my face in daylight, so after dropping the Porsche off at my designated spot, I decided to take a little daytrip out of the city to clear my head and reevaluate the situation. It was obvious that my paranoid theory of her working for some type of law enforcement to take me down was wrong, since during the high speed chase, it wasn't her doing the chasing. Was she really just getting herself off by being some kind of rebel-without-a-cause-thrill-seeker? It still didn't explain the fact that she had been following me. Or maybe there was nothing to explain. If there's one thing the night has taught me, it's that when the lunar goes up, the loonies come out. So perhaps she was just one of those crazy people. Not crazy in the sense that she mumbles incoherently or walks while uncontrollably bobbing her head in spasms, but crazy as in "I'm normal until I get into the shit that I like and then all bets are off".

My initial plan when I got back to my apartment was to give her door a good kick in and try to pry some sense out of the insanity that nearly got me killed. But, I needed a second opinion on it before making a move, so I called Shelly, the one person I could trust to tell, and told her to meet me at my place that night. I really did want to skip Shelly's verbal assessment and go right to my mystery girl, but, I simply only looked in her door's direction when I got back and turned the key into my own. It didn't matter anyway. Because there she was. My mysterious neighbor, standing right by my fucking window in my living room when I walked in. I froze within the threshold, nearly dropping my keys. It was Shelly's voice that snapped my attention. "Hey, you," she greeted as she sipped a beer over by the kitchen counter. "Look who I met in the elevator."

"Oh," I shakily managed to mumble, keeping my eyes on the neighborly goddess of hotness. "H-How... how did you get in?"

"I have a key, remember?" Shelly reminded me, questionably perking her eyebrows in a reminding state as she jingled it. "Anyway, she said she hadn't noticed me on this floor before and asked if I was just visiting. I told her I was your sister. We got to talking, and soon enough, I just invited her in." Shelly casually slinked out from the kitchen into the living room as she went on with, "Apparently she tells me you two have yet to formally meet."

I wasn't quiet sure how to react. It was pretty awkward. I could see in her eyes the entire reoccurrence of last night's joyride, but she played it off with her usual silent and steadily firm expression.

"No, uh... we haven't," I flatly said.

"Well, then," Shelly confirmed, looking between her and I. "Amanda, this is my brother, Adam, and Adam — this is your new neighbor, Amanda."

"Very nice to meet you. Adam," Amanda spoke, eyes deadlocked on me.

"Yeah..." I murmured.

A smirk crept across Shelly's face as she looked at Amanda. "Leave it to me to always be the one who breaks the ice for him," she joked. "You'll have to excuse my brother and his manners if he's failed to make an attempt to ask your name since you've moved in. He doesn't realize that too much late night TV deteriorates the personality."

"No harm done. I've been pretty busy since coming here," Amanda responded. "I'm a bit of a night owl myself."

"And what is it you do exactly?" I sharply blurted out.

"I'm sort of a... people-finder," she answered, crossing her arms.

"Oh yeah? What kinda people?"

"People that need to be found."

Shelly crafted a confused face. "Like a private investigator?"

"Sort of," Amanda shrugged, giving it a quick thought.

"What kinda private investigator people-finder moves into an apartment in the middle of the night?" I then asked.

Shelly surprisingly arched away from me. "Jeez, Detective Adam. You wanna sit her down and use some hot lamplights to grill her while you're at it?"

Amanda lightly snickered. "It's okay. I'm being a little blunt. One of my quirks. I guess you could call me more of a "people archaeologist", really. I don't dig in the dirt for ancient objects but I try to track down local people who are known to dabble in the trading of them.

I work at the museum downtown. We're putting together an exhibit and I'm trying to locate certain items that we can showcase. A lot of my work consists of me doing research late at night finding those people and helping with the set-up. Hence the "people-finder" aspect. Mostly rich scum that want big numbers on a check. Seems like I'm there all hours of the day. Sometimes I don't even leave. I was living downtown but my short-term lease was up. I found a great price on the apartment here and made a deal with the landlord to move it at night because it would better coincide with my hectic schedule."

Shelly turned to me and raised her eyebrows with one of those superiorly silent "I told you so's". I ignored the gloating and darted my eyes back to Amanda, who continued with, "But aside from work, when I have the time, I like to cut loose and go to a good bar or club. You know, the whole nightlife thing."

"Oh!" Shelly remembered, laying her hand on my arm. "Which is what we were talking about before you got here. Amanda's meeting some friends at this great club downtown in a bit and asked if we wanted to tag along. I told her anything at night was right up your alley and to put a checkmark next to our names."

"The place just opened," Amanda added. "It's getting great reviews. Good music, good dancing, the whole sha-bang."

"I'm gonna hit the bathroom and get ready first," Shelly noted. As she turned and passed in front of me, she gave me a playfully hinting wink. "Let you two get acquainted a little better."

She headed for the bathroom. I looked back at Amanda, who returned the stare as she leaned against the window. "Uh, um, you know, Shell," I pointed out, quickly walking to catch her. "The toilet's been acting up. Lemme come in and make sure it's working okay. Excuse us — Amanda."

I turned the corner of the hallway and took her arm, guiding her into the bathroom and lightly closing the door nearly all the way. She flashed a smile. "Play your cards right tonight with my help and you may have yourself a little sleepover," she cunningly said.

"Why the hell did you invite her in?" I quietly snapped, being careful to not raise my voice. "I said I had to talk to you about the fucked up shit that went down last night!"

"Yeah, what were you talking about? Something about crashing a Porsche through a second story level and going a hundred while being chased by the cops? Please, Adam — elaborate."

"I already told you what happened! She was following me on the way to the dealership and she was there right after I had left it! She was driving right alongside me, like she wanted to race me or something," I sternly explained.

"Race you," Shelly repeated with an unbelievable hint in her tone. "While you were being chased by the cops."

"*A* cop," I corrected. "And not race — just — like, I don't know — joyriding. Like she was getting a kick out of it. Like she was taunting me. Look — the point is, she's been following me. I don't know who the hell she is or what the hell she wants with me but you can't stand here and honestly tell me you believe all that bullshit about her working in the museum."

Shelly gave a strong shrug, extending her arms. "I don't know what to believe because I don't know her, Adam! I just met her! If that's what she says she does then to me that's what she does. I have no reason or proof to suspect otherwise."

"So you think I'm crazy," I huffed.

"I think your wiggage needs to be put in check. You've always been... you. And you've always gotten into some kinda mischievous late-night trouble, but lately it seems like things are spiraling out of whack. I mean, come on, Jesus, Adam — a high-speed pursuit in the middle of downtown? You could've gotten busted, or worse. I just..." she stopped herself, taking a light breath as she planted a worried hand across her forehead. "I knew this lifestyle was gonna get out of control for you sooner or later."

"This has *nothing* to do with *what* I do," I said, pointing a finger in her face. "That's what I'm trying to fucking tell you. If it were something like she was working for the cops then it'd be different, but it's something else."

"What? What is it, Adam? Tell me. Please. Because the only thing you're sounding like to me right now is a paranoid delusionist who's been wired on an all-night lifestyle for way too damn long," she threw back at me. She took a deep breath, trying to calm herself as she tossed a hand in the air. "Just come with us tonight. It's the perfect opportunity to get to know her better. Then you'll see that this is all in your head."

"No," I firmly stated, shaking my head. "No fuckin' way. I'm not going anywhere with her. And neither should you."

"Oh, so first she made you hard and now you've gone soft for her?" Shelly wondered. "Ya know what? Forget it. Don't go, Adam. But I'm going, because I wanna have a good time."

Before I could retort any further, Shelly had turned and gone out the bathroom door. I hurried to follow her but stuttered my steps at the sight of Amanda in the living room perusing around some of my desk and cabinet drawers. "Uh, something I can help you find...?" I weirdly asked.

Amanda snapped back to prompt attention, closing a drawer. "Kleenex. Just a Kleenex," she told me.

I bent a suspicious face, reaching over to the small box of tissues right in plain sight on one of the end tables next to the couch and handing it to her. "I'm ready when you are," Shelly said to her.

Amanda turned her head to me as a sly smile spread across her face. "Not coming?"

"Nah. I'm, uh... not feelin' so hot. I'm gonna hang in tonight," I tried to casually respond as I scratched my head.

"That's too bad," she said, handing me back the box of tissues and making a point to lightly rub my finger with hers. "I'm a good dancer."

"Don't have too much fun here tonight, Adam," Shelly snipped, turning and exiting out the door.

Amanda was about to join her when she stopped; eyes drifting toward my chest at my pendant necklace that had popped out from beneath my shirt at some point during the night. "Pretty," she admired, helping herself to reach out and take it in her left hand. She rubbed her thumb over the hieroglyphic-like symbols that were imprinted. "You know what it says?"

"No. My grandfather gave it to me before he died," I told her, looking down at it as she let go.

A smile slowly and broadly crept on her face as her eyes once again pierced into mine like sharpened blades. "Give us a call if you change your mind," she said. "I've got a pretty fast car. I can be back in no time to get you."

With that, she turned and left out the door as I looked back down at the pendant necklace.


It really bothered me knowing that Shelly was out and about with Amanda. In fact, I had tried to get my mind off of it by actually going to bed at night for a change. But aside from my internal clock keeping me from nodding off, I was just too mentally distraught as it was. So I laid there in bed, thinking and going over everything. It pissed me off when Shelly did stuff like that to spite me. That little snivel and bitchiness she gave with each little syllable that came from her Miss-Smarty-Pants mouth. I kept contemplating if I had made the right decision to just let her go alone with Amanda like that, knowing what I knew about her. What I knew. What *did* I know? Nothing, really. Nothing I could describe or analyze, for that matter. Just a chick that liked to follow me and race me amid a police car chase. Nothing important. Nah, nothing big at all. Yeah, sure. Like hell nothing at all. But of course, the jury sitting around the elaborate rationality table of my brain was hard at work once again, arguing defendable cases. Maybe Shelly was right. Maybe it really was nothing to be concerned about. Maybe Amanda was just simply one of those late-night head-case freaks and nothing more. I mean, that stuff does happen. Usually not to me, but I certainly have seen my share of friends who took the wrong girl home at night.

Still, Amanda was different. With crazy people, you can tell they're crazy after a short while, even in their sane periods. They have certain tiny body movements, or tones in their voice, or expressions that give away something much deeper, something just aching to burst out if the wrong thing was done or said to them. Amanda had a cool sense to her. Like everything was under control. A master illusionist of her true agenda. And that is what gave me a sense that there was no fucking doubt in my mind she was solely fixated on me and me alone. I felt like a mouse whose tail was caught beneath her feline paw, and just when she lifted it for me to scurry free, she slammed it back down, trapping me in a twisted game of her play.

Fucking Shelly. She had to go. At about two in the morning, I finally called her cell phone to see if they were still out, or on their way back, since the clubs were closed or in the process of winding down business. It rang a few times and went to her voicemail. I left a message but knowing her didn't expect any immediate response back. So I stayed up for a while longer, watching some mindless late night TV or playing a video game I had only already beaten fifteen thousand times.

It wasn't until I was sitting on the couch with the flicker of the screen in front of me, eyelids heavy and sagging, when the knocking came at my door. And I don't mean that normal little "knock-knock-are-you-home?" interruption. This was a knock of serious drunken proportions. And that's what I figured she was as I rubbed my eyes and sighed, sliding off the couch to my feet to hear her mutter my name. Why didn't she use the key she so gallantly reminded me she had earlier? I figured she was either too blasted to turn the damn thing in the lock or too blasted to even remember she had the damn thing period. "Ya know, I might still be up, but other people on this floor are trying to sleep!" I said as I approached the door.

As I yanked it open, she nearly collapsed right into my arms. For a split second, I wanted to just laugh and shake my head, making some mundane comment that she wouldn't even remember in the morning. But as I held and directed her upward to brush some hair out of her face, my joking instincts were overcome by a sudden wave of seriousness. Her face was dampened by a massive amount of sweat. Her eyes glazed and rolled as they fought to stay open. "Jesus, Shelly — how much did you have?" I asked with concern.

She mumbled a few words that I couldn't make out. I only caught the part where she said, "Don't feel so good." So I slung one of her arms around my shoulders and tried to direct her through the living room. That's when she began to cough. I expected her to upchuck all over the damn carpet, but nothing came out. She just wheezed and began to hack uncontrollably, enough for her to weaken her connection with me as her arm slid off.

"Oh, shit. Shelly," I murmured as she softly collapsed to the floor; body beginning to convulse and shake. "Oh, Jesus!"

My first initial instinct was to dial nine-one-one, but as I turned to leave her and get my phone, her cold, clammy hand caught my wrist and locked me in place. "N-No," she pleaded, jaw clenched tightly. I could see the veins in her neck pulsating from the strengthened squeeze. "D-Don't leave me."

I swiped some of her brown hair from her face, cradling her cheek. "Shelly, what did you take?" I demanded to know. "You have to let me know what happened."

"I... I d-don't... remem-member," she said. Her teeth were beginning to chatter. "I was j-just... drink...ing. I don't... rememb-b-ber."

"Where's Amanda?" I then asked. "Did she come back with you? Is she back in her apartment?"

Shelly's eyeballs swung and swayed as her eyelids dipped open and closed. I gave her a quick look up and down. Her skin was ice cold. Her face was nearly blue. Her lips were stiff and shading gray. "Look — I'm gonna call an ambulance," I told her.

"N-No," she said. "B-Bath — room. Bathroom."

I hesitated for a quick second and scooped my arms beneath her frail body, immediately carrying her into the bathroom and sitting her on the floor next to the toilet. As soon as I flipped the seat up, she leaned forward — and out it came. I don't think I've ever seen someone throw up like that. I mean, it was bad. I couldn't even watch. Christ, I couldn't even *listen*. The awful dry-heaving and gagging as she clutched and braced the side of the porcelain. She must've thrown up for a good five minutes, stopping only to flush a time or two. I couldn't even believe she had that much in her. At that point I could only imagine that it should've been a stomach-pumping situation at the hospital. That she just had a really bad case of alcohol poisoning, or worst case scenario, some asshole dropped a friendly little mixture into one of her drinks.

My tension had eased up just a bit when she had finally stopped, slouched and lazy above the toilet. I grabbed a towel and helped wipe her face, giving one more final flush. And after a short while of silence in what seemed to be the aftermath, she had requested that I help her into bed, so I carried her and buried her within a sea of blankets on the mattress, with a handy empty bucket by her side should the need of external use be called again. And pacing around the room to relax myself with deepened sighs, I thought that she had gotten it all out of her system.

But she began coughing again. That uncontrollable fit of hacking that would seem to outdo the world's worst type of fever. I tried to help with a glass of water, but she only choked and ended up spitting most of it out. Whenever the coughing did manage to momentarily subside, she would lay curled within the sheets shaking and trembling. I didn't know what to do. My gut kept telling me to obviously grab my phone and call for help. It's what I should have done. But instead, I stomped my way out of the room and through my apartment, swinging the door open and trotting down to the hall to Amanda's closed door. I balled my fist and began pounding on it over and over. She didn't answer, and although I knew she most likely wasn't there yet, I continued to thrust my demanding knock until one of the neighbors had decided to pop out and chime in with his annoyance. "Keep it down, asshole!" he angrily huffed.

"Hey, you shut the fuck up!" I barked back as he grumbled and shook his head, closing his door. I looked back to Amanda's door and gave it an agitated final punch, turning to head back into my apartment.

I didn't get much sleep the rest of the night. Actually, I don't think I even got *any* sleep. Shelly had calmed down a bit; her coughing finally let up but she was still shrouded and enclosed in an endless shake. I had the phone in my hand for a few of those hours with my thumb over the "9" button, but I never made the call. I suppose any sensible person would have dialed long before that, and in the back of my mind I was constantly kicking myself for any second lost that would have resulted in something happening to Shelly that I could have prevented by following common human safety protocol. She fell asleep and just kept sleeping, giving a spastic shake every now and then. It wasn't normal. I didn't consider myself an expert in the sort of bar drugs and their side effects, but I knew this wasn't normal. Still, I kept a steady and watchful eye on her throughout the hours of early morning after the sun had started its day. At one point I had nodded off myself in the love seat for what I thought was at least a few hours, but when I came to, I glanced at the clock and realized that the whole day was nearly gone already, and the light that had once briefly ignited the city outside was now cast with purple and pink colors. Stretching and clawing the sleep from my eyes, I stepped over to the bed, peaking at Shelly's face. She was still heavily sleeping, face buried within the pillows. I didn't want to disturb her. Maybe she was getting better. Maybe all the remedy required was a shit load of sleep. I would give her just a little while longer and perhaps try to grill some information from her when she awoke and was more coherent, but until then, I took another tactic.

"I already told you," the balding man said behind his desk only mere minutes later. "If it's an emergency or you got some kinda personal issue with this tenant, then you gotta call the police."

I groaned and ran a hand through my hair, taking a calm breath. "Listen, man — I'm tired as hell. I'm not asking you to get in the middle of it. All I'm asking is that you go up there with me to her apartment and open her door so I can talk to her."

"I can't do that," he snarled. "We got rules around here. Laws. I just can't go opening up people's apartments because you want me to."

"And I already told *you* — she won't answer the door for me. She's in there. I know it. My sister is sick and she might have had something to do with it! She's been following me, stalking me!"

"You know what I think?" he asked with a hint of arrogance. "You could've already gone to the police about this but instead you're down here buggin' *me*. Sounds to me like maybe you don't want them snooping into something *you're* involved in."

Hmm. Clever fella. What on earth was he doing in a life of apartment managing? Still, he had me, and it wasn't until he said it that I actually thought about it myself and realized how true it was. To that, I really had nothing immediate to come back with. He picked up some paperwork and started to go back to his own business, bluntly adding in, "Not — my — problem. Maybe you should take your sis to a doctor. And until you're standing here with the cops at your side with reasonable cause, I ain't opening up any doors for you, pal."

Fuck it. I sighed and turned to walk out of the tiny office, making my bitterness very apparent in my body motions. I don't even know why I bothered wasting my time there with that jackass. I could just as easily have picked her lock. And that was probably the best plan I had going for me that moment, but before jumping to anything that drastic and dramatic, I wanted to get back to my own place and check on Shelly. Then I could make a better assessment of how she was doing after sleeping the entire day, and maybe get her to remember some shit that I could use to build my case on. Or worst case scenario, I could make the judgment call to finally take her to the hospital if I thought she wasn't improving in the least bit. When I got back to the apartment and opened the door, my jaw hit the floor.

It was trashed.

And I'm talking ransacked-up-the-ass trashed. A complete and utter mess. Furniture was flipped over. Glass was shattered. Papers were everywhere. Desk drawers had been pulled out completely. Everything was either broken or turned over. Even the TV. *Even the fucking TV*. Christ, what was I gone, only a half hour? This was unbelievable. After what seemed to have been tornado chaos registered into my brain, my thoughts quickly shifted to Shelly in the bedroom. I turned and raced in there, jumping over the debris in my way. The bedroom was just as bad — things lying and broken everywhere, the mattress flipped over, clothes scattered — but no Shelly. "Shelly?! Shelly?!" I called out in a panic, throwing the mattress over and checking beneath.

I tried to turn the switch to a lamp but the bulb must have been broken, and I was about to hit the main light switch to the room when I glanced over to my open walk-in closet. Sitting within its darkness, I saw her outlined in the shadows that the moonlight from outside cascaded. "Shelly?" I asked, my motions slowing as I made a creeping step toward her. "Are you all right? What the hell happened here? Who did this?"

She didn't answer. She just sat there. I sensed she was awake, as I could see her open eyes watching me within the blackness. But there was something about them. Something void and solemn. Something that made me cautious and careful as I approached the closet and crouched to a lower level. "Shelly, what happened? Why don't you come out of there?" I softly urged. She didn't respond. I cocked my head back to the mess and then back to her. "Did *you* do this?"

That's when she sprang out. I didn't have time to react. I didn't even expect something like that from her given the state she had been in. But from out of the darkness of the closet she came, full force and full of life as she plowed directly into me, knocking me to my back on the floor. "Shelly, what the fuck?!" I yelped as she began to claw and tear at me.

I fought back, smacking her hands and arms away and finally tossing her off as I quickly crawled back against the slanted mattress. "Are you out of your damn mind?!" I yelled.

She sniveled and groaned, coming back at me to clutch my shirt and heave me clear across the room as I crashed into the already-beaten dresser. Grunting as I rolled on the floor, I wondered if it had just really happened. "Shelly..." I started to mumble.

She came back, grabbing me and throwing me against the wall on the other side of the room. We wrestled for a moment, and given her size and her ill state, I should've been able to avoid this ass-kicking easily. I mean, come on — forgive me for being sexist here but this was just plain uncalled for. Maybe the darkness of the room attributed to me having a slow reaction to what was coming, but still — I should've been easily able to fend her off. She just kept coming at me, knocking me to the floor again and clawing at my shirt. I clenched my jaw and gave a strong heave, kicking her off as she collided with the opposite wall. I painfully held my side, squinting my eyes as I tried to push myself back on my feet. I turned my head to look at her. She shook off my defensive blow and looked at me before turning and hopping onto the open window sill. "Shelly, wait!" I hollered, reaching a hand out.

She ignored my plea, leaping out onto the fire escape and disappearing. I coughed and got back on my feet, fumbling a bit as I tried to make my way through the mess across the room, nearly tripping once or twice. I reached the window and poked my upper-body out, looking down the stacked metal fire escape route. No one was there. There wasn't even the noise of someone clanging their way down the various steps and ladders. "Shelly?!" I called out. I glanced to what portions of the street below I could see. No one around. Just parked cars here and there and some steam hissing from a nearby sewer cover. I didn't know what to think. She had just... vanished. There was no way she could get down the entire fire escape that fast. No way. Not without... falling. The horror struck me hard and tightened my chest, but I convinced myself that it wasn't an option. It was plain dynamics. From the point of the fire escape at the window, even if she had jumped or fallen, she would've only landed in the clear radius of the street level that I could visibly see from my spot. And she wasn't there. No body. No sign.

A part of me had wanted to go down there and check just to be sure. Another part of me was itching to just give in and get the police in on it. But for me, it had gone far enough. This whole thing had gone too far without a reasonable explanation. So I did what I had to. I grabbed a credit card and a paper clip or two, sternly trotting my way out into the hallway and down to Amanda's door. I began work, twiddling and tweaking the tools of simple B&E. And if she *was* there behind that door, listening to the snapping and clicking, she could do whatever she wanted to keep me from coming in. But I was coming in whether she liked it or not. And whether she actually had something to do with Shelly's sickness or she merely just ditched her with her friends to leave her to the fate of some evil college frat boy, I was gonna find out who she really was. That was for certain.

I finally cracked the lock as the door barely clicked open. I half-expected it to slam shut in my face, or when I opened it more fully she would be standing there with some kind of gun or weapon at the ready. But there was no one there. I opened it more and quietly crept in. This wasn't my thing. I wasn't used to the tactics that a burglar might use, but I knew I had to be quiet. It was dark as I rounded the corner of the small entrance foyer and peeked around. There was nothing. No pictures or posters on the walls. I thought the darkness might have just been playing tricks on me, so I tried the light switch for the hell of it. Surprisingly it clicked on, illuminating the apartment.

The empty apartment.

And I mean bare carpet empty. No furniture, no TV, no utensils — nothing. I could only stand in the center of the emptiness and gaze around with my baffled eyes. I wasn't crazy. Amanda *was* living here, and any thoughts that I was in some asylum in a straightjacket were put to bed when I went downstairs and had it confirmed. It was one of the night lobby guards that looked into it for me in exchange for a crisp fifty dollar bill, despite the risk of losing his job. "Yep," he firmly said, giving a nod as he came back to the desk. "Records show that the tenant moved out last night."

"Last night?" I unbelievably repeated, giving a confused thought. I thanked him and turned, pacing in the lobby with confused thoughts. Amanda was out with Shelly, so how could she have moved out? I remembered I had been up most of the night, so I surely would have heard the commotion in the hallway. But then again, I did nod off there for a while in the later hours, and being as tired as I had been from the previous night's excursion, I might have slept through it like a rock, especially considering how she moved in without a whole lot of things to begin with. But still...

I remembered what Amanda had said to Shelly and I about working at the museum, and working there late at night. Although I didn't really find it to be credible, I thought it was the best shot I had. I could've waited until its normal business hours the next day to start doing some investigating with the personnel there, but why did that option seem like a senseless lost cause? If she had moved out of her apartment so suddenly, and if she really did have some kind of connection with the museum, then it was also an apparent possibility her time with the museum might have been limited. Maybe she had things there. Maybe she had to tie some things up. Regardless, it was the best chance I had. The only chance I had.

So I hopped onto the subway and took it downtown with thoughts, possibilities and plans racing through my head. The tunnel lights flashed by as the car lightly rocked. The usual late-nighters were all there, tagging along with whatever personal agendas they had in store for them. But as I sat there glancing at them one by one, I realized that this was the first time I wasn't perplexed into wondering where their destinations would be. For some reason, it wasn't fascinating to me anymore compared to my Amanda agenda. I could really have cared less what drugs they were off to buy, what friends they were off to party with, what roads would wind and lead them through their own starry twilight paths.

I had reached the museum stop downtown, and seeing as how they currently weren't accepting general admission at that hour, I had to take it upon myself to find a way in. There's always a way in. It was toward the back in one of the smaller building sections of the greater massive establishment — a window that was jarred just a bit open enough for me to work some petty magic. There were no alarms that went off, and if the place used alarms, they were surely not set as the open window wouldn't have allowed for it in the first place. Surprising, as you'd think they'd be more cautious and wary at these places. I guess most of the things inside didn't really have too much face value to normal everyday people. After all, how many museum heists of ancient cultural artifacts have you heard of? What would the thieves do, try to sell the pottery on the street? It was a little ridiculous to think about. Maybe that's why people only stick to usually snatching diamonds and other precious priceless jewels that have more than an archaeological value.

There were a few overhead lights on here and there, but mostly the museum in its entirety was dark and empty. I figured I would creep in the shadows anyway until coming across someone. I didn't know what she did exactly or where she would be. I just figured that it would be in some kind of research-lab type area or room, so I moved through the big display areas quickly. Tribe statues stared and gaped at me with their eternal stone expressions. Stuffed animals were forever-frozen in their poses of attack or curiosity. The way the light tricked the shadows over them seemed to make them move out of the corner of my eye. It sure as hell kept me alert. At one point I had heard a noise, something that wasn't in my head. I thought maybe it was some kind of electrical issue, like the mechanics of an air conditioner or ventilation system kicking on. Those types of noises that are only too common around us but amplify our imagination, especially when our hearts pound and our nerves are on edge.

She struck me from behind, coming out of the shadows as if she had been there beside me all along. I hadn't seen or heard her coming, but when I flipped over on my back to catch her next move, she was gone. Or maybe she was still there. Somewhere buried deep within the blotchy patches of shadowy darkness floating around the room. And as soon as I carefully got to my feet, she sprung again, kicking me out from under as I landed with a hard thud on my ass. I braced myself and jerked my head, waiting and trying to focus in on the dark. When Amanda emerged next, I caught her off-guard. Hell, maybe I just got lucky. But I caught her arm and slammed her down on the floor, immediately pinning her on her back as she grunted and tried to squirm free. I dug my knee into her neck as she attempted to pry my arms away, but I was stronger than she gave me credit for.

"Why have you been following me?!" I snapped. "What happened to all your shit back at your apartment?"

She didn't answer. She just laid there, trying to choke back the pressure of my clutch. "What the hell did you do to my sister?! Huh?! Answer me, goddamn it! Where is she?!"

"Gone!" Amanda finally shouted, bending her eyebrows down in a state of annoyance as if tired of playing shenanigans. "She's gone. She's living a different life now."

"Gone? What do you mean "gone"? What the fuck is going on?! Why have you been following me? What is this all about?!" I sternly asked, giving her a quick shake.

"This!" she simply answered, managing to pull something out from her pocket as she held it up in front of me. It was my pendant necklace. My lucky pendant necklace. "She was bringing me *this*."

I glanced down at it in shock and placed a hand over my chest, realizing that it was missing. "How... How did you get that?" I wondered. And then it had occurred to me — when Shelly was all over me back at my apartment, she was swiping at my chest. She must've have grabbed it then.

"You ever hear of a guy named "Van Helsing"?" Amanda then asked.

I was a bit confused by the subject of the question and let it show in my tone when I confusingly answered with, "The guy who killed Dracula?"

"The guy who *couldn't* kill Dracula. The guy who only *contained* Dracula," Amanda began to explain. "Safely tucked and stored away in a hidden location, which would've made for the easiest victory in history had he taken it to his grave. But not telling anyone just wouldn't have been as fun, now would it?"

"Wha...?" was all I could manage to mumble in response.

Amanda gave the pendant a firm quick shake to my face. "So he scribed the location onto one of four pendants, three of which were fakes, and passed them down to his family, who in turn kept passing, selling or losing them."

I stared down at the necklace, lightening my grip on her neck as I sat back a little. "We've been watching you for a while, Adam," Amanda calmly added. She pushed the necklace against my chest, allowing me to take it. "But you're not the one we're looking for."

I looked at the pendant as it swung from the necklace in my hand and casually drifted my eyes back down to her. "We?"

A tiny, small grin began to birth at the corners of her mouth. That same sly, irresistibly mysterious and in-control expression that had captured me before. She lightly shook her head and spoke with, "You think you know all there is to know about what happens when the sun goes down."

As her cunning smile grew a little bigger and wider, so did my eyes at the sight of the oddly-curved fangs planted on the top and bottom rows of her teeth. "You still have a lot to learn about the night," she elaborated.

I didn't see her hand as it crept to grab hold of the vase that was sitting nearby.

But I sure as hell felt it when it smashed to pieces upon making contact to the side of my head.


When I came to, Amanda was already gone, leaving me alone in the darkness of that display room with only the fragments of some ancient broken pottery scattered on the floor around me and the pendant necklace entwined within the fingers of my hand. I stared at it for a moment or two, rubbing my thumb over the inscribed symbols. I didn't know what to think about what happened, about what I had thought I'd seen. But I figured if I was still there and she wasn't, then it was most likely apparent she wouldn't be coming back. So I bolted from the museum before coming across any more trouble then I'd like to be given and returned back to my apartment — where all I could do was think.

I did that for a long time. In fact, I don't think I've stopped thinking about it. About everything. I never ended up going to the police about the matter except to eventually file the missing persons report on Shelly, whose apartment laid untouched and messy until the day came where I was forced to clean and move everything out as per the landlord's threats. Any calls I made to her cell phone went to her voicemail until the number was ultimately disconnected by her service. There were no postcards. No letters. No calls or reports on any leads. The picture on her missing persons flyer was just another individual among a sea of infinite others who had just flickered out like a quietly extinguished candle. The days turned to weeks and the weeks turned to months. I hadn't pulled too many jobs. I'm not quite sure the life of a car-jacker is for me anymore. Had to eventually end under some kind of circumstance, I guess.

The night was never the same for me anymore. I wouldn't say that I quit lurking in it altogether, but I certainly began to keep a subtly intrigued distance. When that bright yellow sun had dipped below the horizon, and the purple and pink clouds had whisked away to pop stars one by one, I was only filled with a new sense of wonder. A new outlook that went past the mundane actions and motivations of those who stood as rulers of this world beyond the dusk. That maybe those who used the night as their personal playground had something much deeper to offer than what met the eye of a beholder on a subway or sidewalk. For me, the night was new now. An explorer's utopia. Invigorated with a life of uncharted territory.

Even if I slept during its haunting calling hours, I could still feel the night's essence around me. Enough to wake me up to the presence of feeling someone else in my room with me, anyway. A wake that barely cracked open the lids of my tired eyes so I could see the outline of Amanda's face eerily emerging from the shadows of the darkness toward me, lurking over me in bed as the weight shifted the mattress; her expression briefly lit by the stream of light coming through the window from the neighboring building as her mouth craned open to reveal her set of threatening and mystifying fangs.

I gasped and quickly sat up. The kind of disturbance you might have when you've nearly fallen asleep and the slightest noise jolts your entire body into a state of lucidness. I sat there alone, breathing heavily and scanning my eyes across the dark room until they stopped and stared at the open window nearby. The open window I was sure I had not left open. It was nights like those that made me remember the power of its stretching possibilities.

I had once thought that I knew all there was to know about what happens when the sun goes down.

Turns out I still have a lot to learn about the night.

# About the Author

Award-winning writer Dan O'Sullivan was born and raised in upstate Rochester, New York, home to giant film-processing corporation Kodak. A scribe of feature length screenplays and stories widely stretching across every single genre, he attributes his natural use of wordplay from his mother's scholastic English-teaching roots and his fascination for the science fiction genre in particular from his father. His personal inspirations stem from the work of John Hughes, Quentin Tarantino, Kevin Smith, Stephen King and Kevin Williamson.

O'Sullivan is a graduate of both the New York Film Academy and Brooklyn College in New York City for film production and screenwriting.

Most of his work can be found readily accessible on his official website at www.dan-osullivan.com.